the

HEALER'S DREAM

Gil Meyer

△G△
Greenridge Publishing
Cross Junction, Virginia

This book is dedicated to my wife and the many other medical professionals who strive daily to put caring first in the healthcare system.

PROLOGUE

Time Island interrupts the broad sweep of the Susquehanna River as it flows between granite bluffs during the final stage of its single-minded journey to become the Chesapeake Bay. The island, long and narrow and sharpened on each end, divides the course. It bristles with trees anchored in ancient boulders. Among the rocks, seldom-seen flowers flicker like candles in the breeze. Dragonflies hover, swoop and dart. Adaptable amphibians leave traces of their lives, tiny prints that disappear into lapping water. Birds, great and small, visit but few call it home.

To stand on the east bank of Time Island would be to look across 200 yards of dark water toward the oddity town of Port Deposit, Maryland, a sliver of human existence that clings to life between a granite cliff and an irreverent river. For a local citizen to stand on the east bank of Time Island would be to observe Port Deposit, but no one does.

The sluggish Susquehanna drifts to the northern tip of the island. In wavering light, the current carries yesterday from upstream. In due course in normal times, dreams flow just beneath the surface. But during thin times and in thin places they surface, often unnoticed, like a turtle that peeks above the water line.

Normal times are no longer, and a storm looms. For Nita, there is scant separation between the worlds of sleep and wake. The worlds swirl and eddy as if merged in a flood. The reliable, low-tide mooring for a dream during sleep has detached, now drifting and rocking recklessly. Dreams mix uncomfortably in the wake of the day.

CHAPTER ONE

Nita probed the rock gently, as if it was sacred, which she suspected it was. In the light that filtered green through ferns and moss, chiseled forms stood pale on the cliff side. Primitive animal forms, along with shapes that could have been either arrows or bird footprints were carved in the stone above a set of three concentric circles. Nita's finger traced around the outer circle while a voice hinted of healing, but either the sound of the river below or the primordial language created a frustrating barrier. Through the haze a hand touched her shoulder, first gently, then with greater urgency.

"Miss, you're going to have to leave now. The library is closed."

Nita bolted upright in the chair. A moment passed before her mouth would work. "I'm...I'm sorry. I didn't even know I had fallen asleep." She looked down at her open anesthesiology book. The page was wet where she had obviously drooled. She swiped at the moisture with embarrassment and scrambled to scoop up her books and notebooks. The librarian scowled and pressed against the table's edge with her flabby thighs, indenting them under her faded blue dress. She placed her clenched fists on her shelf-like hips and clucked in disgust at the watermark on the page, "Books are to be respected and cherished."

"I'm sorry," Nita said again.

The puffy and huffy librarian shrugged and tilted her head toward the cleaning people who were leaning on their brooms, waiting to sweep the area.

Nita stuffed everything in her backpack, zipping it as she hurried down the entire length of the room, having arrived early in the evening to secure a choice spot in the far reaches. If the library was closed that meant it was midnight. She wondered when she had slumped onto the book. Panic gripped her stomach. So much material to know for tomorrow.

When she reached the giant glass doors to exit the library, her reflection startled her. One side of her long dark hair was matted together in thick clumps, and her t-shirt looked like she had slept in it. She gave a weak smile. "The truth hurts," she said out loud as she swung one of the doors out.

Nita heard the thick glass door creak closed behind her, then a bolt slammed into place. She turned to see the librarian glaring at her.

Nita stood at the top of the broad stone stairs and surveyed the oak trees along the two walks that outlined Scholars' Green. The evening had cooled considerably. When she entered the library, it had been unusually warm for February. Now she tucked her arms across her chest and wished she had brought a jacket. She chided herself for wishful assumptions of how the world should be. She was ready for spring and so behaved as if it were so. Lampposts along the walks lit the trees like skeletons in X-rays. From the elbows and fingertips of the trees, large drops of leftover rain splattered onto walkways, giving rise to delicate mists that floated up into the night. A moon, waning from its pregnant fullness, watched from above College Avenue on the far side of the Green.

Nita shifted the backpack on her shoulder and was reminded of the weight of medical school. Tomorrow's anesthesiology exam would be impossible. She wondered how much time she had lost after the click, yet another of those tormenting switches to somewhere, sometime else. In some such instances, almost no time lapsed after a click. Even when the encounter was extended and complex, she would click back to catch the end of the sentence the professor was starting as she clicked out. With other clicks, though, large gaps were left in her life. She wondered how much she had lost in the library. She imagined it to be about two hours, far more time than she could spare with an exam on vital organ support during anesthesia threatening at 9:00 in the morning. Add to that, the winding ride to her cottage, and sleep would be sparse tonight. Nita trotted down the remaining steps and jogged the empty walkway toward the parking lot where Little Earl waited.

From fraternity row two blocks away, she could hear slurred singing. Nita felt twin reactions of disgust and jealousy. Didn't they have anything better to do? Nita thought of a detour that would take her past the rowdy fraternity house where she would likely be called to by the young men to join them. She knew only too well that she would be welcomed, a lithe woman in tight jeans and with long black hair. Guys were always trying to hit on her, at least until they found out she was in medical school, which intimidated most of them, causing them literally to take a step backward.

She would, however, welcome the carefree feeling of drinking beer, dismissing any intruding thoughts of the problematic morning. She slowed where a concrete path laced between the chemistry and physics buildings and toward a night of irresponsibility. A rowdy cheer echoed down the path as the song ended.

Then she remembered her hair. Even drunk frat guys wouldn't be attracted to her tonight. She looked like a disheveled witch—a gritty street-person in a crumpled t-shirt. She stretched the front of the shirt down in an effort to iron out the differences. Then she shifted her backpack to her other shoulder and strode toward Little Earl. No doubt he'd be wondering where she was.

Thoughts of enjoying herself faded quickly as she picked up her stride to walk across campus to her car. She didn't feel comfortable walking alone, but she had learned twice not to call the campus escort service. Both times she was escorted by guys exactly like the ones she wanted to avoid. One of them called her for two weeks trying to get a date. Besides, it pissed her off that women had to bow to fear when guys didn't.

As she walked under the dripping trees behind the student center, more pieces of her dream drifted slowly back, floated near and then moved away. She recalled a feeling of damp and gentle green. The vagueness was so frustrating. Her dreams were like bubbles that would bob on the slightest breeze and as soon as she tried to grab one, it was gone, leaving only a faint mist in her mind and little to grasp in her hand.

Gradually she recalled the time and place she had slipped to from the library chair. She knew the place, but not well. She had come to understand that when she went—how she went—these were not dreams, not as dreams were known from any of the extensive reading she had done. These were clicks. There was no fade through alpha, no orderly decline of brain wave frequencies, no slide through a twilight consciousness into a non-linear world. Unlike the familiar, yet still strange descent into dreams, this was a click, a snap, a sudden and uncontrollable fall. Narcolepsy with a purpose.

She knew where she had been, but not why. More than that, she had no idea how all the pieces fit. She knew, though, with a certainty that was perhaps more hope than assurance, that they must fit together. Or was this just another example of why she was out in February with no jacket?

She had been in the woods. Deep soft woods with massive moss-covered boulders and giant logs decaying, woods like those where gnomes might dance. Dark woods with single beams of light here and there finding their way through to the forest floor. The forest floor sloped to a rock wall where she had climbed out and around to petroglyphs that were carved into stone high above a river. Other details dangled out of reach. There were people. She could feel their personalities but could not see their faces clearly. Through the haze, a dark-skinned hand reached and gripped her shoulder. The back of a woman's hand bore the lines of a life's journey etched by worry and want. From this ledge Nita was jerked by the pale and puffy librarian, shattering the connection.

Other details were just beyond her recollection. One article on dreams suggested writing down details immediately upon wakening. Right! How could she make time to write down her dreams when she hadn't had time to do laundry for three weeks? Oh, and should you also write them down when you slump over in the library? "Ah, excuse me, but you'll have to wait to sweep this area because I need to record my dreams." The only dream she needed to worry about was getting through medical school, not creating notebooks of bedeviling fantasies.

Despite the foul scowl of the book lady and Nita's flight from the building, the connection was nonetheless logged. In contrast to the common and confusing dreams of sleep wherein they flee from the waking world, the connections Nita made after a click did not completely fade. Rather, they rattled around in her head as if looking for a place to rest, to wait for something further. Pieces, unfocused and unassembled, waiting.

Nita's sneakers crunched on the gravel path that led to the student parking lot. Her little red Toyota was one of just three cars left in the vast space. Six hours ago, this was all prime real estate jammed with cars. As she opened the car door, another piece of the dream bubbled up. She was kneeling near some boulders. Actually, beneath some of them. It was more like a cave, a low passage.

She turned the key, and Little Earl coughed into action. Nita patted his steering wheel and thanked him for his loyalty. It was at times like this that she regretted the half-hour drive home. The little stone house in Maryland on an acre of land that bordered Rock Run had seemed like a great idea back in July. Now the drive to Port Deposit from the University of Delaware ate up time she couldn't afford. The only redeeming value was a little bit of sanity away from campus.

As she checked the rearview mirror, she caught another glimpse of herself. The dark eyes, which people talked about as being so beautiful, had big black circles under them. She looked terrible. Her skin was chalky white, and her hair was a disaster. Unfortunately, looks were not deceiving, in this instance. Another night of having to wash underwear in the sink, and then picking through the hamper to decide which pair of jeans was least dirty.

Little Earl must have driven himself most the way home, because suddenly they were pulling through the gap in the low stone wall and into her driveway. She thanked him for his help and dragged her backpack out of the back seat. In her little house Nita carefully avoided looking at the pile of dishes in the kitchen sink. She put her backpack on the desk chair and pushed papers aside on her desk to open a space to work. But after fifteen minutes of staring at the anesthesiology book without any cognitive connection regarding the neural synapses and organ function, she decided to allow herself four hours of sleep with the promise that she'd get up at 5:00 to hit the books before heading back to campus. This was why she didn't like to study at home. Her bed called to her like a Siren luring her onto the rocks where she would crash and burn and flunk out of school.

To save the precious minutes of rooting in the hamper, she decided just to wash what she had on. She flipped off her t-shirt and squirmed out of her jeans. Then she took off her bra and panties and threw them in the sink, where she ran water and poured in some detergent. She looked in the mirror as she scrubbed. She had an ink mark on her face. How long had that been there?

Might as well take a shower now. Naked and next to the tub was as efficient as it was going to get. As she ran the water to get it warm, another bubble of her earlier dream floated by. She was wearing some sort of a hide or fur. It was long, and she had nothing on under it. It was rough, especially against her shoulders and her nipples. And it was baggy. It kept getting in her way as she knelt and…

The bubble drifted away.

The warm shower felt wonderful. She washed her hair twice and let the gentle stream of water run through it. She bent her head forward and hid inside the shiny black strands that hung a foot beyond her face. It was the straight black hair along with the black eyes and high cheekbones that made everyone guess she was American Indian. Actually, that was just a small piece–an eighth Cherokee. Nita got her looks from her mother who was Japanese-American and her long thin body from her father who was mostly of Welsh descent.

Nita was almost asleep when she remembered to change the alarm time to 5:00. That would give her almost three and a half hours of sleep. Better than last night at least.

An obnoxious car advertisement blared her awake in what seemed like a moment after she'd closed her eyes. A man was ranting that you could get a brand new 1987 Ford Taurus for only $11,800. She squinted one eye open and was disappointed to see that it really was morning already. She hit the snooze button for just ten more minutes and turned over. But remnants of another dream, a disturbing click, caught her attention and raised her brain waves enough to pull her awake. Another weird dream. Or was it the same one? Maybe prolonged sleep deprivation did this. She had to keep having small parts of the same dream since she was never asleep long enough to have a whole dream.

CHAPTER TWO

The anesthesiology test dimmed her confidence that she really would make it through the final year of med school. Details on signal transduction to vital organs, material she knew she had studied, hovered out of reach. She would be lucky to have passed the test.

At the end of the day Nita turned down an invitation to attend a birthday party for one of the other med students. "Come on," Paul Alvarez badgered, "just for a few beers. It's Friday. Lighten up."

She just shook her head. "I bombed that test. I just need to go home and die."

"We all bombed it. Why go home and die when you can stay here and party and drown your sorrows? I will write you a script for three Miller Lites. It's an ideal pharmacology solution, along with maybe a few shots of Jack."

"Now that would kill me," Nita laughed.

"Perfect. Why die alone at home?"

Nita's smile faded. "I can't. I wish I could."

Paul ran his fingers through his curly dark hair. He started to say something, then stopped. Finally, he shrugged and offered, "There is more to life, my friend."

Nita shrugged back and mindlessly stroked her hair. Paul was handsome and gregarious, the kind of person she both wished she could be and resented at the same time. She touched his forearm and turned away.

Nita headed home with Little Earl. Halfway there she flipped on the radio and heard the female disc jockey introducing the next song as "Respect" by Aretha Franklin. "It was twenty years ago this year in 1967 that Aretha released this iconic tune, which not only became a big hit for her but also became an anthem for the feminist movement. Now, this year her song is being inducted into the Grammy Hall of Fame. What's more, in January of this year Aretha became the first woman inducted into the Rock & Roll Hall of Fame. She's getting the R-E-S-P-E-C-T she deserves." Nita sang along with Aretha and felt a little uplift. She wondered about the pharmacology of music. It certainly was a powerful force in all cultures.

By 8:00 Nita was dead to the world—at least the current one. She could tell as she lay in bed that tonight would be another busy night. Her head floated slightly, a signal that a click was waiting.

Nita climbed a steep bank among giant boulders. She struggled to keep up with two women who were dressed in leather robes. The older one, who appeared to be in her forties, had long black hair with streaks of silver. The younger was a black-haired teenage girl. The older woman paused as they climbed. "Chee-na-wan, notice this tiny plant with three leaves growing in the crack of the rock. There are others in this area as well. They will flower white in the summer. In the autumn we will return to gather their seeds, which hold special medicine to help with the pain of childbirth."

Pulling themselves up by hanging onto rocks and trunks of trees, they reached the top of the cliff. Nita struggled to catch her breath. She turned and looked out over a wide river, strewn with huge boulders and small islands. The older woman pointed to a long thin island. "After the spring floods, we will take a canoe to that island. There are special roots to gather there. Today, let us gather some gifts from the early greens that sprout up here. Then we must head back since light is still short." She looked to the western sky over the opposite ridge, across the river from where they stood. "We still have a little time," she nodded.

When the two had gathered some leaves from near the precipice, they started walking back away from the cliff, but a call came from below. "Kanianguas, Kanianguas," called a male voice. "Can you come? It is Sarangararo. He has broken his leg."

They hurried back to the edge of the cliff. Halfway up the steep path that they had climbed stood a tall, lean Indian man, who was panting. Apparently, he had run a great distance.

The older woman responded immediately. "Certainly, Shae-e-kah. How bad is it?"

"The bone is sticking through the skin of the lower leg. The others brought him back to the village. He is in great pain, and the wound is bleeding."

"Tell Cantowa to go to my pots of medicines. From the smallest pot she is to take out two pinches of the leaves, being sure not to get any seeds. She is to warm some water and put the pinches into it. Let it stand for twenty heartbeats then give it to Sarangararo to drink."

"Also, near my mat are some pieces of birch bark. Tell her to soak them in water and then strap them around the wounded leg until we arrive. And have the women warm much water."

Shae-e-kah repeated the instructions and nodded his understanding.

"Go, now. Be swift and safe. We will hurry behind you."

Nita watched the man bound down the slope like an antelope and disappear on a path that ran along the river bank.

"We are fortunate to have runners like Shae-e-kah to serve us," Kani said to Chee-na-wan. "This is why we always tell others where we are going in our search for plants. They must be able to find us if the need arises. In coming weeks, we will travel much farther, and our people must know where we can be found. Our people rely upon us, and we must serve them well."

Nita struggled back down the slope behind the other women. The climb up had been grueling, but the slide down was worse. Slick mud between the boulders threatened to toss her headlong down the slope, crashing and bashing into rocks. When they finally reached the base, she paused.

The sun felt warm on Nita's face. She opened her eyes and found the sun streaming in the window of her bedroom. It was so bright it hurt. She flipped over on the bed to look at the clock. It was almost 9:00. She had slept more than twelve hours.

After breakfast, Nita walked out on the small front porch of her cottage. What a delightful morning. Cold, crisp and clear. The sun warmed the yard so that frost only remained in the shade. Minute white crystals on the grass filled in the outline of the cottage where the rays were yet to reach. She listened to the water of Rock Run babble over the many rocks that gave the creek its name. This was why she moved here, she reminded herself. This was the therapy that would allow her to keep her sanity through the final stretch of med school. The stream's gurgle spoke to her in ways her fellow students could not.

Med school. Her stomach tightened at the thought of everything that was piled on her. It was suffocating. Just the current material on metastatic skin cancer was overwhelming, and that was just a small slice of all she needed to know. She was about to head back inside when a bird in a bush by the porch suddenly opened up a cheerful song. She turned and looked as its small brown body with a flipped-up tail trilled amazing notes. Janie would know what kind of bird it was. She got her degree in ornithology.

Janie was like the bird herself, tiny and always chirping about something. Her chirping became annoying the second year they roomed together, and by the end of their sophomore years they agreed to try different arrangements. Nita made a mental note to try to find Janie's phone number. They hadn't talked for almost a year.

For now, Nita decided that she could spare a little time to work the garden, which was off to the left of the porch. She wanted to have the soil ready to plant some lettuce in another few weeks. Right now, the soil looked dry enough to work, and there was no telling when that would happen again. Apparently, the rain that hit the campus last evening had missed the area around Port Deposit.

Fighting back the side of her brain that demanded so much of her, she put on her old blue jeans and a denim jacket and headed to the little shed in back of her house for some tools. She would study later at the laundromat.

To the side of her house was an open area, beyond which were a small stand of trees and then the surging Rock Run. Last summer she had started to clear the weeds for a small garden and had even planted a few things for the fall, but they didn't do well. This year she would dig deeper and expand the plot to make it larger. When she stepped on the heel of her shovel, it broke through a half-inch of frozen crust and then sunk easily into the dark soil. A rich aroma rose to welcome her involvement. She imagined that for ages the river had deposited soil here. The thought reminded her of where she had gone last night.

The big river in her dream was obviously the Susquehanna, which was where Rock Run emptied out another hundred yards down its tumbling path. The crashing brook flowed from a crack in the cliffside up and out of sight on the other side of Susquehanna River Road. The stream was funneled through a pipe under the road and the railroad tracks. Past the tracks it flushed into the wide river, paying its small but timeless tribute to the larger whole.

Rock Run was something of an outer boundary of Port Deposit to the north of the town. Port Deposit—an odd name. She wondered where it had come from. Nita's mind continued to wander as she dug in the garden, turning over the soil from last year and then cutting into the dead weeds that bordered her little patch. Her mind meandered, and her arms worked, until she heard a vehicle pull into the gravel driveway to her house. She walked around to the front to see who might be visiting, since no one ever did. She saw her landlord's gray head coming out of a little red pickup truck, and she walked toward him. "Morning, Nita," he called when he saw her. "I'm going to fix that burner on the stove, if that's okay with you. Shouldn't take long."

"Sure. That's fine, Henry. Thanks."

Henry looked at her with the shovel. "Getting a jump on the season?" he smiled.

"Yeah, I couldn't wait."

"Just like my wife. Bessell loved to go out there and work the soil." He smiled again. "I figure somewhere in heaven, she's digging in some dirt." His smile dimmed a bit, and Nita could see that he missed her. He quickly erased the look and asked what she was planning to plant.

Together they walked back to the side of the house to look at the garden. "Lettuce, probably Black-seeded Simpson. Some spinach. Some onion sets. Sugar Snap Peas – I love Sugar Snaps. What did your wife plant for her spring vegetables?"

"Greens and onions. And radishes. You know what grew well here was potatoes. Bessell used to grow some great potatoes. You gotta dig deep, but it's not too tough since the soil is so rich." He reached down and picked up a handful of the dark brown soil that Nita had turned over. He clamped it into a ball and then bounced the ball in the palm of his hand. It broke into loose clumps. "Yep, perfect tilth to be digging. His eyes drifted out into the trees in the distance. "Bessell used to say, 'You gotta dig till you're wise.'"

Nita watched him move back in time to gone days. Rock Run's song chattered in the background, and a cardinal flew in an undulating ribbon of red into the brush where a few stubborn leaves from the previous year still rattled in the breeze. Henry snapped his head back down and continued as if there had been no pause, "Plus you'll find some treasures."

"Treasures?" Nita wasn't sure if he was kidding her.

"Oh, arrowheads and things like that. Bessell got excited when she'd find things, and I kind of enjoyed it too. In fact, just last night I got out a box of them and was looking at them."

Nita was curious. "You mean you found them here? Right here in the garden?"

"Well sure. This is where the Susquehannocks lived. All up and down the river, mostly upstream, north above the Pennsylvania line, but they used to have a fort about a mile north of here where Octoraro Creek comes down. You pay attention while you're digging, and you'll probably find some. Unless of course Bessell already collected them all," he laughed.

"You like that kind of stuff too?" he asked.

"When I was an undergrad, I took an archeology course and really liked it. I even went on a dig at an Indian camp that they found when they were putting in a shopping center in Delaware. We found some pieces of pottery and arrowheads—projectile points they made us call them—and stuff like that. They were from Lenni Lenape Indians."

Henry nodded. "Well the Susquehannocks lived near the Lenape, but they weren't really related. The experts say the Susquehannocks were related to the Iroquois from farther north, but there is actually very little known about them. Next time I come I'll bring some of the stuff we found." Henry looked down at the soil and again got lost in his thoughts. Finally, he rubbed his balding head and looked at Nita, "Listen, I'll let you go back to your digging, and I'll get going on my project. Nice talking with you."

Henry turned and headed toward the front door. He walked with a slight shuffle, his shoulders rounded forward. He moved slowly kicking lightly at the grass and weeds. When he was almost to the house, he turned back around. "And another little trick. Since you've turned this soil over, come back out here after the next rain. You might find a few things washed off and sitting right on top. You know, arrowheads and the like."

Nita thanked him for the tip and went back to digging the section she was on, keeping a close watch for anything interesting. The search for treasures slowed the process since she was now constantly stopping to pick up each little rock. She thought it would be fun to find something, but she didn't and decided she really needed to get going on her studying. Henry was leaving as she headed into the house to gather up her laundry and books. "Burner's all fixed," he said.

"Great. Thanks. I thought you said you weren't able to find that part you needed."

"Hate to say it, but I got it at that big new store they opened in Aberdeen. It's called Home Depot."

Nita looked confused. "Why is that so bad?"

"My prediction is that in ten years, or certainly by the time the calendar flips to the next century, that kind of store will put a hardware store like where I worked out of business. You can find darn near anything in that place."

Back inside, Nita opened the top drawer of her desk and shuffled through scraps of paper stuffed in front of a tattered brown notebook that constituted her phone book. She found a piece of a Christmas card she had saved with Janie's new phone number and address. She lifted the receiver from the beige phone on the corner of the desk and pressed the buttons to dial. After three rings, she heard Janie's cheerful "Hello."

"Hi, Janie, this is…"

"Nita! I was just thinking about you. In fact, at breakfast I told Frank I was going to call you. How are you, kid? What's up? How's school… Dr. Nita?"

"School's hard, but I guess I am doing okay."

"I'm sure you're doing more than okay, but are you having fun?"

"Well, I wouldn't call it fun exactly."

"Do I need to come down there—wherever the hell it is you moved to—and straighten your ass out? Are you getting any? You're not, are you? You need to get laid."

"I miss you Janie."

"I miss you too."

"Listen, I called about something important. So, what is a little brown bird with a flipped-up tail that chirps really fast?"

"Is this a dirty joke? Good, I need to hear a dirty joke?"

"No, it's not a dirty joke. It's a question for my favorite bird lady. I saw the little guy when I was out working in my garden."

"Kind of chocolate brown on the back and light underneath with a cocked-up tail? No neck."

"Yeah."

"Probably a Carolina wren. If it was singing, it was a male. Same notes over and over—like most males," she laughed. "He's a horny little guy. Always wants to climb on a female, like most males," she laughed again.

When Nita asked how married life was treating her, Janie shared that she and Frank were trying to get pregnant, but it wasn't working. "After all those years of trying not to get pregnant, now I find that I can't. We're looking into going to an infertility specialist, but it's really expensive. Hey, why don't you become that kind of a doctor, then you can help me get knocked up?"

"Actually, infertility is a big, emerging field. Lots of stuff happening in endocrinology and in vitro fertilization. I just went to a special lecture on it. In fact, the lecturer was a doctor from right there in Pittsburgh."

"Really? What was his name?"

"Dr. Samuel Archer."

"Yeah, there was an article in paper about him. The problem is that it can cost tens of thousands of dollars, and there is no guarantee that it will work. That's why I need you to be that kind of a specialist."

Nita sighed, "The sad thing is that I don't even know that I want to be a doctor anymore."

"What?! Are you kidding me? After all the work you put into this? It's your dream, Nita. You can't stop now. What's wrong?"

"Well probably the most frustrating part is that this whole thing isn't taking me to where I want to be going. Turns out med school is more about technology than about healing. Each year I've imagined that soon the caring part would start, but here I am in my final year and I have yet to see it."

"That can't be right."

"Even worse, at a couple points instructors have actually said you should avoid caring—don't get tied in with the patient. You need to be objective, they say."

"They really said that?"

"Maybe med school wasn't the right choice for me. Maybe nursing would have been a smarter option. Sometimes I think the nurses have it best because they get to actually care for the patients while the docs just bounce through on the surface. Maybe I was wrong when I thought that being a doctor was the real heart of healthcare. I thought that was how you could make a difference. I don't know, maybe I'm just exhausted," Nita let out a deep sigh. "I don't know, maybe the caring comes later. I just don't know when."

"Holy shit, Nita, you sound really depressed. I know you. You can do this. You've always wanted to be a doctor. You're making it happen. Really, kid. You gotta hang in there."

"I'm sorry. I didn't call you just to whine. Plus, it's the anniversary of my dad's death. That doesn't help."

"Yeah, I remember that you always circled February 21 on the calendar. How old were you when he died?"

"I was five. He was just thirty-five. I had no idea what an aneurysm was or how that could kill someone who was so healthy. Now I understand it only too well," Nita paused. "I'm sorry. I'm whining even more. Guess you're really glad I called to brighten up your day."

"Hey, you can call me anytime you want, whether it's to whine or just to find out the name of a horny little boy bird. Remember, I have a degree in hornithology."

Janie giggled at her own joke, and Nita laughed with her. "Janie, you can always make me laugh."

"It's the best medicine, as they say. Just what the bird doctor ordered."

When they hung up, Nita went to her closet and got out a shoe box full of photos. She flipped through them until she found one of her and Janie with giant beer mugs at an Octoberfest party. She propped up the picture on her nightstand.

CHAPTER THREE

At the bustling Port Deposit Laundry Basket, Nita managed to get one washing machine and a chair near it. She quickly immersed herself in the pathology of the skin, tuning out the fussing children, gossiping women and Teenage Mutant Ninja Turtles cartoon on the TV that hung from the wall in the corner. Nita worked to grasp the differences at the cellular level between seborrhea, psoriasis, and eczema, while monitoring for another washer to come free for her whites. When it did, she stuffed a large assortment into its mouth. Upon returning to her chair, she found a guy in greasy blue jeans staring down at her book. He looked over at her as she walked up. "Yer a pretty thing to be looking at such ugly pictures." His dark eyes nodded toward a photo on the cover of the book of small pox on an Asian man.

"Studying," she said as she picked up the book and sat down.

The man, who was wearing a black Harley-Davidson t-shirt, continued to stand at the chair facing her with his grease-stained blue jeans too close to her knees. Nita squirmed inside but calmly opened the book. She retrieved her Hi-liter from the crease in the book and used it to point to a section she was not actually reading.

"Studying what?"

"Pathologies of the skin."

"What's that?"

Nita looked up at the man. His mouth hung open revealing a line of yellowed teeth with one top incisor missing. He had a large uneven scar down the left side of his face. "Skin disease."

"You a nurse?"

"No."

"I mean you studyin' to be?"

"No."

"Then what?"

"Med school."

"Well shit. You wanna go get a beer?"

"Nope. I need to study so that the next time you lose a fight there will be someone in the ER to stitch you up." Nita smiled an insincere grin.

The man's confused eyes looked at her, trying to assess whether he had been insulted and if so what to do with it.

"And by the way," Nita added, "you better get that cut on your arm looked at. It's infected. That red line running up from it is a very bad sign."

The man looked at her a moment longer, then looked at the two-inch cut on the inside of his right forearm. He touched its puffy red surface and winced.

"Told ya," Nita snarled. "Now I need to study." She tilted her head down toward the book but actually watched the black motorcycle boots that remained next to her white Nike's. Out of the top of her eyes she could see only the man's right hand, which indicated his left was probably still probing the wound. "Dumb shit," she muttered.

"Huh?"

She looked up, moving her insincere stare to his stubbly chin and crooked nose. "Oh, I'm sorry, are you still here?"

The guy gave her a look that said she was within one comment of getting smacked, and if she had been a guy, it would already have happened. "Thank God your mother taught you something," she smiled.

"What?" the man squinted at her, his left eye drooping a little lower than the right, by virtue of the ragged scar that extended above it.

"I said that if you don't mind, I am trying to study." She cocked her head to the side and gave him a look that wondered, just short of being out loud, "Why aren't you getting this?" It was a look she was sure he had seen often, at least since the first grade.

The left side of his upper lip lifted, and his squint narrowed further. People seated and standing near them sensed conflict rising and the buzz of conversation rapidly dropped off. The man's right hand twitched.

A large woman with curly blond hair stepped over to them and inserted herself between Nita and the biker. A little girl clung to the woman's gray sweat pants. The mother looked at Nita, then looked at the man and sniffled as if to keep a running nose from dripping. She looked again at Nita and said, "Can I borrow some of your Tide?" She pointed to the yellow and orange box of detergent sitting next to Nita's chair.

"Sure," Nita reached down and handed her the brightly colored carton. "Measuring cup's in the box."

"Can you show me how much you use?" The woman handed the box back to Nita, then she turned to the man and said, "You'll excuse us, won't you."

When Nita and the woman got to the woman's washer, there was a full box of Bold detergent sitting on it, and the washer was already running. The woman winked at Nita and said, "I just didn't want you to bust him up and get blood all over everything. You know them blood stains can be hard to get out. Bold works though, if you ever need to borrow some." The woman winked again and smiled, then nodded slightly to her left as the biker went over to check on his washer, which was apparently done because he was pulling black t-shirts and blue jeans from it and shoving them in a mesh bag.

"Ain't seen you in here before," the woman said to Nita.

"I guess I don't wash my clothes enough," Nita said with a laugh. "Actually, I usually come late in the evening, when it isn't so crowded."

"Sounds nice, but this is our one time when we can come do our worsh, isn't it Kitten?" She tussled the blond curls of the little girl who was still clinging to her sweat pants.

The little girl looked up and smiled. She was missing the same tooth as the biker.

Nita set her yellow plastic laundry basket on the ground next to Little Earl and opened his trunk. She paused to look north up Main Street at the odd configuration that was the core of the town. Houses, many of them more than 150 years old, stood shoulder-to-shoulder along undulating sidewalks like old soldiers lined up for a muster they could no longer pass. Porches, contorted with arthritis, clung to downspouts that leaned like rifles about to be dropped. A rusty pickup truck wove toward her through the pot-holed street.

Port Deposit was sprinkled heavily with a lower-class white population of mostly underemployed people who had settled into a comfortable relationship with that lot in life. It was also peppered with black people who seemed to mingle seamlessly with the whites. Segregated at the south end of town was an assortment of wealthy people buying into a strip of real estate that had the potential to become the next hot spot developing along the Chesapeake Bay and its tributaries. Port Deposit's setting along the lower Susquehanna River just above the place where the wide water sprawls into the Chesapeake Bay made it a desirable location for the boating set. Holding Port Deposit back from becoming the next St. Michaels, though, was the lack of flood control. Nita had already experienced it once. Certain houses and lots, which were well known to long-time residents, were periodically inundated by the muddy waters of the Susquehanna. Quietly and relentlessly the river would spread beyond its assumed boundaries. The water, carrying a wide range of debris, slipped up the sloping riverbank, over the railroad tracks and climbed onto Main Street. From there it journeyed at will into the basements of long-suffering row houses on the west side of the street where it might remain for hours or days then leave behind a slimy and slippery residue of mud on everything it had touched.

On the east side of the street sat similar row houses interspersed with churches and larger homes, all nestled up against the granite cliff that jutted steeply up hundreds of feet above the river. Also on the east side were businesses such as the laundromat and some diners. Down on the southern end of Main Street, where more of the boating set had infiltrated, there were some antique shops and nicer restaurants. American flags sprouted from almost every home, north and south, west and east, as if the flag was an indigenous flower of the area.

On Sunday, Nita's plans for going to Mass and doing some gardening in the interest of her mental health were washed out by a steady rain.

While her coffee pot brewed, she chided herself for again skipping church. Instead she put in a productive day of studying.

By Monday Nita was feeling a little better than the week before. Just catching up on some studying, sleep and laundry seemed to give her a renewed feeling that she could actually get through the semester and graduate. She even allowed herself to eat lunch with some of her classmates. Normally if she ate lunch at all, it was with a book not a person. When two of the guys waved to her in the cafeteria and pointed to an empty chair at their table, she smiled and joined them.

"You missed a good party Friday," Patrick Atkins told her. He was a muscular student who was totally committed to becoming an orthopedic surgeon. Nita envied his focus.

"Really? Who all went?"

Paul Alvarez answered, "Actually there were probably twelve from our class, but lots of other friends of Bill's." Paul seemed to function as the informal social director of the class and was a frequent companion of Patrick. "It was a good crowd, but pretty rowdy."

"Rowdy? I guess I only see the people here when they're in student mode."

Paul laughed. "Yeah, well you should have seen Sarah Mellis dancing on the kitchen table, then."

"No way. Sarah seems like the most conservative and serious person there is." Nita thought Sarah was the prettiest woman in the class. She dressed sharply, often sporting a colorful dress that flattered her figure but with a modesty that enhanced her attractiveness.

"During the day she may be tame, but at night she turns out to be an awesome dancer," Patrick said. For less than a moment Nita thought she would have liked to see Sarah dancing, wondering what she was wearing, but she quickly pushed the thought away.

"At least until she fell off the table," Paul chuckled. He picked up his hamburger and moved it in an arc toward the floor.

"No way!" Nita laughed in disbelief.

"Ask Patrick. He's the one who caught her."

Nita looked at Patrick for his comment.

"Right place at the right time," he pretended to lunge for Paul's hamburger.

Paul grabbed his burger away from Patrick. "Seriously, she would have been hurt if Pat hadn't been there."

"Sounds like I missed a good time."

"Well there will a party at my place in three weeks," Paul said. "You need to be there."

"I'll try."

"Try?"

"Okay, I'll be there," Nita said.

"Great."

"Probably," Nita added.

"No 'probably' about it. I'm gonna hold you to it."

That evening Nita stayed in the library until it closed at midnight. She congratulated herself on staying awake the whole time, and even said goodnight to the librarian who had given her a wake-up call the last time. When she got home, she washed her breakfast dishes and straightened up her desk. She resolved to try to stay on top of things and maybe even dress a little nicer.

Nita dropped abruptly to sleep and quickly found herself back with Kanianguas, who was unwrapping the bark that had been applied as a temporary bandage around the broken leg of the young Indian man. When she took off the first leather strap, Sarangararo asked for it. He put the thick band in his mouth and bit down hard. Kani noted it carefully. She leaned to Chee-na-wan and advised her that it was particularly important with the young warriors to observe carefully how much pain they are in. "They will try never to show it. You will hear no sound from Sarangararo."

Kani finished unwrapping the leg and revealed the tibia jutting out the front of the leg about halfway up the shin. The wound oozed blood onto an area of skin where more had already coagulated. Nita looked at the young man who lay on the woven mat. He was about her age and remarkably tall. She estimated him to be almost six and a half feet tall. He was extremely muscular and very handsome. Clearly, he had almost no body fat. She checked herself as she realized her thoughts were probably not appropriate for a medical professional. She shuddered to think what brutality was about to occur to this young man. She figured the chance of saving the leg was slight and that he might even die of infection.

Kani went to the wall of the long narrow building Nita now realized they were in. There were many other Indians in the space. Most were tall and lean. They each wore leather clothing with a leather necklace displaying some decoration, often large claws or teeth. There was no expression on any of their faces. Dark eyes peered calmly from above high cheekbones. She couldn't decide whether to call them fierce or solemn.

Kani called Chee-na-wan to her side apart from the others, and Nita followed. Kani explained that they must first deal with the pain. She barked an order to two young men standing near the arched doorway, and instantly they darted outside. She then continued to explain to Chee-na-wan what they would be doing.

"We can certainly fix the broken leg, and it will be like new," she said as she selected leaves and other plant materials from various leather bags and clay pots. "Of bigger concern is to watch Sarangararo so that his spirit stays with him." Nita was still wondering at her extreme level of confidence in what would be a fairly complex surgery, when she realized that Kani was explaining the risks of having the patient go into shock. Kani told Chee-na-wan how

they would monitor his spirit, which obviously meant his vital signs but perhaps there was more than that.

The two men who had run out returned carrying a large clay pot with steam rising from it. Kani instructed them to set it near Sarangararo and then commanded them and the others to stand back from him.

Kani knelt by his side and grasped his large hand and thick brown forearm. She spoke to him quietly and calmly. He nodded when she was finished and opened his mouth. She removed the leather strap and accepted a small earthen cup from Chee-na-wan.

Kani called a man standing near to help her lift and support Sarangararo's shoulders as he drank from the cup.

When he had drained the liquid, she gave him a piece of root to bite on. They laid him back on the mat, and she touched his eyes to close them.

Kani went back to the wall and slid out a stone that looked like a flattened football with an indentation in the center. She took small seeds from a clay bowl on a shelf and placed them in the indentation. When she picked up a long, thin stone with a rounded end, Nita realized that this was a mortar and pestle. Kani seemed to speak to the seeds as she slowly pulverized them into a tan powder.

Kani tilted the rock and poured the powder into Chee-na-wan's hand. Together they moved to Sarangararo's injured leg and knelt down. Kani spoke to him, and he did not respond. She touched the wound lightly, and he still did not react. She nodded to Chee-na-wan, signaling that they were ready.

Kani dipped what looked like deer hide into the pot of hot water and gently cleaned the area of the wound, including the protruding bone. She then sprinkled the tan powder on the area. She looked around the room at the observers. She selected one particular man and one woman to assist her. With the man providing tension by pulling on Sarangararo's foot and the woman stabilizing the leg, Kani manipulated the bone back into place, actually reaching her fingers inside to assure the fit was exact. When she was satisfied, she *closed the skin over the wound. She wiped her bloody fingers on a separate moistened deer hide.*

Another command from Kani sent a young woman scurrying from the room. Nita went with Chee-na-wan to the side of the long house to get what looked like a sliver of animal bone as a needle and gut as thread from a woven basket. The materials were not unlike what Nita had used in training for suturing wounds. Kani stitched the wound with great skill, lacing through the perimeter skin and pulling it tight. She instructed Chee-na-wan in the final cleaning of the leg. As she finished, the young woman she had sent out returned with a bowl. When Kani dipped her fingers in, Nita realized it was honey, which Kani carefully smoothed over the wound. Together Kani and Chee-na-wan took birch bark from a water trough and worked it to create a cast, which they form-fitted to the leg and strapped on with hide. When they finished, they said what seemed like a prayer.

As they cleaned up their materials, those who had been watching came to Kani and thanked her for skills. In response to each comment, Kani acknowledged the spirits and that she was pleased and honored to be responsible for something as important as their health. To this they each replied, "Long Life."

Nita gathered from people's comments that Sarangararo was actually the son of the chief, Harignera. She also learned that the chief was not there. He was off in some sort of negotiations, which seemed to be a point of controversy. She listened to conversations among those in the room, and the words became more heated. Some in the group objected to selling more of their land to the white settlers. Others valued what the transactions brought them, especially guns and rum. Nita saw that Kani was becoming increasingly agitated by the discussions. She sat beside Sarangararo, periodically touching his face and speaking to him. He was beginning to stir slightly from the anesthesia. Kani pointed out to Chee-na-wan, "We cannot heal a wound unless we touch the spirit. Our spirits connect first through our fingers."

Chee-na-wan sat beside her, taking in all the surrounding conversation as well as Kani's handling of the patient. Suddenly, Kani rose and with a sharp word, silenced the gathering. "The spirits of our ancestors are in this land. The good and generous spirits of the trees and rocks and water are all we need for happiness. Guns and rum are evil spirits. They destroy what is good."

A young man in the group began to argue with her, but an elderly woman cut him off and sent him outside.

Nita watched the stress crack over Kani's face. Kani wished she had not had this outburst. Others too saw the reaction. Most slipped quietly out of the long house. One older man stayed and came to Kani. He told her that Sarangararo and some other young men had been drinking rum earlier in the day and were then wrestling on the large rocks above the village. "Kanianguas, that is how Sarangararo broke his leg."

Kani nodded and said she knew. She could smell the rum on his breath. She said that this was not the first injury she had treated since rum had arrived. Her bigger concern was what it did to the spirit. "Cousin," she said, "I can heal the body if the spirit stays whole and healthy." She squatted down and traced three concentric circles in the dust of the floor of the long house. "We must guard the spirit of our people and our land, or all will be lost. Do you believe this?"

"I do," her cousin nodded, "but I fear that many are being blinded by the wonderful blankets and tools and bells and glass. I am worried."

"Today will be cloudy with a chance of ..." It took Nita a moment to realize that her clock-radio had come on. "Showers will become heavy late in the day." A cloud of concern for the plight of the Indians lingered over Nita. She knew well what eventually happened to many tribes. Part of her angst involved the healing arts that were lost in the process of the white settlers overrunning the Indians and their lands.

CHAPTER FOUR

Nita usually enjoyed the times they got to go to the hospital. Despite the overabundance of steely fluorescent light and the smell of disinfectant, she tried to find the warmth in patient interaction. It made all the theoretical information in the books and lectures real. Finally, in the fourth year, the students could pick clinical rotations they might like. Nita settled on orthopedics, but she wasn't sure it was where she wanted to end up.

Every time Nita was on the ortho floor, her mind went back to the wrenching days when she was eight. She wanted to be like Dr. Clark who cared so much that he even cried with her when her sister died. He cared for Carly, really cared. Carly was six when the accident occurred. The police said their mother was at fault for rolling through the stop sign, but her mother said the man in the pickup truck had been drinking. Nita struggled to try to forgive her mother for the accident and for never really being her mother again. Her mother had been badly injured in the wreck, and when she died ten years later, the doctors said it was partly due to the accident. During high school, Nita sometimes wished she had been in the car too so she could have died when Carly did. Now she still had terrible memories from that time, especially related to hospitals and her mother's slow decline. She hated all the time she had to spend in those horrid places, yet now she was working so she could spend much of her life in the hospitals. Some days it made sense, and some days it made no sense with the recollections almost too much to bear. During those times, she forced herself to focus on the present. Certainly, there was plenty to focus on.

The docs who escorted med students around often made it look easy, but it was clear how interwoven and complex all the issues became. It wasn't just that the patient had a specific illness or injury. There were always other factors. Did they smoke? Were they overweight? How was the patient's mental health? This was the challenge Nita loved. How do you sort through all of that to make the right diagnosis and develop the right treatment plan? Then you have to factor in other aspects such as family support and, of course, the all-powerful insurance companies and what they will be willing to pay for. How do you integrate all that?

She also was intrigued by the differences among the docs. Some tried sincerely and creatively to reach out to the patients, to really touch them, like Dr. Clark did with Carly. Others were so lacking in bedside manner that the patients seemed to be mainly a means to status and money. Last week they had gone with Dr. Charles Baines, who talked more about himself than his patients. Instead of attempting to instruct the students about the medical conditions they were seeing, he talked of his possessions. "All of this makes possible my short office hours on Friday when I can zip in my 'Vette down to Tilghman Island on the bay and cruise out on the water with a drink in my hand. You work hard," he said, "and you can have all of that. If a kid who grew up in a rough part of Baltimore can live like this, you can too." Nita looked at the middle-aged woman lying pale in bed who had been informed that morning that she had bone cancer in her jaw. A tear trickled from the woman's eye as she watched the doctor.

When they parted ways with Dr. Baines and were on the elevator, one of her classmates suggested that instead of Dr. Baines' specialty being Ear, Nose and Throat it was actually Car, Clothes and Boat. All laughed, but Megan Connelly chimed in that certainly money was one of the benefits. "I mean face it—one of the reasons we're all here is for what being a doctor can get you. Who wouldn't want his lifestyle?" Nita looked at her as they stepped off the elevator but did not comment. Instead, she wondered what part of her own desire to be a doctor was really the status piece. Certainly, the doctors had more power than anyone else in the hospital. Her intentions were to use that power for the patients. But there was a nagging worry that she, too, would be worn down and ultimately corrupted so that it would become a money and status thing.

The following day they were with Dr. Pamela O'Neill. She was not particularly warm with the patients but nonetheless showed caring, if only in her eye contact and how she listened. Her specialty was geriatric orthopedics. When Nita mentioned to Dr. O'Neill that she found her specialty particularly interesting, Dr. O'Neill paid extra attention. "Understand," Dr. O'Neil explained to Nita as they walked down the hall to see the next patient, "that mobility is everything. Hips and knees are not just conveniences. They are independence, and they are the fork in the road between viability and decline." She explained that the next patient was ninety years old and that she had had to fight with the insurance company over whether a hip replacement was really called for "at his age." Dr. O'Neill used her fingers to emphasize their point with quotation marks.

"Elmer is a wonderful man with a remarkably active life. He goes dancing twice a week and works at a food pantry two other days. If you had an antique car, like my brother has a '34 Ford, you'd think nothing of replacing parts. No one ever questions my brother when he spends money keeping that old car in good condition. With humans, though, apparently when we get old, we aren't worth the investment."

In the room, Nita found that Elmer was everything Dr. O had said and more. First, he wanted to know the names of each of the five students, who were all dressed in white lab coats, and proceeded to use their names in the conversation. Next, he was challenging Dr. O to speed up the rehabilitation period. "There are lots of ladies out there crying their eyes out because I'm not there to dance with them. Have a heart, Dr. O, the ladies need me."

Elmer winked at Dr. O'Neill. "Do you dance?"

She smiled and replied, "I think if I tried, then I'd be the one needing a new hip." Nita had never considered too much about Dr. O'Neill beyond her medical skills. She looked to be about forty, a gaunt woman with wiry red hair. Elmer pushed the issue with her. "Oh, don't worry that you're too old to learn, doc. I can teach you. It's good for what ails you," he winked. He turned to Nita, the only other female in the group, "How about you, Nita? You dance?"

Dr. O'Neill stepped toward Elmer and held up her hand. "Down, boy," she chuckled.

He then turned to one of the male students, "Okay, Tom, here's your assignment. You got to liven this group up. A positive attitude is the whole trick. You got to have fun. As soon as Dr. O here lets me kick that damn walker out of the picture, I'm going to show you folks how to do it. Did you ever try the Texas Two-step? Every day you need to do something a little out of your ordinary. I can tell from right here that you're all chewing up precious days by being too serious. So, your prescription," Elmer beckoned to whole group, "is that before the sun sets, do just a little something you don't usually do. Then write in your notebook how it made you feel."

The warm glow imparted by Elmer stayed with Nita throughout the day. She found it ironic that he saw the need to heal the healers. And he did it. When she finished her afternoon classes and went outside, it was raining. A cold wind pressed on her blue denim jacket, and the rain stung her face. One part of her said to just go get Little Earl and head home. But her other self grabbed her by the backpack and pulled her toward the library. She couldn't risk going home and falling asleep when she had so much to learn. Of course, there was no assurance that she'd be safe from the tormenting dreams, even in the library. Plus, there was the added risk of irritating the librarian.

Before heading to the library, she decided that a cup of coffee would boost her enthusiasm for studying. Coming through the line in the cafeteria she grabbed a honey-nut muffin as a toast to Elmer. A little something she didn't usually do. With her mug of coffee and muffin on her tray, she looked for an open table. She wandered around looking without success, and finally asked a young man who was seated alone and reading if she could use the other chair. He nodded and kept on reading.

Nita slung her backpack off her shoulder and pulled out her neurology book. While picking on her muffin and sipping her coffee, she reviewed the role of acetylcholine in synapses.

"Neuro?" said the young man.

"Yeah. Interesting but tough."

"Med student?"

"Yeah. You?"

"Grad student in neurophysiology."

"Wanna take my test for me?"

"Not sure I could pass for you." His dark eyes and straight black hair actually were similar to hers.

"Hmmm, guess not. What's your name?"

"Doug," he reached his hand across the table toward her to shake.

"Nita," she took his hand.

"Yeah, I'm not sure I would pass for a Nita."

Nita feared getting dragged into a conversation. She wanted to look at her watch, aware that she was wasting precious time. Then she recalled Elmer's use of the word "precious" to describe how they wasted their days by being too serious. She decided that he would be proud of her doing two things unusual, eating a muffin and chatting aimlessly with a stranger. She gave herself permission to linger a little longer.

"Hello, Nita," Doug waved his hand in front of her face. "If you went away, you left some parts here."

"Oh, I'm sorry. I was just worrying about my test."

"Yeah, I know the feeling. I lose sleep pretty much every night worrying about all the work I have to do. The irony is that my research is on the neurophysiology of dreaming. Kind of sad that I don't even get to do much dreaming myself," he shrugged.

"Sort of like all the med students who make themselves sick trying to become doctors and heal other people."

"Exactly."

"Your research sounds interesting, though."

"Yeah, but forget it," he held up his hand to stop what he knew was coming "I can't tell you what your dreams mean. Everyone wonders that. Even my mother. She asks, 'So what good is it?' She tells her friends that I am going to be a doctor but not the kind that helps people."

Nita laughed. "You don't have a class in dream symbolism?"

"You sound like my mother."

Nita laughed again, and put the last piece of muffin in her mouth. "You must think about it, though."

"Sure. That's why I was excited about the research being done in my department. So much goes on in the dream state, yet we know so little about it."

Nita finished her coffee and closed her book. "So, I can't talk you into taking my test on the biochemistry of signal transmission?"

"Sorry, but I will brush up on dreamology so next time I run into you I'll interpret your dreams for you."

"Sounds scary."

"What, running into me again or learning what your dreams mean?"

"The latter," Nita smiled as she stood. "Thanks for sharing your table with me."

"My pleasure. This is my usual spot, so stop by anytime. I also read palms and Tarot Cards." Doug stood to shake her hand, and Nita realized that he was about an inch shorter than she was, maybe five feet, five inches tall. On the walk to the library, she silently thanked Elmer for pushing her toward simple joys. Her conversation with Doug was fun.

When Nita finally left the library, she walked out into a cold, dreary world. Her shoes squeaked on the sidewalks as she sloshed through the residue of what obviously had been heavy rains. At the crosswalk by the student center, the traffic light reflecting in the wet, black roadway looked like a blood red streak stretching halfway down the block. A single car came through the cross street leaving in its wake a spray that splattered the blood into the air.

Nita crossed against the light.

By the end of the week, Nita was dragging almost as badly as the previous Friday. Although she had indicated she would go out for beer with some of her classmates, when the last lecture ended, she begged off. Her brain felt like it was out of kilter and certainly not ready for socializing. She had gotten a little more sleep than usual during the week, but she was tormented by the strange dreams. Or maybe it was more accurate to say tormented by pieces of the same dream.

As she pulled into her driveway, she realized that she had again missed most of the trip home. Little Earl had done the driving himself.

Now his lights shone on the stone side of her house. She wondered how old the house was. Henry would know. It was a stone cottage, an enchanting little place with fieldstone all around its single story. The thick wood of the front door made her think the dwelling was pretty old. The shed out back might have been a carriage house at some point. In the dark distance she could hear the waters of the Susquehanna surging by, carrying the week's rains from far up in Pennsylvania. Rock Run added its voice to the chorus.

The interior of her house looked like a flood had just receded, leaving debris everywhere. It resembled her life. The week was over, but more problems were piled up. Her nerves were frayed from the pressures of a paper on brain chemistry she hadn't even started to write but that was due on Wednesday and then there was a pediatric oncology test Thursday. Deep down, Nita knew she didn't have what it takes to get through med school. She was faking it, and she knew the cracks were starting to show. She wasn't the smart student she pretended to be. The end of the charade is near, she admitted.

Nita forced herself to do the dishes and straighten up the kitchen, but her mind departed while her hands and arms performed the tasks. She found herself standing, staring at the kitchen window, but with the darkness outside, the window served as a mirror that forced her to look back inside. Staring at the truth was staring into an abyss, gazing into the bottomless fears of her inabilities. By 9:00 she couldn't hang on anymore. There was every reason to go to bed and no reason not to.

CHAPTER FIVE

Kani spoke directly into Nita. "You must respect these young trees. They give their lives for our health. Just as we respect the plants that give us medicine, we thank these for their sacrifice." Kani dug a small pit next to a sapling and placed a handful of brown material into the hole from a pouch around her waist. "Tobacco is the symbol of appreciation and balance."

Kani explained the importance of a positive attitude in all healing. "We consciously work to maintain hope in the person who is ill or injured. It is also critical that the healer believe. Truly there will be doubts, but we must trust in ourselves or no one else will. And beyond that, those who surround the ailing person must also remain positive. Spirits and healing travel together, in either good directions or bad." After she covered the hole containing the tobacco, she drew a stone hatchet from her waistband, and with just a few skilled strokes felled the small tree.

Chee-na-wan caught the falling tree as it came down and held it steady as Kani swiftly used the hatchet to eliminate all the branches. Chee-na-wan placed it with others like it.

"That will be enough. One pole for each of the twelve levels of heaven."

Kani and Chee-na-wan buried the bottoms of the long sapling trunks in holes in a circle and bent them, lashing the tops together. This was apparently going to be some sort of hut. But it was not in the village. At a distance down by the river, Nita could see the palisade that surrounded the busy cluster of long houses and huts. The gate was open and people moved in and out.

"Building a sweat lodge is a special honor," Kani instructed Chee-na-wan. "You must learn the exact way so that it works well, both in how it creates heat and also in how it aligns with the spirits. It must honor the creator through fire."

"What is wrong with the people of the east long house?" Chee-na-wan asked.

"Some say it is the bad spirits that have come to those families because they talk loudly about wanting to trade more land. Perhaps that is true. I have given them our best medicine, but it was not able to cool their fevers as it usually does. Some of them have now begun vomiting."

"If your strongest medicines do not work on them, does that mean it is an illness of the spirit?"

"That is my fear. Their bodies hurt from within, and the fire burns throughout. Even the young and strong lie on their mats in pain."

"Will the sweat lodge work against the evil spirits?"

"It is our next hope. It is not our last hope, but I do not want to have to resort to that."

"What?"

In Kani's eyes there was a brief flicker of fear that she quickly hid by looking away. "Here, lash this hide across the poles."

They each held an end of a tanned hide and used a fibrous cord to secure it. Soon the coverings were all in place, with one hide forming a flap that opened.

"The opening must face north or south."

As they built a fire in the center of the lodge Kani said, "We must use twelve logs for the fire."

Chee-na-wan persisted. "Kanianguas, if the sweat lodge does not heal them, what else can we do? You mentioned something that you did not want to do. What is that?"

Kanianguas' eyes narrowed to slits. Her gaze moved from Chee-na-wan to a space far away. "There is a man who has powerful medicine. Powerful, but dangerous. The man himself is dangerous. Tong-quas is his name. He can kill animals with his eyes alone. They say he has killed men too with them."

Kanianguas repeated, "There is great danger and great power. He is a large rock that is balanced on the edge of the cliff."

Chee-na-wan's black eyes were wide in awe. "Do you know him? Have you met him?"

Kanianguas nodded. "I know him. Too well perhaps. I knew him when his name was Wa-a-shen, before he was Tong-quas." The look in Kani's eyes struck dread into Nita. Her heart thumped in her chest.

Nita kicked back the blankets on the bed. Her pajamas were soaked with sweat, and her pulse was pounding. She looked at the clock and saw it was just midnight. She rolled over, afraid to sleep, then turned the other way afraid not to. She reached for the lamp, but her fingers wouldn't turn it on. She looked up toward the window, but darkness was pouring in.

The wind blew Nita's long black hair as she followed Kanianguas down the slippery bank to the edge of the wide river. Nita looked around but did not see Chee-na-wan. Large round rocks were strewn along the riverbank and out into the water. Kani pulled a canoe from where it had been lodged in some bushes near the river's edge. She motioned for Nita to grab the opposite end, and together they carried the remarkably light craft to the water where Kani pulled it in behind her. When it was all the way in, Kani moved to its side, keeping a firm grip. She signaled for Nita to get in at the front of the canoe. When Nita hesitated, Kani said, "Move boldly into the trial. Stride with the grace of the doe into the storm."

The cold water stung Nita's legs as she moved into the river. She slipped and shuffled on the rocky and slippery bottom until she was near Kani. With some difficulty Nita lifted one leg into the unstable craft. More tumbling than stepping, she lifted her other leg into the canoe. Swiftly Kani pulled the canoe deeper until she was behind Nita and then slipped gently on board. From the bottom of the canoe, she retrieved two paddles handing one to Nita and keeping the other for herself. With a powerful stroke Kani launched them out into the river. Nita knelt in the bottom of the canoe like Kani. She could feel the rough bark of the outer covering through her wet blue jeans. Across shallow water by the shore, they glided until they were in a deeper channel and Nita could no longer see the rocky bottom. They were aiming toward an island slightly upstream from where they had put in. Nita attempted to help paddle with what technique she could remember from Girl Scouts, but her strokes seemed to splash and slurp more than propel. Kani provided most of the propulsion with such smooth entry and exit that the water surface was sliced as if by a scalpel.

As they neared the island from the east, Nita observed that it was long and narrow with some trees and brush. To their right at the north end of the island, the water of the river parted to go around it. Perhaps a hundred yards downstream, the waters rejoined at the south end.

Kani slowed the canoe as they approached the shore, steering it carefully to a small sandy area about halfway along the island's length. With a slight scraping sound, the canoe came to a halt on the little beach. Kani bounced out and held the boat steady as Nita clumsily managed to get out. With each woman lifting an end, they carried it completely out of the current. They continued up the slight slope until they rested at a large log, the remnant of a tree that had fallen victim to a long-ago flood. Its naked trunk and stubs of arms lay headless among the rocks of the shore. After a minute, Kani again took the front of the canoe and pointed to the back for Nita. They lifted it over the log and carried it well into the middle of the slender island. Kani used leather thongs that she pulled from the pouch on her back and bound the canoe securely to some trees.

When Kani was convinced the canoe was tightly tied, she led Nita back to the water's edge where they had landed. Nita shadowed Kani down the eastern side of the island until they reached the southern tip, which was a clutter of rocks that jutted out to where the channels from the two sides of the island rejoined. Kani and Nita stood looking out into the expanse of water flowing away from them. On each side of the broad river the land rose sharply for a hundred feet, giving the river tree-covered shoulders. Above the dark green shoulders were somber gray brows of clouds that reached from one side of the river to the other. The clouds were riding on a stiff wind up the river toward them. Different layers were traveling at different speeds, which caused a disorienting vertigo feeling. The angry lower layer of the gloom reached its fists down toward the counterflow of water surging down the river. Nita thought she heard thunder moan in the distance.

Trees on the island and the banks of the river turned their leaves silver sides up, and the winds whipped them into a frenzy. Nita's eyes followed the banks down the river until the shoulders faded into the distant mists. Thunder rumbled, and the dim daylight darkened even more.

Kani began searching among the trees for something. She periodically picked up a stick and then discarded it. Eventually she found one that seemed to satisfy her and then another to match it. Each was about four feet long, slightly bowed and thick as her forearm. Taking the hatchet from her waistband, she cleared each stick of any side branches. She then handed one of the sticks to Nita and led her to the point just in front of where the first trees stood on the southern tip of the island.

The growling thunder seemed to object to their presence, and the clouds began to spit at them. Kani stood on the rocks with her legs wide apart, glaring up in defiance at the menacing sky. A sheet of rain whipped across her face. Kani spat back at the heavens and turned her back, ignoring the response of the thunder that rolled up the river valley and straight up her back. Kani examined the trees that faced the river and selected two oaks adjacent to each other. Both trees were tall and thin and lacked branches on the bottom eight feet. They tilted a few degrees backward from the pressure of the wind, but they held their ground. Kani leaned her stick against one tree and moved a flat rock to the base of the tree on the side facing toward the wide water, now bristling with white caps along its surface. She carried a similar rock to the base of the other tree and seated it firmly.

Suddenly she turned to Nita and said, "Achonhaessti—woman must face the storm." At that moment a bolt of lightning dove from the clouds and split in two above the trees on the riverbank on their left. The simultaneous blast of thunder almost knocked Nita to her knees. She used her stick to catch her balance on the rocks. This was a pretty stupid place to be in an electrical storm. Kani glowered at Nita and commanded, "Woman will falter, but she will not fall."

Nita turned her back to the wind as it hurled a thick spray of water, soaking her t-shirt and blue jeans. Kani moved toward one of the selected oaks. The branches higher up were being twisted against their will. She stepped onto the rock at its base. She motioned for Nita to go the other tree. They stood with their backs braced against the tree trunks, facing the storm, which Nita had begun to fear was nothing short of a hurricane, a hurricane that could wipe this island from the face of the earth and all things on it.

Kani placed one end of her stick in the crook of her right elbow and moved it behind the tree then slipped her other arm over it. She adjusted herself until she was positioned straight into the face of the torrent and braced firmly so that she would not be swayed. Lightning exploded simultaneously onto both shoulders of the river. Nita trembled at the power. Kani seemed not

43

to notice either the detonation nor Nita's response. She signaled for Nita to use her stick to brace herself with the tree. Nita slipped as she stepped onto the stone, her legs quivering as lightning cracked and snarled beside the island. She managed with some difficulty to get into the same position as Kani. She now stood with her arms back and chest out toward the rising storm. Down the river lightning cleaved the blackened world with blinding streaks. One bolt zapped straight into the water a few hundred feet from them. As if it had boiled the entire river, the water near them lifted up onto the wind and splattered their faces. Kani let out a disdainful laugh that seemed to live on the edge of evil, although Nita could not be certain which side. Nita failed as she tried to stifle her fear, and tears dripped into the deluge.

Kani spat into the storm, and wind and rain hammered down upon them in response. A violent gust ripped up from the river and slammed Nita's head back against the tree. The wind then turned and tried to tear her sideways from her mooring. She could feel the skin at her elbows grinding against the branch that kept her strung in place.

Nita could barely see Kani even though she was less than ten feet away. She could also no longer distinguish between sky and river or the wind's howling and Kani's wailing. The world had become one angry mass mobilized against itself. She hung her head to deflect the sting on her face. But the battering would not relent. Cold whips of water stung her cheeks, her breasts, her thighs. The wind flattened her shirt against her belly, and water poured down her jeans. She broadened her stance on the rock to keep her balance as the wind began to whip side to side in addition to its frontal assault.

The tree that supported her groaned and twisted as it fought to live against the potentially lethal onslaught. Lightning sliced into the water all around, and thunder crushed her eardrums. The sky and river combined forces to lash her with wave after wave of cold stinging blasts. Her face felt as if sharp crystals were being flung at it. She squinted to avoid having them hit her eyes. The pain over the entire front of her body was so intense that she thought her cheeks and her chest must be bleeding by now. Her back shoved *against the tree with such pressure that she could feel the bark imprinting on her spine. She wondered how long Kani intended to have this punishment go on. But when she looked over, she saw that Kani's stern visage was hardening into impervious rock. The wind plastered her leather dress against her broad body, and water shards stabbed her face, but she stared unflinching into the storm. Rain streamed from her raised chin and cascaded from her black hair.*

Nita lost track of time and consciousness. She moved through phases of pain, numbness and fear until they became one. Gradually she sensed that she was rising above the raging tempest even as the water rose on the island first around her ankles and then almost to her knees. And though lightning flailed and thunder screamed, they became more a distraction to her thinking than a threat to her being. Eventually the thunder tumbled northward, and the dome overhead lightened slightly. Though the rain continued to arrive in wide ribbons, the drops were warmer and softer compared to their fleeing cousins. Nita knew she could survive. Kani looked at her and nodded.

CHAPTER SIX

Nita looked out the window and saw the first gray rays of light bringing the morning. Unlike some other dreams, last night's did not fade in the dawn. It wrapped like a cocoon around her, and she lay in her bed wondering about these torturous apparitions. Despite more than eight hours of sleep, she was exhausted.

She considered looking up something at the library on dream interpretation, but the more she pondered, the more she began to suspect she was just going crazy. She decided it would make more sense to research dreams as evidence of mental illness than to study their symbolism. Quickly she put that out of her mind. If she was going to read anything, it would be for the brain chemistry paper that was not going to write itself.

She made some coffee and instead of showering, decided to put on some old jeans and allow herself a little Saturday gardening time before getting cleaned up to head to the library.

The dew was thick on the grass as she walked to the shed to get her tools. Her old shoes and the bottoms of her jeans quickly became covered with droplets of water.

When she got to the garden, she squatted down to test the soil to see if it was too wet to work. The rains had stopped on Wednesday, but they had been heavy to that point, plus there was dew every morning. She used Henry's trick to test the soil, grabbing a handful of soil and squeezing it in her hand. She then bounced the ball of soil on the palm of her hand a few times. It crumbled slowly apart. Good enough. If it had stayed in a ball it would have been too wet to work.

As Nita was about to stand back up, she noticed small rocks in the soil she had worked last week shining in the early sun. Apparently, the rain had washed them loose just like Henry had predicted. She wondered if she would find any projectile points.

Some of the pebbles actually perched on tiny towers of soil. The rain had flattened the soil around them, but they shielded the soil directly under them. Nita had never noticed this before. Her eyes scanned the soil for anything of interest. Mostly the rocks were small and round. Anything big she had already tossed to the side while she was digging. Then her eye caught on something white out in the middle of the plot.

When she walked out to retrieve it, it turned out to be a triangle-shaped piece of white china. She was about to toss it into her rock pile, when she saw another and then a third, all of them white with some faint blue markings. She picked them up and found that two of them fit together. The third was part of the same item, probably a teacup, but pieces of the puzzle were missing. She kicked around in the soil and found a fourth piece, which fit with the one lone piece.

She went to the edge of the garden and got her rake. She gently probed the area and found other parts. "Yes!" she shouted when she found the cup handle. She made a little mold in the soft dirt and started fitting the pieces together. Eventually she had almost the entire thing. But much of the bottom was missing. She raked more, finding one more small chip, but not the base.

As she started to gather up the pieces to take them to the porch, she wondered if last week she had tossed any chunks into the rock pile as she had nearly done just this morning. She had a vague recollection that she had.

She placed the collection of white chips on the gray weathered floorboards of the porch and then headed over to the rock pile. Each time she dug in the garden, she tossed the big rocks to the side. Now she was digging through them. An orange sliver moved as she lifted a rock and then stopped perfectly still. It was some sort of a salamander. Nita carefully worked around it so as not to harm it. She remembered reading in a zoology course that salamanders are the number one predators of some woodlands. Collectively they ate more than any other predator. The little orange guy strode off and crawled under a nearby log.

Nita sorted through the sizable array of rocks using both hands to move them into a new pile. Her eyes scanned for white. She was about to toss a rock with her right hand when the different texture caught her attention. She looked at the item in her hand. Although it was about the same potato-size as many of the others, and roughly rounded, this one had a narrowed middle. And one end was chipped. It could have been a hammer or something with a handle attached in the middle. Nita set it to the side to continue the search for white china. As she neared the bottom of the pile, a flash of white stopped her from tossing aside the last stones. There was the base of her cup. The piece was a little thicker than the others and it had some sort of marking on it. Her heart raced as she took it and her other find back to the porch. She tested the base with a couple of the other pieces and it fit. It would take some doing to put it all together. She wondered how old it was. She laughed at herself. *It's probably just twenty years old, and somebody bought it at K-Mart.* She rubbed the other item. This rock had definitely been worked. No K-Mart purchase here.

These discoveries pushed her to resume looking for arrowheads. She went back to where she had started, intending to branch out from there. But as soon as she looked down, she spotted a small brown triangle right where she had already looked. She picked it up and examined it but wasn't sure at first whether it was an arrowhead. The ones she had seen in archeology class had a fish-tail cut into the end. This one was just a triangle, cut cleanly across the bottom. Both sides of the triangle were perfectly symmetrical, and their sharp edges came to a precise point.

She put it in her pocket, energized to find more. Slowly she walked up and down the garden soil, periodically stopping to examine something, but without any further luck. She only put one other rock in her pocket, which she wasn't sure about. It was about the size of a silver dollar and had a sharp edge. The archeologists with whom she had worked in Delaware had found items like this that they called scrapers. They said had been used by the Lenni Lenape for scraping hides to preserve them. She thought they looked a lot like every other rock, and so did this one, but she put it in her pocket just in case.

Nita looked at her watch. Originally, she had intended to spend just a couple hours working in the garden and had hoped to expand one edge into what was currently tall weeds, but her search for treasures had used up about half the time.

As she dug into the original task, she found it a little easier going than it was last week. The rains had further softened the soil, so the shovel went in easier. She dug out chunks of earth where the weeds grew, shook the soil off the roots and threw the weeds into a pile. Chunk by chunk she moved down the row. Her mind wandered to a wide range of topics as her arms and legs did their work. She thought about Elmer, the ninety-year-old dancer, and what an inspiration he was. Their geriatrics course indicated that the single greatest indicator of longevity was a positive attitude, and Elmer certainly exemplified that. She hoped she could be like him when she got to that age. Hell, she wasn't like him now. Yet she really had nothing to complain about. I mean damn, she thought, I'm about to graduate from medical school. Hospitals are contacting me about doing a residency in their programs. In a few years I could be practicing medicine. She had worked hard and was on the right path.

The path. She thought about Kani and Chee-na-wan. They were often on a real path. They were constantly in search of medicines. What was it they were doing? Their fear was rising, but it was not clear why. Nita struggled to bring back a piece of a dream from earlier in the week. She fought to try to retrieve it. She leaned on her shovel and stared up at the trees on the edge of the field. It was so frustrating when she couldn't recall pieces of her dreams. Why was that? She tried to remember that from the memory chapter in her neuro class. Great, she smiled to herself, I forgot the memory part. Wait, it was something about headaches. Kani and Chee-na-wan had hiked out to a stand of willow trees and had carefully removed some bark. They had buried tobacco first near the trees and talked to the trees about their appreciation for the gifts of their healing bark. Kani had then shown Chee-na-wan how to soak the bark in water and extract something that would cure headaches. Nita wondered if that really worked.

She was back to digging. She had developed blisters on her left hand and tried to adjust her technique to ease the pain. She would put some antiseptic and Band-Aids on them when she went inside. She just wanted to finish this one row. She wondered what Kani had in the way of antiseptics. All Nita had to do was open a tube and squirt Neosporin on. Kani would have to go make it first, just like she was basically making an analgesic like aspirin out of tree bark. Nita thought nothing of popping an aspirin out of a bottle, and never really wondered where it came from or how someone first figured out that aspirin cured headaches. She just knew it had been around for a long time.

That evening she was booted once again from the medical school library as it closed. It was aggravating that it closed at 6:00 on Saturdays, but this was actually an hour later than the main campus library. She walked out into Saturday night, alone and lonely. Alone and lonely seemed to be teamed on Saturday nights. She created her own word, *alonely.* "I'm alonely tonight," she said out loud.

God, I am losing my mind. The torment of the dreams and the distress of struggling through school were giving her no relief night or day. Her persistent fear that she was going crazy grew even stronger. She needed do something to stop the chronic sinking feeling. Where was her positive attitude?

Then she had a great idea. She'd go see Elmer. She pivoted in her tracks and headed over toward the hospital, which was next to the medical school library building. Surely, he wouldn't mind a visitor. The sidewalks were almost empty, and the hospital lobby area was vacant except for an elderly lady who was reading a magazine at the reception desk. She didn't look up as Nita got on the elevator to take it to the ninth floor. The ubiquitous fluorescent lights had been dimmed, and the linoleum squeaked against her Nike's.

She entered Elmer's room slowly. "Knock, knock," she said, pretending to knock on the green curtain that divided Elmer's bed on the window side of the room from the other patient, who had two visitors.

"Nita!" Elmer exclaimed when he saw her. "You changed your mind about dancing," he grinned. "Fortunately, my dance card is not yet full for this evening." He used the remote control to turn off the TV.

"How are you?" she said cautiously.

He coughed slightly and straightened the white bedsheet over his pale blue hospital gown. "Doing much better now."

She suspected he was making a reference to having a visitor.

"They work you students late, don't they," he commented.

"Oh, I'm not here on official duty. I just stopped by to say hi. I was at the library studying and thought I'd stop in. But I didn't want to bother you. If I'm bothering..."

"Nita," Elmer interrupted, "you are definitely not bothering me. When you get to my age, what friends are left are not doing so well themselves, and almost nobody can drive at night. Frankly, being lonely is one of the toughest things to deal with. I swear it kills more old folks than anything else. Of course, that's not what gets documented, but that's what it is," he nodded to affirm his research. "When there's nobody to play with, you quit playing."

"That's an interesting point."

"I don't mean to complain, but that's just my observation from a front-row seat, which is a good seat to have, because I don't see so well anymore," he chuckled, which turned into a cough. When the coughing stopped, he asked, "So what's going on with you, besides wanting to learn to dance?"

"Not much. Studying mostly. A little gardening."

"Gardening. I used to love gardening. So did my wife. What do you plant?"

"I'm thinking some greens, and sugar snap peas, and I might try some potatoes."

"Hey, you can sit down if you want. I mean if you want, you don't have to stay if you need to get going." Nita reached to pull a tan vinyl chair from near the window. The window sill was devoid of cards, flowers or pictures.

"Can I get you anything?" she asked.

"Have any beer in that backpack?"

"Sorry," she shook her head. "I thought they were giving you something better than beer."

"Ain't nothing better than beer."

"How's the new hip doing?"

"Actually, pretty good. I think I'll keep it. You know they wouldn't give me anything on my trade-in."

Nita laughed. "There's no justice."

Elmer shrugged and nodded. Then he said, "Actually the search for justice begins in your garden. Keep digging and the earth will speak to you."

Nita cocked her head slightly to the side. "Not sure I understand that."

"You will someday. Keep searching and listening. The answers are there." Elmer's head dropped slightly, and his smile faded a bit for the first time. When he looked back at her, he put the smile back on, "Getting too deep I suspect," he coughed again.

"Are you getting a cold or something?"

"No, I think it's the air in these places. Dries me out."

"Make sure they listen to your lungs, okay?"

"Yes, doctor," he smirked. "Seriously, though, you're gonna be a really good doc, Nita. The world needs more like you."

They chatted for a while longer and then a nurse poked her head in to announce that visiting hours would be over shortly. Nita said she'd better get going. When she stood to leave, Elmer thanked her for coming in. Then he held up his hand, "but wait, before you go, I have a prescription for the doctor. Take two beers and get a good night's sleep. It's good for what ails you." He extended his hand, and she took it for a moment. "Thanks for coming, Nita. You have a nice evening."

When Nita walked out into the hall, she was surprised to find tears running down her cheeks. The hospital floor on a Saturday evening was a much different place than the hurried hive of a weekday. The hallway lights were dimmed, and the air was quiet except for faint beeping of monitors from the open doors of the patient rooms. Serenity flowed through the area.

"Little Earl," she said as she got in her car, "We need to make a stop on the way home. I have to pick up a prescription," she smiled.

When she got home and went to put the six-pack of Rolling Rock in the refrigerator, she noticed water leaking from under the kitchen sink.

"Henry, this is Nita. I'm sorry to bother you. But I have a leak under the sink."

Henry had her check to see where it was coming from and then told her how to use the shut-off valve. "I'll come out tomorrow to work on it," he offered. "I'll go to the 9:00 Mass at St. Teresa's and then stop over if that's okay."

"I've gone to St. Teresa's a couple times," Nita said. "I like the priest there."

"Yeah, if you can deal with his bad jokes," Henry chuckled.

Nita opened a beer, then rifled through her CDs and found Tattoo You by the Rolling Stones. She opened the tray of the little player, popped in the disk and selected the "Start Me Up" cut. She turned up the volume, remembering how Janie would dance around their dorm room pretending she was Mick Jagger, using a dildo as a microphone. Nita shook her head. That girl was crazy. While Nita drank her first beer, she rearranged her little living room and hung some pictures that had been sitting against the wall since she first moved in. Janie used to drag her to flea markets looking for treasures, and she actually found some. One was an old painting of a stone cottage, not unlike her own. She stared at it, wondering at the remarkable similarity.

Nita listened to more music that reminded her of those college days and drank two more beers. Those days had their problems and stresses too, but now they had acquired a nostalgic glow. She missed Janie.

After finishing the third beer, Nita decided she better go to bed. She went to the bathroom to pee and then took off her jeans and her bra. In bed she remembered a technique Janie had taught her for dealing with the spins, a sensation she hadn't experienced since college when she would occasionally drink more than she should. For fun and old-time's sake, she put her hand on the wall above her head, as Janie had taught her. Nita determined by the end of freshman year that Janie's technique yielded minimal results. A better approach, she found, was to limit her consumption of alcohol.

Nita and Janie roomed together their freshman and sophomore years, and their different personalities proved to be a good fit. Janie was carefree to the point of recklessness, as Nita periodically told her. Nita was careful to the point of endangering herself, as Janie in turn counseled her. Nita was never quite sure what that meant. "See!" was all Janie would explain.

Their sophomore year ended with Janie dating Frank, the guy she eventually married after they all graduated. Nita was a bridesmaid and met a guy named Michael at the wedding. For a few months they had a good thing, but she ran out of time. School beckoned.

CHAPTER SEVEN

Nita stood with Kanianguas and Chee-na-wan inside the long house where Kani had repaired the young warrior's broken leg. They were alone, dimly illuminated by a fire whose faint ribbon of smoke sought a hole in the roof above the fire pit. Kani looked at Chee-na-wan and saw that she had frozen in place. Nita felt terror burning from Chee-na-wan's wide black eyes. Her lower lip trembled like a birch leaf in advance of a storm.

Kani stepped close to Chee-na-wan, but instead of a compassionate touch or a question to inquire what was wrong, she spit stern words in her face. "Never, never allow your fear to leak from your soul, such as you do at this moment. My heart and my soul shudder at the thought of this journey just as yours do, but I will never show my inner demons on the light of my face. Tong-quas would smell your fear at a great distance and would either vanish into the forest like the copperhead or strike you out of spite like the rattlesnake. We must confront him, but first we confront our own selves. He demands nothing less, and nothing less will we give him. You must conquer your demons before we set out. I will know if you are worthy, and worthy you must be. It is time for the girl to become a woman."

Nita felt her own shoulders shift back and her spine stiffen at the rebuke of the young Indian. Chee-na-wan sniffled back her tears. Kani looked with disappointment at her protege, then turned on her moccasin heal and moved to some clay pots that were lined along the side of the long house. There she knelt and lifted the stone lid from one.

"What should I bring?" Chee-na-wan asked, pointing her chin out in the direction of Kani's back.

"Bring a bed roll, mat and blanket. Also, bring a pouch of psinda-moakan. The corn bread will allow us to keep going without having to stop. Psindamoakan nourishes the body and the spirit."

"Will any warriors escort us?" Chee-na-wan asked.

Kani stood abruptly and faced her. "We must go alone," she hissed. "Tong-quas will not receive us if there are warriors with us. He may not receive us well anyway, but certainly not with warriors."

Nita saw fear leak from Chee-na-wan's eyes, "What about the Seneca raiding parties? You know what happened to the Conestoga village north of Conowingo."

Kani nodded. "The scouts say the Senecas have departed with their prisoners. We can only hope for their quick death." She paused as she thought about what she had just said. Nita saw lines of apprehension start to form at the edges of her eyes, but the lines withdrew back inside her. "We will be quiet, and we will build no fires. The spirits will protect us. Go now, my friend, but be quick, we must start on our journey." She touched Chee-na-wan's arm. "Gather what I told you and say good-bye to your family. Tell them we hope to return in three or four days. They understand the importance."

With their rolled mats and blankets strung across their backs Kanianguas and Chee-na-wan started north along the river. Nita followed behind. People from the village watched solemnly and bid them safe journey. Wisps of the morning fog twisted like snakes along the water's surface, and some crawled toward their path.

Soon they climbed off the main trail up a trace that ran next to a large stream, which Kani called Octoraro. It was a boastful and violent stream that plunged recklessly toward the river. Nita's feet slipped on the untrustworthy rocks, slick with moss and mist. The roar of the water taunted them with the peril of their climb. Leaning trees and precarious stacks of boulders added to the treachery.

When they reached the top, the land leveled out, and the stream broadened. Its calmness here belied the fury just a few dozen yards farther in its journey. It was as if the flow was gathering its rage before hurtling off the edge.

They continued to follow the path along the stream's bank until Kani paused and pointed to a large angular rock submerged in the water. "Not all of importance is at the surface. Note the swirls on the water's skin even though the rock lies below. So it is in our lives where forces below the surface of the day and time cause ripples and even torrents. If we are not attentive, we may never understand why there is turbulence. On a hot summer day when the flow is low, this rock will protrude into view, a clear warning for all to see. For some, though, it will be too late. Those that travel in higher water if they are not attentive to the smaller signals will see their canoe smashed and its bark sides left to return to the land."

The trail led them as a narrow hint that turned away from Octoraro and slipped deeper among the brooding trees. Thick roots made looking up dangerous. Dense silence, punctuated only by periodic buzzing of insects, merged with damp odors. Giant ferns glowed among the enormous black trunks. Nita felt that she had entered an ancient cathedral. Her senses were humbled by the scene, and she was pressed upon as if by a religion that was one with her spirit. Churches always seemed sterile, walled off from God's world. Here, there was nothing to separate her soul from God's true nature.

The three walked, first Kani, then Chee-na-wan, then Nita. All abided in the pious gloom.

After a long while, Chee-na-wan reached forward and touched Kani's shoulder. "Did you check on the sick people this morning?" she whispered.

Kani nodded.

"Were there improvements? Did our tea of last night help?"

"The pain was less, but some had developed red spots on their arms and legs."

"What is that? What illness do they have?"

Kani slowed in her steps and turned to look at Chee-na-wan. "I have never seen this before. I do not know. It frightens me."

"Is it evil spirits that come from the plans to trade more land?" Dread seeped into Chee-na-wan's voice.

"That is my fear. I am afraid that it is connected to the white settlers. Their ways are different than ours. They tear out the forests to build their houses and farms. The spirits of the forest and land with whom our people have lived since ancient times are angered by our disregard." A large pileated woodpecker drummed on a hollow trunk off to their left. The noise trailed off, followed by the silent flight of the bird with its red, black and white plumage.

They walked on in silence for a long time. The path rose slightly and trended roughly to the northeast. Twice they came to intersections with other paths, where they would stop as Kani quietly considered their way. Each time, she paused, sensing the air, looking at clues that Nita could not see, then confidently chose and strode on.

After another hour of walking in silence Kani said, "I have not traveled here for many, many years, but so far I have remembered the way well. Soon we will come to a small river where many elk are often to be found. We will walk the path north along the near bank until we come to a place where two *large Sycamore trees guard the opposite bank. The river is shallow there, and we can cross."*

Eventually they came down a slope and found the river as Kani had remembered. "Yes, this trail is the one I took. This is the Shawnah. We will walk north and until we find the Sycamores."

After a while, Kani told Chee-na-wan to start watching the other bank for the large white trees. "Sycamores are the peeling-bark trees. Their brown skin peels away and reveals white flesh beneath. "They should be easy to spot from a distance. I believe we may be able to see them from the top of this next rise."

Their pace quickened as they moved up the incline. Without turning Kani asked, "Chee-na-wan, what do we use the bark of the Sycamore for?"

"It is for..." Chee-na-wan's voice hinted that she was not sure. "It is for... it is for sore throat."

"Correct." Kani said over her shoulder. They wove through a narrow section among the trees. "How is it prepared?"

"It is prepared...," Chee-na-wan slowed and looked down at the path. "I am not sure. I forgot."

Kani stopped and turned around. "Three chips of bark are taken from the east side of the tree. They are steeped together with red oak bark and sweet flag root to make a soothing hot drink."

"I am sorry. I know you have told me before."

"You are learning. It takes time."

They continued up the long slope until they saw smoke rising in the distance on the other side of the river. "Could that be Tong-quas' hut?" Chee-na-wan asked with the faintest thread of fear in her voice.

"No, we are still far from his home. And Tong-quas would not build a fire with so much smoke. I don't know where that smoke could be coming from. Be very quiet as we reach the top."

"Could it be the Senecas burning another village?"

"I do not know. We will be quiet and stay hidden." Kani held up her hand in a call for silence. As they reached the summit, Kani slowed and signaled to them. They followed her off the trail into some laurel bushes that lined the path. Kani guided them through the thicket so they could approach for a better view while staying concealed among the foliage. They pushed aside branches and brushed through spider webs that caught in Nita's hair and on her face and arms. Kani picked up a laurel branch from the ground and used it to quietly sweep the webs ahead of them.

They emerged from the laurel, and Kani halted. Chee-na-wan and Nita followed as she stepped quickly and silently into the next tangled stand and opened a narrow view. Across the river they could see what was burning. White settlers had cut the trees from a section of the land. The slope to the stream bristled with ragged stumps. Workers were using horses to drag giant sections of trees to a huge pile where they were attempting to burn them. Kani gasped. Another group of men with horses was working on pulling a stump out of the ground. Kani and Chee-na-wan crouched inside the bushes and watched. Nita crouched and stayed hidden as well. In bending down she realized that she was wearing the same hide dress as the others.

After a long period of scowling at the sight, Kani spoke. "Those two large stumps along the river. See the white bark? Those were the Sycamores. Our path was to follow down the bank, across the Shawnah and into that area where the men are."

"What will we do?"

"We must find a way to go around. The hills far beyond them are still wooded. That is where we need to go. Tong-quas lives beyond those hills."

"What if the white settlers are there? They will take us prisoner and kill or scalp us?" Chee-na-wan was trembling. Nita could feel the fear of both women, and she realized that with her straight dark hair and hide dress, she looked very much like an Indian too. If they were in danger, so was she. Her heart drummed in her chest.

"We must be brave," Kani said, but she was looking more at Nita than at Chee-na-wan. For the first time on this journey she seemed to acknowledge that Nita was with them. "Life is not a level and clear path," Kani said to both of them. "Life is a journey with obstacles. When we deal with life's challenges, new parts of our spirit emerge. Always the seeds of growth are beyond where we are comfortable."

They watched for a while longer and saw a huge tree fall at the edge of the clearing, tumbling in the direction of the fire. Apparently, there was yet another group working there, blocked from view by a thousand-year-old forest. A black bear lumbered from the far side of the trees and down the bank, splashing across the Shawnah. He paused as he exited the water and looked straight at where Nita hid in the bushes, seeming to make eye contact with her, seeking her help. He stood to his six-foot height on his hind legs and sniffed. A gunshot blasted from within the trees the bear had just fled. He staggered, tried to regain his balance then fell back into the stream. Blood tinged the current.

"We cannot stay here," Kani said. "There are many white men, and it will be getting dark soon. We will go back to where we can be secure and stay there until first light. Guidance will come in the night. There will be no moon tonight to allow us to walk, but the signs will arrive nonetheless."

They retraced their steps back down the river to a point where a small stream came toward the Shawnah. They found an area among some large rocks and set out their mats and blankets. Nita followed their lead with a mat and blanket from her own back.

When Chee-na-wan unwrapped her mat and took out her blanket, Chee-na-wan saw the look of disdain on Kani's face.

"I am sorry," Chee-na-wan seemed to plead with Kani. "It is so warm."

"*You do not understand the power and the symbol. You do not understand that spirits live in all things.*"

"*It is just a blanket.*"

"*You wrap yourself in that which was given by those who destroy the forest. Little by little our people exchange themselves until nothing will be left,*" Kani hung her head in sadness.

"*I am sorry. I should have known.*"

"*Their fires will slowly consume the biggest logs until there are just ashes left.*"

Chee-na-wan looked at Nita and whimpered, "I should have known."

Even though the sun was only now disappearing, the air was getting cold. They each ate from their pouch of psindamoakan without talking. Nita discovered that she had a pouch too. She dipped her hand in and pulled out a roughly shaped corn biscuit. She examined it before putting it in her mouth. It was grainy and dry but tasted sweet. They went to the stream, squatting at the water's edge and cupping their hands to draw some water.

In the morning they rose and had another piece of psindamoakan and some water.

"*How will we get around the white settlers?*" *Chee-na-wan asked.*

"*In a dream, smoke came over the land to the south, blocking it from my view. To the north there was no smoke, and the sun was shining. The sun lit a path as it reflected in the water. We will go north along the river and look for the place to cross.*"

Upstream the river was rougher, with rapids, small falls and deep pools. It looked dangerous to attempt a crossing. They kept moving north and were back into an area where heavy forests lay on both sides of the river. Gradually the river narrowed, and they hoped for a place to cross. Then through the tall trees on the opposite bank, a ray of sunlight shot through and illuminated a portion of the river. Clusters of light danced on the surface. "This is where we are to cross," Kani said with confidence. She moved quietly to the edge of the water and looked up and down before stepping out onto a rock that was exposed above the moving stream. Nita saw that she was wearing the same footwear as her companions. The soft but sturdy moccasin bottoms allowed her to grip the slippery rocks as she hopped from one stone to another, following the course Kani and Chee-na-wan took.

They climbed the opposite bank where the terrain was flatter than what they had come through. The trees were so tall that little sunlight reached the forest floor. The ground was mostly clear of an understory except for giant rhododendrons and laurels here and there.

If they were on a path, Nita could not tell it. Kani would pause periodically and then point to a direction for them to take. As best Nita could discern, they were moving generally southeast. Although the moccasins were comfortable, her feet and legs were tired.

"We need to find an opening in the trees," Kani said as the afternoon wore on. "You see that this land is flat. Soon we should be able to see a hill that stands alone. Tong-quas lives on the other side of that hill. It is called Marettico, the Hill of Hard Stone. The white settlers have named it Iron Hill because of the metal they take from it. We are once again close to where white men may be. Or Senecas. Danger prowls in the shadows."

Chee-na-wan's eyes grew wide with fear. "Marettico? We are going to Marettico?" She froze in mid-stride.

Kani turned and looked at Chee-na-wan. She waited.

"Marettico?" Chee-na-wan stammered. "That is the place where warriors from one of our northern villages killed three white men. That was Marettico, was it not?"

Kani nodded.

"Can there be a more perilous place for us to go? If not the Senecas, then other tribes stopping to get the stone for strong brown points. And if not those warriors, then white men looking for vengeance. And even if we find Tong-quas while we are still alive, he himself is a danger."

"All that you say," Kani stepped close to Chee-na-wan's face, "is quite true. You are right to fear. The dangers are real, and it would be difficult to say which fate is worst."

"Then why? What I have heard that the Senecas would do to us—women traveling without warriors—is..." she shuddered and could not finish her sentence. When she continued, her voice came like the squeal of an animal caught in a trap, "They say it goes on for days what they do to their prisoners—that they are masters at keeping their victims alive."

Deep distress creased Kani's eyes. She nodded.

Nita's knees felt weak as the desperation of their plight seeped into her soul. The capacity for cruelty among humans, had always disturbed her. When they had to read the Diary of Anne Frank in high school, she could barely finish it, then had nightmares about the fate of this innocent young girl and so many others.

Kani looked from Chee-na-wan to Nita. "Life presents us with situations where all paths lead to terrible places, yet we must walk onward. Our people are reaching such a circumstance."

She looked again at Chee-na-wan. "Could you smell it? As we left our village, could you smell it?"

"Smell what?"

"The scent of fear and the scent of death. They were entwined in the air. They are sometimes so close that they are hard to distinguish. Even the leaders are afraid. They fear for the end of our people."

"The end of our people? What does that mean? For years beyond counting we have been here, feared by our enemies and respected by all."

Kani shook her head. "What has been true for all the yesterdays may not be true for even one tomorrow. That is what Tong-quas warned years ago.

Now people dread that he was right. We have no choice but to see him—if he will see us."

"But why us?"

Kani shook her head. "Because it can only be us. Medicine takes many forms. Soon you will understand more. Now we must go. I am not certain how much farther to Marettico, but I know that danger stalks our flank." As she stepped forward to continue the journey, they heard rustling high above them. Chee-na-wan cringed.

Without turning around, Kani assured her that it was rain in the tree tops. "In a forest such as this, most rain will be caught far above us in the tight cover of the leaves. It will be a lonely drop that finds its way to our path."

As they walked, the patter in the leaves above continued, but few beads of water fell all the way to earth. Eventually an opening in the canopy was created by a stream flowing across their route. There the rain splattered into the water and on the rocks. Then all of them looked up. Immediately ahead was Marettico, alone and dark with ribbons of gray mist draping its shoulders. It flared toward the storm clouds with spikes of trees. Black boulders were its feet.

Nita gradually regained consciousness, but her brain lingered on Marettico. She knew the place by its current name, Iron Hill. It was only about ten miles south of the UD campus. She had visited the museum there during her archeology class at the University of Maryland because there were still clear sites where Native Americans had quarried stone and worked it to make projectile points and various types of tools. In fact, the stone they used was now called Iron Hill jasper. Later, the white settlers mined iron oxide deposits on the hill.

CHAPTER EIGHT

Nita looked out her bedroom window and saw that it was still dark. Her clock confirmed that it was almost 2:00. She rolled over and was rapidly back to the base of Marettico.

Kani raised her hand and without speaking motioned them back in the direction they had come. When they retreated a couple hundred yards, she signaled them to the ground behind a clump of four tree trunks, a cluster of oaks that sprouted seventy feet in the air from an ancient stump. The carcass of the original tree lay stretched into the distance. Green moss carpeted its length, and orange fungi lined its ridges. Even lying on the ground, it was more than six feet high. Kani scouted the area and then guided them to sit near the four trees. She again peered carefully all around them. When she seemed satisfied, she too sat down.

"Many tribes use this place for its stones, which make fine points. There may be warriors or hunters from various tribes in the area. White men now

dig here too." Nita was surprised to hear Kani repeat what they already knew, then she realized that Kani, too, was having difficulty containing her fear.

Chee-na-wan looked at Kani for a long moment and then whispered, "If Tong-quas is so brave, why did he leave our people?"

Kani hung her head for many minutes, so long that Nita assumed she either had not heard or chose not to answer. When Kani spoke, it was with quiet breath, "Tong-quas left out of frustration and fear, fear that what the others refused to believe would nonetheless happen. He told me, 'What one believes is not what determines the truth.'"

Kani's hand stroked the moss on the log behind her. "Tong-quas was both brave and afraid. Bravery and fear are cousins living in one hut." Kani squinted behind her cheekbones and shook her head. "I have seen Tong-quas boil water with the hate from his eyes."

"Is that true?" Chee-na-wan asked in awe. "I have heard the legend that he could boil water with his gaze."

"That and other amazing powers," Kani nodded with assurance. Then her eyes narrowed, "Powers to be respected and feared, even by Tong-quas."

Kani looked up into the trees, and Nita's gaze followed her lead. Broad arms of oaks and maples joined to create a dark roof speckled with deepening blue beyond. Kani said, "It is getting late. We must decide whether to approach Tong-quas now or wait until morning." Her eyes moved back down to the forest floor as she rolled the options around in her head. She scanned the area around their resting place. Hollow flute calls of wood thrushes echoed in the trees. "We will wait," she said. "I am not sure I can recall precisely where his hut was, and I do not know if it is in the same place. To find him as darkness comes would be a mistake. We will wait. We will walk with the first light." With minimal movement, they unrolled their mats, ate sparingly, then slept.

Nita was already listening when Kani touched them to rise. The final gray of night was still fading, and distant birds pulled the dawn toward them. They quietly rolled and wrapped their mats and blankets. Chee-na-wan stumbled as she slung her blanket over her shoulder, snapping a twig under foot. With stern signals, Kani warned her to silence.

"It was an accident," Chee-na-wan whispered.

Kani stepped close to Chee-na-wan and hissed, "An accident could get us killed—or worse. There can be no accidents here." Chee-na-wan's lower lip quivered, but she held back the tears. Nita judged her to be perhaps fifteen, but at times she seemed younger, sometimes older. Kani moved to within a breath of Chee-na-wan's face, "You must also wrap that blanket completely inside your mat. Nothing must show." Chee-na-wan did as she was told.

The strain of the journey had not been soothed by their sleep. Kani motioned for them to join her close to the ground as she squatted and rubbed the dirt smooth. With barely a word, she indicated where they were and then she marked where she thought Tong-quas' hut would be. As she placed her finger on that spot, a large, moccasin smashed her finger to the ground.

Chee-na-wan shrieked and stumbled backward into a sitting position. Nita leaned back to see a muscular giant who held a club in his left hand and a stone knife in his right. His fierce eyes threw fire down at them from deep within black braids hanging over broad brown shoulders. Around his neck was a necklace of large claws.

Nita looked down at Kani's hand, which was being crushed into the dirt with the full weight of the man. Kani strained to remain calm despite her pain. She tilted her neck to look up and then looked back at her hand. She did not try to pull away.

Nita was frozen three feet from the man's thick leg. His brown calf looked like a tree trunk. She tried to scoot back slightly, but he swiftly brought the bent head of his club behind her neck and grunted.

Chee-na-wan, who was trembling visibly, started to sob quietly. The quartet stayed locked in place, with only the tiny chirps of Chee-na-wan's throat interrupting. Even the birds halted their songs.

Finally, after an excessive time of no movement, the man spoke. "Why do you come, Sister?" His voice was rolling thunder.

Kani remained still, as if he had said nothing.

"Why?" his question boomed through the forest and bounced off the lone hill.

Still, they remained. Even Chee-na-wan's crying stopped, although her shaking continued. Nita's knees ached from holding her squat position, but the edge of the club dug into the nape of her neck, and she knew any movement would be ill-advised.

After another extended silence, the man abruptly lifted his foot and stepped backwards. In the same motion, he slipped his club from behind Nita's head.

"I will not help you," he said to Kani. "I will not help you and your pitiful band of blind cowards."

Kani rose and stood facing him. She looked deep into his eyes, and he returned the stare, looking into her soul. Tension rose and fell like the painful breaths of a dying person.

The man spoke again. This time, a bit of the edge was gone from his voice. "I cannot help them. They have dug their grave. They have dug everyone's grave. It is too late." He shook his head, and his braids drifted slowly.

He paused and stared at Nita, his eyes penetrating her thoughts. She stood in response. Her impulse was to step back, but she held her ground. When the man spoke again, his voice was even quieter than before, but somehow this only made Nita more afraid. The bass vibrations entered her and would not leave. "You know it in your heart. I see it. It is the disease of all death. No healer can heal this." His voice was rising again, "Not even Tong-quas."

Suddenly Tong-quas looked at Chee-na-wan where she cowered, now kneeling on the ground with her hands tucked in below her chest.

"You," he bellowed, pointing his club at her head. *The thick shaft with a gnarled ball at the end seemed to be an extension of his bronze arm. Nita looked at his triceps, which stood out a full three inches from the back of his upper arm. The muscle of his forearm was a twisted root that flowed down to the massive brown hand, grasping the threatening club. The entire system pulsed with buried rage.*

Chee-na-wan tumbled to the side and fell into a fetal position.

"What do you have? What did you bring it to this sacred place?" *He sniffed the air like a dog.* You are wearing the clothes of a white woman. I feel it."

Chee-na-wan was whimpering again and shaking uncontrollably. "I'm, I'm not wearing any white clothes," *Chee-na-wan managed to stammer out.*

"Take off your clothes, White Serpent," *he commanded.*

Kani stepped forward, but Tong-quas shoved her back. "This evil creature has brought the disease to this sacred place, and she lies."

He continued to point his club at her, but now he extended his right arm as well and aimed the knife at her. Take off the white woman's clothes, or I will cut them off," *he ordered.* "Or perhaps I should burn them with you in them."

Kani stepped forward again. "Brother, you are right. But she is not wearing them."

"Chee-na-wan," *Kani turned to her where she lay cowering on the ground,* "unwrap your bed roll."

With trembling difficulty Chee-na-wan took off the roll, which was slung across her back. She then began to untie it.

As soon as the blanket was partially exposed, Tong-quas jumped backwards. "No!" *he shouted.*

He pulled Kani and Nita with him as he stepped back away from Chee-na-wan and her blanket. "Do not go near her or the evil blanket."

"Evil Serpent," he commanded, "build a fire. You must burn the blanket."

Chee-na-wan looked at Kani with a question on her face.

Kani nodded, "Do as he says."

Chee-na-wan stood and began to gather sticks from the area.

"No!" Tong-quas howled again.

Chee-na-wan looked pitiful in her bewilderment.

"You must build it of birch. The white branches must burn the white man's evil. On Marettico at the very summit, you will find an evil tree that was felled by lightning. Bring back its pale branches and build a white fire."

Chee-na-wan hesitated.

"Go, Serpent. There is no time to lose."

"But, but there may be warriors."

"Then let them have you as you deserve. Go!"

Kani nodded.

Chee-na-wan moved off, stumbling into the forest in the direction of the dark hill.

Tong-quas stood with his legs apart. He turned his head to stare in the direction of Kani and Nita, yet looked far beyond them, perhaps to another place or time. Then he turned to look at the blanket still tangled with the roll.

The entire time Chee-na-wan was gone, Tong-quas stood and stared at the blanket as if it might lunge at him. Nita guessed it was well more than an hour before Chee-na-wan returned dragging two large sections of branches, Tong-quas instructed her with elaborate details exactly how to build the fire. He would scold and scoff at her when she made a mistake. Always he kept his distance, and he forbade Kani and Nita from helping.

Eventually he pronounced the fire ready to start. He took a piece of flint and a stone from a pouch on his waistband along with some tinder. With almost no motion, he struck a spark and had a flash burning in the hair-like tinder. He built a small fire beside a rock, away from Chee-na-wan's pile of branches. When he had it flaming steadily, he secured some of the burning material between two sticks and handed it to her. "Light it from the west," he instructed, pointing to one particular part of the pile.

Quickly the fire roared into a sizable pyre. "Now take out the evil blanket and feed it slowly into the flames."

Chee-na-wan did as he said. The blanket burned slowly at first but soon flames cut into it, and then it was gone, leaving a cloud that hovered as black lace before it drifted to the east.

"Now, the mat that touched it."

Chee-na-wan looked at Kani, who nodded.

The mat went up quickly.

"Now your clothes."

Chee-na-wan's young eyes grew wide in fear.

Kani turned to Tong-quas. "We have a long journey."

"She is dying anyway." He said it with such cold certainty that Chee-na-wan's head shuddered as if it had been hit with his club.

"Your clothes before the evil fire departs."

Without looking at Kani, Chee-na-wan pulled her hide wrap over her head and placed in on the fire. Nita saw that she was wearing some sort of hide underpants but no other undergarments.

"Everything," Tong-quas said, as if he were tiring of the whole ordeal.

Chee-na-wan removed the undergarments and her moccasins and placed them on the fire. She now stood naked in the cold morning. Nita saw that her body was much like her own, tall for a woman and well formed. She estimated that Chee-na-wan might be perhaps eighteen or nineteen, rather than younger as she had assumed.

Tong-quas did not look at her, but turned to Kani. "Kanianguas, you know that we should burn her."

Kani looked back at him. Nita saw what she almost thought was a look of agreement from Kani, the slightest of nods.

Tong-quas spoke again. "Strong medicine and sacrifice must fight great evil."

Nita looked at Chee-na-wan. She had stopped trembling despite the cold. She stood straight and tall with her legs slightly apart. Her chin was up and proud. Her long black hair hung straight over her shoulders to her chest, which was heaving with courage. The nipples on her round breasts stood out. Her arms were at her sides with fists slightly clenched. She stared firmly at Kani and Tong-quas as they considered her fate.

Kani looked at Chee-na-wan and saw the transformation. She motioned for Tong-quas to look. His eyes examined her body neutrally. When he glared into her eyes, Chee-na-wan did not blink or flinch. Nita watched as Tong-quas' eyes bored into Chee-na-wan's. She stood unmoving and unmoved by the attack. His eyes challenged hers, but she withstood the assault. Silence stood witness all around them.

Finally, Tong-quas turned back to Kanianguas and nodded. He stepped toward Chee-na-wan and knelt on one knee near her feet. He drew three concentric circles in the soil. Tong-quas stood and walked away from Chee-na-wan motioning for Kani to follow him. Kani signaled to Chee-na-wan that it was over. Kani slipped off her bedroll and handed it to her friend, then followed Tong-quas.

After a while Kani returned alone. Without speaking she helped Chee-na-wan fashion a garment out of her own blanket to wear on the return trip.

For the first part of the journey, no one spoke. Finally, Chee-na-wan asked Kani if Tong-quas was really her brother.

Kani nodded.

"Why is he like that?"

Kani halted and pivoted on the trail. Her eyes flashed at Chee-na-wan, "Tong-quas is a great man. He has great power. Do not mistake him." She turned and strode rapidly down the path. Nita followed Chee-na-wan as they hurried to keep pace. The route slipped slightly downhill into one of the sections of giant and solemn trees. They walked in a silence that was much heavier than before.

When they came to a small stream, Kani turned and addressed them both. "Tong-quas has great power. Great power is a great burden. People do not understand it. Some fear it. Some even ridicule it. His power was too great to be contained in a village." Without waiting for a reaction, she spun around again and stepped onto a rock and over the trickle of water, then bounded up the steeper bank on the other side.

At the top of a small rise, the forest opened into a flat meadow where flowers of orange and white mingled. The meadow eventually slanted upward, where the path slithered through brush, up a long slope and into a dim hall of trees. A noise in the shadows to her right snapped Nita's attention in that direction. Out of the blend of grays and browns, a small herd of elk pranced away.

Again, Kani picked up her line of thought, this time not stopping but speaking over her shoulder. "Tong-quas is like lightning. Power and danger come straight from the creator. Tong-quas carries both."

Nita watched Chee-na-wan's lips move. She wanted to ask more questions, but was afraid.

Kani knew it, and she strode on, continuing to explain. "Dreams of great terror haunted his nights when we were children. During the days, even as a young teen, Tong-quas spouted warnings, but the people ignored him. He began to confront anyone who came near, even the elders. He fought with other young warriors, and though he always won, it did nothing to convince anyone to listen. Soon everyone shunned him, which left him bitter and angry. I thought perhaps the years would allow that to fade, and it has somewhat. Some of the anger has aged into wisdom. If what happened today had happened when we were young..." Kani shook her head and did not complete her sentence.

As they started down in the direction of the Shawnah, she started up again, "Anger is a very powerful force, but it is poison. Like our medicines that come from the mushrooms, a tiny piece is all that is needed. Even a small amount more can kill the person. Anger well directed and in the right time is powerful. It is the lightning of the spirit that can open the night and split evil in two."

A long time later into her fierce walk, Kani slowed, turned, stopped and talked once more. "Tong-quas has the greatest strength I have ever seen in a person, but he lacks the strength to control his own power."

She paused to let Chee-na-wan think.

Finally, Kani spoke again. "So, what is there that can harness that power?"

Chee-na-wan didn't realize that Kani was waiting for her to answer until she grasped her by the arm and pulled her close to her face.

"What is your answer?"

"I, I don't know."

"I ask you again: where is that power?" Kani released Chee-na-wan's arm, nodded her head and then pointed her finger at herself. And then to Chee-na-wan's amazement, she turned her hand and pointed the finger at her. "You and I. You and I have the power."

Kani nodded as Chee-na-wan looked unbelieving. Chee-na-wan's mouth moved for a few moments before making a sound. Eventually she spoke in a soft tone, "Kanianguas, for most of the trip back I have chastised myself for my childish mistakes and my cowardly behavior. How can you say that I have something that could harness the fearsome power of Tong-quas?

"What matters is what we do with our mistakes." Kani stepped close to Chee-na-wan's face. "Today you stood the test of lightning when you *withstood the power of anger. Your spirit rose and grew. You will need that spirit and strength for the trials ahead."*

Sunlight slanted through Nita's bedroom window and forced her awake. She pulled her pillow over her head. Her heart ached for the plight of Kani and Chee-na-wan. She shared their fear for their future, but like Tong-quas, she felt she already knew the outcome.

CHAPTER NINE

Nita could tell by the sound of a rushing stream that they were nearing Octoraro when Kani suggested that they stop to rest and talk. After they had eaten some psindamoakan and had a drink of water, Kani grew solemn. She looked at the ground near the rock she sat on and scratched it lightly with her moccasin. Still looking down she said, "Tong-quas can foresee the future. He is not always right, for the future like a river does not travel in a straight line, but in most instances, he is correct. Foreseeing the future is another source of his anger. Can you imagine the frustration of knowing what is to happen, and even with all your powers you cannot change it?" She picked up a piece of a twig from the ground and began rolling it between her fingers. "Yesterday he told me that from the time he was a child his dreams were of these days that we now walk through. When he was young, it was far into the future, but now the river has flowed through many seasons and has come to the point of his dreams." She stopped moving her moccasin and brought her feet together near the base of the rock. She put the twig back where it had been and rested her hands lightly in her lap.

Kani looked at her hands as they lay still on the leather of her worn robe. Her brown skin seemed to be a part of the leather. Finally, her gaze came up, and she joined her eyes to Chee-na-wan's. "Dreams are passages. Often, they are but tiny openings through which we glimpse a larger understanding. The small streams we passed today come together to form the tumbling Octoraro. And the Octoraro and its cousins like the Conowingo each contribute to the broad-shouldered Susquehanna. In turn the Susquehanna and its cousins provide the blood waters of the great shellfish bay, the Chesapeake. So it is that your dreams flow into your life to guide and nourish you."

Kani lowered her head again, and Chee-na-wan waited patiently.

After long minutes Kanianguas seemed to summon her strength. "And now I must tell you the future." She looked into Chee-na-wan's dark eyes. Chee-na-wan looked up and met Kani's eyes. She was ready. "The illness in the village will kill our people. All of our people, one-by-one. Even those who try to flee will be chased down. Evil spirits have grown down into our land. They have taken root and have spread through many parts. The evil red eyes are about to appear and begin claiming their victims. Our people have lost their balance and have fallen from their high place."

Confusion washed over Chee-na-wan's face. "We are feared and respected. We are the Susquehannocks—we are known for our power. The stories as far back as anyone can remember are of deeds of noble strength. That cannot just disappear." Her voice was pleading more than disagreeing.

"You and I will be strong. We will be the final story of strength. This will be the last and greatest service we can provide. Tong-quas assured me that the spirits will be with us."

"Are you saying that the Susquehannocks will no longer be? How can that happen?"

Kanianguas nodded her head and looked at the ground. "The Susquehannocks will live on only in the mists of dreams and stories."

Kanianguas and Chee-na-wan stood and looked into each other's eyes. Chee-na-wan's shoulders drew back.

Kani motioned for them to move on, and they walked in silence and thought. Late in the day as they neared the cliff above the village, Nita heard drums in the distance. Chee-na-wan looked at her mentor, "Kanianguas, those are the drums of mourning."

Kanianguas nodded, "It has begun."

The drums grew louder as they approached the bluff. When they got to the top of the cliff, Nita looked down at the long houses and saw torment flowing among the people as they ran one to another in panic. Now the drums pounded even louder.

"Anybody home?" Nita jerked awake. She heard someone coming in her front door. "Hey Nita, you here? I been knocking and knocking. I saw your car out there, but nobody answered." It was Henry.

Nita's heart continued the drumbeat from the village. "Ah, yeah. I'm here," she called from the bedroom, trying to shake her head awake.

"Sorry to barge in," he yelled from the front door. "Nobody answered so I used my key. You okay?"

"Yeah, yeah, I'm fine."

"Okay if I look at that sink?"

"Yeah. Sure. What time is it?"

"Almost 10:30?"

The terror of her dream clung to her, fogging her eyes and ears. She put on her robe and came out of the bedroom. "I guess I was just really tired."

Henry stuck his head halfway under the kitchen sink and continued talking to her. "Hey, when I was trying to get you to answer the door,

I walked around on the porch. Looks like you had some luck with finding artifacts."

"Yeah, I found a couple things. I'm not real sure what to look for."

"Well you found that cup."

"Yeah, for all I know that came from K-Mart." Nita rubbed her face in an effort to force the sleep and dreams out of her head.

Henry slid out from under the sink and looked up at her, "Well I don't think they had K-Marts in the mid-1700s." He rubbed his shoulder. "This old seventy-two-year-old body don't twist and turn as well as it used to."

"The mid-1700s?"

"Did you see that mark on the bottom? There are people who could give you a better read than me, but I'm guessing it was made in England somewhere in the mid-1700s. Probably brought over here by an early settler."

"An early settler? Here?"

"White folks been living here since around 1700, even before."

"You're serious? That cup is that old?"

"Now I could be wrong. An archeologist could tell you for sure." He picked up a monkey wrench from next to him and turned its wheel to open the gap in its jaws. "Listen, I brought my shovel in case you wanted a little help digging in your garden."

Nita could tell that Henry was excited about the prospect. But she absolutely could not waste any more time. She had to make progress on the brain chemistry paper that was due Wednesday.

She was still deciding how to respond when he put his head back under the sink. Nita tucked her hands into the pockets of her faded blue robe and went back into her room and put on some old jeans. She could hear Henry fussing under the sink. Something went thump, followed by a muffled "son-of-a-bitch."

As she finished getting changed, Henry yelled through the bedroom door, "All fixed. She won't leak anymore."

"Thanks very much," Nita called back. "I really appreciate you doing that."

"Yeah, she's good now. Pipe just came loose a little."

She heard Henry go out the front door, and she slipped out of her room and into the bathroom. When she came out, he was sitting in the living room, holding his shovel. Nita tried not to look disappointed.

"I've been thinking about this all week. I used to like helping Bessell out in the garden."

Nita tried to smile. "Well I have to get to my studying, so I can just do a little gardening today. I'll meet you out there as soon as I get some toast." While she waited for the toast to pop, she fretted over Henry. He was such a nice guy, but she worried that she needed to separate him better from this place. It was hard to know how to say something without hurting his feelings.

The sun's rays hung nearly straight down as they started into digging. Henry was now sporting an Orioles baseball cap. "They already started spring training, you know," he said pointing to his hat. Nita said she wanted to add another line to the edge of the garden. She figured that would be a defined objective and then she could get going on her school work. Henry started from one end, and she started from the other so they'd meet in the middle. The row wasn't very long, and they chatted back and forth. Periodically Henry would stop and lean on his shovel and tell her some detail about what Bessell used to do in her garden. "And all that stuff she did that I used to try to correct, like how she would weed by hand when it would have been easier with a hoe, that's the things I miss the most." His eyes moistened at the edges, and he quickly went back to digging.

With each shovel-full Henry was like a little kid looking for treasure. He sifted and shook the dirt as he searched for arrowheads, making his progress slow. When he finally found one, he started hopping like a kid on Christmas morning. "Yep, that's one," he said rubbing the dirt from it. "Yep it's a beaut," he stepped forward and held it up for Nita to see.

Nita had to agree that it was a nicely formed projectile point complete with the tail, as she called it.

"You can have it," Henry handed it to her.

"Oh, I couldn't. You found it."

"Naw, it will be part of your collection. I forgot to bring ours, but you'll see that we have some of them already."

"I don't really have a collection."

"This one's a good place to start, plus all that good stuff on the porch."

"But it's your land."

"Listen, Nita," he smiled, "I'd be pleased to have you keep whatever you manage to find out here. Besides, if you think about it, any of us just happen to be here at this moment, so it's not really my land, even though you call me your 'land lord.' I'm certainly not a lord, and it isn't really my land. This land belongs to all the people who have lived here over the ages. We count too, but we're just the latest in the parade. I guess you could say the land connects us all together over time."

When they were almost together in the middle of the row, Nita's shovel struck a rock. The solid thunk told her this one was bigger than most. It took a couple minutes till she was able to clear the soil from around it. Henry stepped over with his shovel to help her pry it out of the ground.

When they had the edges loose, he lifted it out of the hole and was about to carry it over to the rock pile when she stopped him. "Wait, let me see that."

He set the rock on the dirt near her feet. Nita bent down and touched it.

"It's pretty heavy," he warned.

Nita rolled it over and had to catch her breath. She dropped to her knees on the soil.

She brushed away the soil that remained in an indentation in the middle of the odd-shaped rock. She recognized the rock. It was the mortar Kani used to prepare her herbal medicines. Nita felt dizzy. She wasn't sure why her head was spinning, but she knew enough to remain kneeling.

"You okay?" Henry asked.

"Yeah, yeah," she muttered, wondering what to tell him.

"Look at this," she said. "See this impression in the rock. Could this have been a mortar for grinding things?"

Henry bent down and rubbed the center of the rock. It does have a strange shape. "I suppose it could be. The Indians ground acorns and corn and other things in holes like this in rocks or logs."

Henry carried the rock to the porch while Nita turned over the last couple shovels of soil. She looked for a pestle but didn't see one.

Henry was still looking at the rock when she got to the porch. "I have some books that were Bessell's. I'll see if they have any pictures of things like this."

As soon as Henry left, Nita hurried inside to shower. After a quick lunch, she sat down on the floor to study.

CHAPTER TEN

*P*anic screamed from the faces of everyone in the village. A woman carrying a lifeless child staggered from a long house. Another child lay crying in the mud. Pustules covered the little girl's face, arms and legs, but people ran right past her. Nita stooped to try to help, but someone knocked into her. She fell and could no longer reach the little girl.

Cold rain hit her face as she lay on the ground. She looked up to see Kani slogging toward to a young woman with a scarlet rash on her face and arms. The woman dragged her limp son, his heels making tracks in the wet ground. He looked to be about twelve and would not likely get any older.

"Lay him here," Kani instructed.

"Chee-na-wan, more tea," Kani called over her shoulder. Chee-na-wan was busily stirring a brew in a large earthen bowl near a fire.

"Can you help him? You must help him. He is my only son," the mother wiped tears from her cheeks.

Before Kani could respond, the mother suddenly spit venom at her. "You cannot help us. You have failed us. Look at what has happened to our people." She swept her arm around. Bodies lay all over. Some lay still in contorted postures, and others writhed on the muddy ground, moaning. Nita stood and went to Kani's side.

Near them, an old and deeply wrinkled woman sat hunched over, cradling an unconscious young man. She swayed slowly forward and back, chanting. A man and woman were tearing down a hut and lashing together the poles to form some sort of apparatus. Nita guessed that it was to carry their goods as they tried to flee.

The forlorn mother of the limp boy continued to berate Kani. "Your medicine is worthless. Where is your power? You are an evil spirit, not the healer you pretend."

The woman crumpled to the ground at Kani's feet with her son halfway on top of her. Kani gathered both of them, and held them close to her. She surveyed the scene of chaos and pain.

"Chee-na-wan, come here," she said gently.

"It is not ready yet."

"No, just come here. I must tell you something."

Kani laid the mother and son down and arranged their bodies to be comfortable together. Neither was moving.

She drew Chee-na-wan and Nita close to her. "We must recognize this moment. This is exactly what Tong-quas described to me when we were there. While we will continue to try to do all that we can, we can also see that evil spirits are consuming our world. For those who have reached that point beyond which we can do nothing to save them," she looked around at the destruction, "then we will ease their pain and help them on their journey."

Kani led them into her hut. There she dug in the ground with her hands near where the rest of her medicines were stored. Slowly she unearthed a clay bowl with a dark leather cover. From it she took a leather pouch that was bound with a leather strap. She unwrapped it.

"This medicine is both terrible and kind. The tiniest amount holds powerful healing, but even a little more and the person will die." She looked at Chee-na-wan. "I will show you how to carefully make something that will help our people on their journey. But for you and I, we will never take it. We must hold on until all is done that we can do. Tong-quas told me when we were leaving that you and I are to be the last embers of the Susquehannock fire."

"But what about him?"

Kani looked past Chee-na-wan into a deep pain. "Tong-quas is dead." Her eyes needed to cry, but she would not let the tears come. "Our world today was already known to him from the earliest moments. That is the terrible truth he tried to tell but which most people looked at only with blind eyes.

"The river flows and we may sit on any rock along its course, but always we know that there is more, even when we do not think about the many turns. Tong-quas traveled the full river, aware at each moment of the whole story of its flow. He could see in each drop of water the entirety of his life and all lives. His sacrifice when we departed was to drown in a drop."

Chee-na-wan nodded her understanding. "Tong-quas was the river, was he not?"

Kani smiled and tears flowed from her eyes. "He is. Still today, he is," she agreed.

As Nita watched them work, she felt nausea and agony sweep over her body. Kani added a brown powder to a thick paste-like material that Chee-na-wan stirred in a bowl. Nita saw that the rash was now appearing on their arms too. She gasped. Clearly the small pox epidemic was to kill them all. Their symptoms looked precisely like the pictures in her pathology book.

The text even mentioned the devastating effects the disease had on Native American tribes.

Kani turned toward Nita and looked into her eyes. "Power travels as wisdom through dreams. You must carry on."

Nita groaned in pain. Kani used a piece of corn stalk to spoon out a barely perceptible amount of the brown paste. She put it on Nita's tongue.

Nita fell into a deep sleep.

Again, the drumming in the village woke her. This time she was a little quicker to recognize that it was someone knocking on her door.

"Just a minute," she called. She got up from the floor where she was slumped on her books. She shook her head as she realized it was Sunday evening. She opened the door to see Henry standing there with a cardboard box.

"You sleeping again?" Henry looked at her. "You don't look so good."

"Well I guess I am dragging a little. I kind of feel like I am coming down with something. Here, come in and put that down. It looks heavy," Nita pointed to her desk chair.

"Listen, I didn't mean to bother you. I had just promised to show you our collection. Maybe I'll just leave it here for you to look at when you're feeling better." As he set down the box, he added, "Hey, I looked in Bessell's books for something like that big rock with the hole in it, but I didn't see any pictures that looked like it."

Henry looked at Nita, "Can I help you? Can I get you some medicine or something to eat? Maybe some chicken soup?"

"Oh, thanks Henry," she smiled. "Actually, I did make some soup for lunch. I think I'm okay. I guess my body was telling me it needed some more sleep."

When Henry left, Nita spent a few more hours studying and then went to bed. Monday evening, she worked on her brain chemistry paper.

Tuesday, she joined a group of classmates on rounds at the hospital, this time in the critical care unit. They hurried down the hall after the doctor, listening to him spout his knowledge.

"Let's hit one more. This is typical of what you'll see. I should warn you that this old guy is CTD. He was brought here from another floor this morning. We see a fair amount of this, so it's a good example."

One of the students asked what CTD meant.

"Circling The Drain," the doctor replied with a smirk and a tilt of his head. "It's an irreverent term, but you will definitely hear it."

The doctor led them into the room, where Nita was shocked to see that the old man was Elmer, the dancer from the orthopedic floor. He was sleeping when they walked in and was jarred awake by the sudden activity.

"Pneumonia," the doctor announced. "Often fatal in the old. This patient came in for a hip, I believe."

The doctor noticed Elmer stirring in the bed. "Oh, you're awake. Good."

The doctor flipped back the covers and exposed Elmer from his feet to his navel. His hospital gown was pulled off to the side and most of his body was left open for everyone to see.

Elmer struggled to cover up.

"The hip operation went well as you can see," the doctor said as he pulled the blanket back over. "Unfortunately, pneumonia can set in post-op, and some strains are particularly resistant." He looked at the students and then at Elmer. "We're trying to fight it, though, aren't we?" He patted Elmer's ankle through the blanket.

Elmer looked at the students. The spark in his eyes had dimmed. He looked much older than when Nita had stopped to see him just a few days earlier.

Suddenly Elmer saw Nita in the group, and his face lit up. He coughed and a weak smile struggled to his lips. His eyes seemed to apologize for his condition.

As the group turned to file out of the room, Nita stepped forward to touch his arm. "You take care of yourself."

Outside the room, the doctor looked at Nita and then said to the group, "I want to point out that it is inappropriate for students to touch or talk to the patients unless instructed to do so by the attending physician. In fact, touching is a good way to spread disease or catch it, particularly dangerous with resistant pneumonia."

Nita started to respond by saying, "I recently read an article about the importance of touch and …," but the doctor burst into a fury. "Are you arguing with me? Are you contradicting me?"

"No, I was just going to say that I actually knew…" Nita couldn't get out that she knew Elmer.

"You were going to say that you already know it all. I have seen lots like you. I'm here to tell you that you have a lot to learn. You're not going to come in here and decide after a few years of med school that you know everything."

"That's all for today," the doctor turned to go, and then whirled back around, "unless anyone else wants to teach me about medicine."

Nita and the others looked stunned as he stomped off.

An older nurse who had been observing the incident caught up with Nita as she walked down the hall to leave. "Honey, just a friendly warning. Don't get on the wrong side of Dr. Warner. When he blows up like that, don't even try to say anything. We've all learned that lesson a time or two up here. He explodes at the slightest provocation. And on the other side, no matter what one of us does for him, he will never thank you for it. The only time he'll pat you on the back is if he knows you have a sunburn." She winked and patted Nita on the shoulder.

The following day while in a pathology lab, Nita was working with her lab partner to get the microscope properly adjusted to examine cancerous skin cells when the lab instructor called her name. "Nita Thomas, a message for you." He handed her a note telling her to see her faculty adviser by the end of the day.

"This is weird," she showed the note to her partner, a tall black man named Terry. "I never hear from Dr. Burns. I see her once a semester to get my course schedule signed." She put the note in her backpack and continued with the lab work.

"Just be careful with her," Terry warned.

Nita turned toward him, her hand still on the large silver knob of the microscope. "What do you mean?"

Terry leaned forward and whispered, "She's my adviser too, and I was told early-on that she has a habit of disliking students." He raised his eyebrows.

"But I haven't given her any reason to dislike me. I hardly ever see her."

"I haven't had any problems myself. Of course, they say it's mostly female students that have problems with her." Terry talked in a slight drawl that hinted at his Alabama roots. "Just sharing what I heard."

After the lab was completed, Nita headed over to Dr. Burns's office. On the way up the stairs, she could feel her heartbeat rise. I hope this doesn't take long, she thought, wondering again what sort of bureaucratic item she might have missed.

"Excuse me," she said to a woman at a desk outside a suite of offices. This was a different assistant than last semester. "Is Dr. Burns in? She asked to see me."

"You must be Nita Thomas. She told me to go get her out of her meeting when you arrived. Just a moment." The short stocky woman, who appeared to be about forty, immediately rose and clomped down the marble hallway. In two minutes, she returned with Dr. Burns who was wearing a stern gray suit with a stiff red collar. Nita had noted previously that her manner of dress made her look older than the mid-forties, which she guessed to be her real age. Her short brown hair was always forced tightly back along the sides of her head.

With curt formality Dr. Burns greeted her and motioned her into her office then closed the door.

"You can sit there," she pointed to a chair facing the large wooden desk, which was rimmed with stacks of papers.

Dr. Burns opened a file in the middle of the desk and read quickly. Nita could see that she was looking at some sort of a memo on school letterhead.

"Can you explain to me what happened yesterday?"

Nita was baffled by Dr. Burns's question. She scanned through her cluttered recollection of the previous day. She quickly lit on the incident with Dr. Warner.

"Are you talking about what happened at the hospital?"

"Let's not get cute here. I suggest you tell me exactly what happened."

"Nothing, really. Dr. Warner said something to the group because I said something to a patient."

"And then you attempted to contradict him."

"No, I simply tried to discuss something I had read."

"Well, you are potentially in serious trouble. You have picked the wrong person to get into a conflict with. Are you aware that Dr. Warner is the same Warner as the Warner Wing of the hospital? His grandfather was the patriarch of this facility. Now, I am trying to help you. Please tell me everything that happened so I can."

"I'll be glad to tell you, but this whole thing seems to be blown way out of proportion."

"That will be for others to decide."

Nita recounted what little had happened. As an after-thought she added that she actually knew the patient.

"Is that right, Miss Thomas? And how did you come to already know the patient?"

Nita explained that she had met him previously while doing rounds on the orthopedic floor and then had stopped in there Saturday evening to say hello.

"Now let me get this straight," Dr. Burns's eyes narrowed and her sharp cheekbones seemed to protrude even more than normal. "You went in to see a patient on your own without authorization?"

When the words came back at her from Dr. Burns, it sounded much different from what she intended. Nita's mouth moved as she tried to reformulate what had happened, but Dr. Burns spoke first and fast. "This was not your patient. You are not even a resident. You do realize, I hope, that this is in direct violation of our procedures, do you not? I do hope that you have familiarized yourself with the policies and procedures that have been developed here at the University of Delaware Medical School over its 103 years of existence and which allow us to operate efficiently and appropriately." Dr. Burns sighed and pursed her lips. She leaned over her desk toward Nita. "Miss Thomas, I do want to try to help you, but this is even bigger than I had feared." Dr. Burns paused and looked at Nita with a quiet stare that was hard to read. Finally, Dr. Burns continued, "Is there anything else I need to know."

"No." As soon as the word shot from her mouth and her mouth clamped shut, Nita realized she had responded too abruptly. Dr. Burns's eyebrows rose.

Nita took a breath and tried to regroup. She struggled to get words that would explain the whole situation without sounding defensive. She looked down at her backpack, which sat across her lap.

"Seems like maybe there is something else," Dr. Burns poked at her. "My advice would be to come clean on everything. Trying to cover up is not going to be helpful."

Nita's eyes flipped up in honest surprise. "Look, I may have made a mistake with that patient, but I didn't mean to violate any procedures. I never even thought about that. I made a mistake, but I don't think I did any harm."

"You still haven't answered the question of what else you have done."

"Nothing," Nita replied earnestly.

"I would advise you to think hard about that. Again, you have picked a very formidable opponent."

"Look, even a nurse on the floor told me that this Dr. Warner is a problem."

Dr. Burns's eyebrows rose even higher than before. Nita immediately realized that she had again stepped onto a landmine.

"You talked to a nurse about this incident."

"No, she talked to me. She saw him yell at me in the hall, and she said something to me."

Dr. Burns tapped the pointed red fingernail of her index finger on her desk and stared at Nita. "My advice to you is to think about everything else you have done and get it all out at once." Dr. Burns let the ensuing silence bear down on Nita. After long moments she asked, "Do you have anything further to say?"

"No," Nita murmured.

"Then let me explain what will happen now. As your faculty adviser, I will be your advocate in the process." Nita thought about what her lab partner Terry had said about Dr. Burns's reputation for disliking female students. She struggled not to let her concern show on her face. While she tried to subdue the panic, she missed the next couple sentences of what Dr. Burns said but did not dare to ask her to repeat them.

"Is that clear?" Dr. Burns concluded.

"I think so," Nita lied.

"In the meantime, try to stay out of trouble."

Nita stood, understanding that she was now to leave. She did so slowly, desperately wanting to ask Dr. Burns to repeat what was to happen next.

As she neared the door, Dr. Burns added, "You will receive a formal notice of this in the mail."

CHAPTER ELEVEN

With dark anticipation Nita waited for the piece of mail to arrive. She wondered how much time was added to mail delivery because she lived in this remote outpost of Port Deposit. Each evening she stopped at the mailbox as she pulled in the driveway, but each time there was no letter from the university.

During the wait she found it very difficult to concentrate. She wondered what the consequences would be. Surely, they couldn't expel her. Or could they? She re-read the Policies and Procedures Manual, but it was very general in its list of penalties for violations. Disciplinary actions ranged from a mild warning to a formal sanction letter to expulsion or even criminal charges for some offenses. She worried that Dr. Hunter Warner the third could do what he damn well pleased. Well if they tried to expel her, she would sue. Surely, they couldn't expel her. She wondered if she should get a lawyer at this point. She really didn't have the money for that. And what if Dr. Burns found out she hired a lawyer?

Nita wished she had spent more time cultivating relationships. She really didn't have any connections on which to draw. She knew a few of the students fairly well but none of the faculty. She focused all her time and energy on schoolwork and not on socializing. She mentally scanned the list of professors or doctors she had encountered for possible people she could consult with. Dr. O'Neill, the specialist in geriatric orthopedics was the one possibility, but she really didn't know her well. Dr. O'Neill had simply paid special attention to her, and she seemed nice. Knowing little about the inner-workings among the faculty, it all seemed full of risks. She needed help and had no idea where to turn.

Once again on Friday when she got home, she opened the mailbox, but the letter wasn't there. She sat on the couch and tried to concentrate on studying, but her mind wandered away. She would periodically catch her thoughts wallowing in dismal outcomes like getting kicked out of school. What would she do then? All she had ever wanted was to be a doctor, to heal people.

She remembered drawing a crayon picture of herself in an operating room when she was in second grade. She still had the picture somewhere. Actually, she recalled, when she drew the picture, she had assumed she would be a nurse. After all, back then all the doctors on TV were men, and the nurses were all women.

Nita recalled the day years earlier, not long before the car accident, when she had learned that maybe that didn't need to be so. The memory was crystal clear. Her mother had taken her and her little sister, Carly, to the doctor for their check-ups. On the way home, Nita and her sister were in the backseat of their big blue car. She had made the idle comment that she wished she was a boy.

"Why do you say that, Nita?" her mother asked.

"Because if I was a boy then I could be a doctor when I grow up."

"Oh, Nita, you don't have to be a boy to be a doctor."

"Really?"

"Absolutely. If you work hard and get good grades, you can be anything you want."

"Even a doctor?"

"Absolutely, and don't let anyone ever tell you differently."

"Carly, do you understand that, too. You can be anything you want to be when you grow up."

"Anything I want."

"That's right, Carly. Have you thought about what you might to be when you grow up?

Nita watched Carly think for a little bit and then her sister said, "I think I'll be a big black dog."

Mom and Nita both burst out laughing. When Mom caught her breath, she apologized to Carly for laughing and said that they would need to talk more about it when she got a little older. Carly didn't seem to mind and even helped retell the story about the funny thing she had said.

That had been a wonderful day. Before the accident, Mom often reinforced the point about hard work and dedication making things possible. But Mom never said anything about jerks getting in the way and screwing things up.

"Hey lady, you getting on or not?"

Nita realized the man in the red t-shirt was talking to her. He was holding open an aluminum gate that controlled admission to an amusement ride. His arm sported a tattoo that read "Hell on Earth." Above the words, a demon rose from a split in a globe.

"Come on, lady. You're holdin' tings up." The man's greased back, black hair framed his pockmarked face. A cigarette bobbed between his lips as he spoke. The smoke curled into his squinting eyes.

Someone behind her, whom she couldn't see in the haze, nudged her.

Nita moved up the ramp to the open teacup that waited in front of her. She slid in around a central round wheel and found that she had joined others in the cup. The piece of the cup that had been open was closed behind her by the attendant.

"You's enjoy youselfs," he said in a monotone that told her he no longer realized he was talking.

As the ride shifted slowly into motion, she saw that one of the other occupants was Dr. Hunter Warner the third. His face bore a plastic smile, and though he looked at her, he seemed not to recognize her.

Their teacup followed other teacups along a circular track. Soon the track started to undulate. The cups rose and fell like small boats on a stormy sea. Then the tea cups each started to spin, slowly at first but accelerating constantly. Faster and faster and faster the cup spun. Nita looked around at the other half-dozen people in the teacup. They all clung to the central wheel trying to steady themselves and attempting to keep from touching the others. Nita's knuckles looked like stubs of chalk and the tendons in the backs of her hands bulged against her skin.

She looked up at those who shared the cup. Their faces reflected her unease, except Dr. Warner whose plastic smile was glued perfectly to his face. His arms were sprawled across the back of the cup's rim in a gesture of patronizing ownership.

Fear rose to replace unease as the centrifugal force of the spinning drew each of them against the back of the cup. One by one they released the wheel and gave up the struggle against trying not to touch the others. Two people opposite her found themselves under the outstretched arms of Dr. Warner in a happy portrait of companionship. One was Dr. Burns whose head rested near his armpit. The other was Dr. Malkowski, Nita's Ob/Gyn instructor from the previous year.

Except for Dr. Warner, who grinned like a wax figure in an arcade, the skin of the other faces was pulled back toward their ears, flaring their nostrils and exposing their teeth. Their eyelids strained to stay in place, but soon they too gave up the fight, and they all glared at each other with eyebrows halfway up their foreheads.

Faster and faster came the whirring in Nita's ears. The world outside their teacup became a streaked watercolor of lights in a rain that was soaking only their ride.

A cracking sound was the first signal of disaster. The noise erupted, then painful light seeped through the base of the teacup as it began to break apart. Looking down was like gazing into the face of the sun. Golden shards stabbed up from between their feet as the cracks widened. One crack formed a ragged split up Dr. Warner's neatly pressed suit. It continued to separate up his neck and into his face. At his lips his smile cleaved in two. The crack continued up until it parted his waxed hair.

Suddenly with a loud retort the cup shattered from its base, and the pieces flew off into a painting that surrounded them. In slow motion each piece rose up and out of the ride and lodged itself in the surrounding painting. Nita's piece contained the handle, which became impaled near the top of the canvas, giving her a seat above the scene.

As the rain continued to fall, the colors ran down over the world, causing the hues to bleed into countless shades of grief. Nita cried with it, and her tears streaked a garish rainbow onto her white t-shirt. The sound of her sobs caused her piece of the teacup to rise. Gradually she came out the top of the canvas where gray morning light forced it all to fade.

Rain smeared down the window. With what little strength she had, Nita pulled herself out of bed.

CHAPTER TWELVE

Saturday, as she ate a bowl of oatmeal, she was thankful for a sunny morning even though she would not have time to work in the garden. She took her coffee to her desk and started to read over her notes on cancers of the eye, but she listened as each car went by out on the road. Where was the letter?

Finally, a small white van with red and blue lettering pulled up to the mailbox out at the road by the stone wall. She jumped up and ran out. The envelope she'd been waiting for burned in her hand as she hurried back the gravel driveway. As soon as she was inside, she pushed her finger into an edge of the envelope and tore it apart. She read through it quickly. It wasn't what she had expected. She assumed there was going to be a meeting or a hearing of some sort. Apparently, that was being waived. The letter was very formal, almost legalistic. She had to read it twice to get the gist. Nita surmised that she was being put on probation and that she was to meet with Dr. Burns for more details.

Nita went to the laundromat on Sunday and then pressed her best outfit to wear.

First thing Monday she went to Dr. Burns's office. In a starched discussion, Nita learned that due to Dr. Burns's heroic efforts, her medical career was salvaged. Dr. Burns presented her most stern expression as she pointed her red-tipped finger at Nita, "I hope you appreciate what has been done for you. Your grades are good, and we want to see you finish here. It is now up to you to stay out of trouble."

Nita thanked her for her assistance and hoped the threads of insincerity didn't show through.

As she walked down the hall from Dr. Burns's office, Dr. Warner was walking toward it.

"Ms. Thomas," he greeted her, extending his hand. His manner was a confusing mix of friendliness and formality. Despite guidance from most parts of her brain, Nita's arm extended her hand to shake his. He held it just a moment too long. She gently retracted it from his grasp.

"Listen," he said looking at her eyes, "I'm glad we were able to help you out of your little problem."

"Yes, I certainly appreciate that," she forced the words through her teeth.

"Let's just chalk it up to a female mistake, shall we?" He pasted a practiced smile on his face.

Nita matched his smile by pasting one on her own face and nodded.

"I mean, no harm no foul. The old gentleman did die by the way."

Nita felt like she had been kicked in the stomach. "El...I mean the patient died?"

"Yep, just as I feared. These resistant bacteria are becoming more and more of a problem to manage. Especially in the elderly, they can be very difficult."

Nita fought back tears.

"Listen," Dr. Warner said, "I've got to run, but if you ever need anything else, don't hesitate to call on me. I know how to get things done around here," he winked at her and patted her shoulder.

Although she attended her classes, she missed much of what was said. At the end of the afternoon she blew off going to the library and went to her car. There she cried onto Little Earl's steering wheel. "He died. And nobody cares." she told Earl. "He just died, and that's that."

Nita bought a newspaper on the way home. She opened it at her kitchen table and was disappointed to learn that Elmer's funeral had been that morning. The brief and bland paragraph seemed to be an inappropriate end to a fine man. After she read the obituary, she turned off the light and sat in the dark. She wanted to cry, but anger put fire in her eyes in place of tears. A good man is gone, and Dr. Warner and Dr. Burns remain. Her mouth tasted of bitter medicine.

At her desk, she tried to read but was retaining nothing. She decided sleep was a better option.

Nita was looking into a fire. A single blue flame danced slowly along the shimmering red coals of a large log. The flicker swayed gently to an air of its own making. Waves breathed among the bed of embers that throbbed under the log.

"I love this time of evening," came a fragile voice next to her.

Nita, seated in an upright chair, turned her head and saw the pale, etched face of an older woman. Long strands of gray and black hair, the consistency of steel wool, framed the woman's pensive look. From her angled chair, she stared into the fireplace with ice blue eyes. She raised the palms of her hands toward the heat. The backs of her hands showed fine wrinkles, like used tissue paper. Nita guessed that the woman was in her late fifties, but her old-fashioned dress and cushion hat made her look sort of like Betsy Ross.

"Most people fear the night," she said in a soft Irish brogue. "Darkness is when the evil spirits come out – don't you know, don't you know?" she smiled to underscore the mild sarcasm.

She sighed. "Alas, people fear what they don't understand, which is easier than working to understand. Soon, their fear becomes hate."

She continued to stare into the fire, speaking comfortably to Nita in a lilting voice. "One might imagine that since we have come to this land with the God-given chance to carve out a new way that we would be working to engender understanding – we who suffered the results of failed ways – but instead the old fears seem to have secured an unwarranted passage like the rats in the holds of the ships."

The fireplace was large and charred. Heavy andirons supported the long log over the embers. A crude hook on a pivoting iron arm held a black kettle near one side of the fireplace. A poker leaned on the stones that began as a hearth floor outside the fireplace and wrapped back inside the core.

The woman stood and walked to the door. She lifted a thick wooden plank from beside the door and slipped it onto black metal brackets on each side of the doorframe. "I bar the door, not for security from my fears, but for security from theirs."

Nita looked around the windowless, one-room log cabin. It smelled heavily of dank wood smoke. The room was a mix of both primitive and elegant furnishings and possessions. A table in the middle of the room, about four feet long and two feet wide, was just a slice of tree trunk supported by branches attached at each corner. A beautifully crafted chair sat next to it. The chair matched a hutch against the wall. Both had obviously been made by a professional furniture maker. Nita stood and walked over to examine the hutch more closely. The doors on the lower part had lighter woods inlaid in a red-toned frame around the panel. The open shelves on the upper portion held a fine white and blue china tea set and numerous china canisters. The canisters were of various sizes and shapes, some cylinders, some more globe shaped. Most were white to match the china set. Some had blue markings. A few were buff-colored with blue writing and designs.

The woman returned to the fire and used the poker to adjust the big log. With some difficulty, she picked up a three-foot log from a stack near the fireplace and placed it on the andirons next to the other log. With the poker she nudged it to where she wanted it. When she was satisfied, she returned to her chair, which matched the one by the table, propped her feet on the hearth and again stared into the fire. Nita returned to sit beside her in yet another matching chair.

Eventually the woman continued her thought. "So much that we do in life is moved by fear in one way or another. A powerful emotion tis fear. Fear and insecurity, the woven fabric of lives and society. Powerful emotions. Emotions that drive motion. Tis a horse moving in the wrong direction to be sure, but the rider imagines progress nonetheless." She looked up and raised her brown eyebrows, "If one is using the wrong measure or is not particular about the direction of the motion, he can cipher any motion as progress. But in the night, the thoughts of right come riding and disturb his slumber. At his peril he ignores them, but he does so nonetheless. The deeper the commitment, the deeper the blindness. Some folks expend their vigor wrapping themselves in darkness."

Nita looked at the woman. She seemed equally wise and weary. Her pale blue dress was made of a thick, coarse fabric. The weave was worn in places. Behind the woman some sort of musical instrument stood against the wall. It looked like a small version of a piano or organ. Beside the instrument was a bed against the wall. What appeared to be a homemade quilt was draped across the bed. At the head of the bed, hung a cross made of split twigs. At the other end of the bed a small spinning wheel sat on the rough-hewn floor. Two wooden buckets full of water rested near it.

The log she had just placed on the fire popped and shot a burning ember out onto the stone hearth near the woman's laced leather boots. The woman watched the red glow gradually fade. "Nothing is all good or all bad. The same force that gives us heat can cause us great pain. The world is always a balance of forces. The strongest sunlight creates the deepest shadows."

She stood and picked up a broom, which was a tree branch with stiff grass tied onto one end. She swept the ashes from the hearth back into the fireplace then returned to her seat.

"Even love. The most powerful source of warmth and yet all the lang since, the source of greatest pain. Seamus was the light of my life. He gave music to my years," her eyes moved off in time. "But now that he is gone, there is an emptiness that can never be filled. My bell has no clapper," she sighed again. "A high price to pay, but worth all the pence in the puddle."

The fire popped again.

"Oh, Seamus," she looked into the fire, "where are you, my love?"

She smiled as tears rolled down her face. "'Rachel,' he would say, 'I'll be as close as the red rose of your cheeks, most notably when you smile.'"

Nita looked at the red glow of Rachel's cheeks. Her skin was so pale that blue veins could be seen as if veiled only by frail lace.

Nita woke moments before her alarm and punched the button to prevent its same rude commercial from blaring at her. " No, I don't want to buy a brand new 1987 Ford Taurus," she said defiantly.

The following days moved more smoothly. The workload was as heavy as ever, but she managed to achieve some balance. On Saturday with the help of Henry she planted potatoes, lettuce and peas. "We're a bit late on the potatoes," he said. "Bessell always said to plant them on St. Patrick's Day, but that was Tuesday. Just a few days late, though, so it should be just fine." They each found an Indian arrowhead to add to Nita's collection, which now took up a small corner of the porch.

Nita went in to get cleaned up, but Henry said he wanted to do some more digging. When she came back out, he said that his efforts to expand the garden into some thick brush had encountered an area full of large stones. "They all seem to be set in a row," he pointed out. "May have been the foundation for some old building." While Nita watched, Henry cut back more of the brush and found additional rubble. Even the stones that were not in rows had clearly been chiseled into blocks. "Stay back from this area unless you like snakes," he cautioned. "My guess is that they'd like this place. Of course, they're probably still hibernating, but it's still a word to the wise." He used his rake to push over one stone that sat on top of two others. It tumbled away from them, but nothing crawled out. "I guess it's still too cold for the snakes to be out and about."

"That's good," Nita said. "I don't mind them too much, as long as they keep their distance and aren't the venomous type."

Henry was examining the stones. "See how these are black on one side? I bet they were from a chimney."

Nita wasn't paying much attention. "Well, Henry, thanks for all your help today. I'm glad we got started with the actual planting. It's supposed to rain some tomorrow, so hopefully God will do the watering for us. Listen, I've got a ton of studying to do, so I am going to head to the library. I do much better there."

"No problem. I'm done for now too."

Thursday afternoon in dermatology lecture, Nita scribbled rapidly to catch what was on the overhead transparency about basal cell carcinoma. Dr. Reed, who was affectionately known as Dr. Speed among the students, was very knowledgeable but also very difficult. He carried a large mug of coffee everywhere and raced through his lectures, which were not necessarily fully aligned with what was in the book. Before she had the last sentence transcribed, he shut off the projector. "That's it. Better know it," he said in a threatening tone as he strode to the door.

"Hey, Nita," Paul Alvarez pulled on her arm as she attempted to bolt out the door after Dr. Reed. "There's another party this weekend. Tomorrow night at Sarah's. You coming?"

Before she could answer, he continued, "Or are you going to blow it off like you did mine…even after you said you were going to come?"

"Paul, I did intend to come. I wasn't feeling well."

"Oh sure. That's not even an original excuse."

"It's the truth."

"So, what's your excuse this weekend?" he smiled.

She paused as reasons not to go ran through her mind. Severe pressure to be studying was even less original than being sick, but no less true.

"Come on," he prodded, "think up a good one. Let me guess, you were planning study."

"Actually," she admitted, "I was. I am just so far behind, and…"

Paul gave her a stupid grin. "We're all behind. It's med school. Come on, everybody's going to be there." He began surveying people as they tried to file past them out the door.

"Susan, you going to Sarah's party?"

"I think so."

"Jesse, you going to Sarah's party tomorrow night?"

"Probably."

"See everybody's going."

Rich Arnone was next in line. "Hey Rich, you going to Sarah's party?"

"Well I wasn't planning to. I really need to study."

Nita laughed, and Paul let out an exasperated sigh.

"What's so funny?" Rich asked.

"I told him I couldn't go to the party because I had to study, and Mr. Social Director told me I was the only one not going."

Paul put his arm around Rich's shoulder. "Rich, you got to come. The whole thing is on you."

Rich's eyes responded to the drama. "OK, I'll sacrifice," he said with a chuckle, "but only if Nita goes."

Nita looked at Rich, "Hey, thanks a bunch," she made a fist and gently poked him in his upper arm.

"Great," Paul said, "Sarah lives at 449 Overhill Street. It's the third left up Stewart Street."

Paul started to strut away a winner, then spun momentarily and pointed at Nita, "and Nita, if you aren't there by 9:30, we're coming to get you. And if you're sick, we'll heal you," he laughed.

Nita looked at Rich as they walked down the hall. "Sorry to get you into this. Are you really planning to go?"

"I suppose I have to now, thanks to you," he returned the punch to her arm.

Nita was secretly pleased that she had been cajoled into going out. It gave her something to look forward to. Now that her early garden was planted, her social life would be slower since even Henry might not be around as much.

On Friday she stayed in the library till it closed at 8:00. As she was going across the lobby past the Circulation Desk, she ran into Rich who was coming from the opposite direction.

"There's the party animal," he smiled. "You still going?"

"I guess so," she replied. "What about you?"

"I have to. I was just headed over to the student center for a piece of pizza before the party. One of the more useful things I learned as an undergrad was not to drink on an empty stomach."

"Hey, I got that same lesson," Nita smiled.

"So, you want to go grab a bite?"

While they ate their pizza, they made small talk about the workload and the stress. Rich looked at her and said, "Speaking of stress, I hear you got crosswise with TD."

"TD?"

"Yeah. You know, Dr. Burns."

"Why would you call her TD? Her first name is Barbara."

"It's just what everybody calls her. TD is short for Third Degree."

"I had never heard that before, but it sure fits."

It then registered with Nita what Rich had just said. "How did you know about that?"

"Everybody heard about it. Hey if I heard about it, everybody did. I'm the last leaf on the grapevine."

"Well I suspect I'm past you. I must be one of those little twirly things trying to reach out and grab something to hold on to." Nita took a drink of her iced tea. "I guess in reality I am pretty much disconnected from the whole vineyard."

Rich looked at her as if he was thinking whether to say something. His lips moved then stopped then moved again.

Too late he realized that she was watching him. "What?" she asked with a small smile. "What are you trying to keep from saying?"

"Oh, nothing really. I'm the last one to talk about someone who doesn't socialize."

"Is that what people say about me?"

"I think people don't know what to say about you. All you ever do is study and keep to yourself. They..." he stopped himself.

"Go ahead," she said although her voice said that she wasn't sure it was something she wanted to hear.

"It's nothing really. I should just shut up."

"You can't now."

"Really, it's nothing. Some people just wonder if you're stuck-up, you know, that you think you're better than everybody else. I mean I don't think that, but I've heard others ask it. I mean because you almost never to talk to anyone and you get good grades and you're so..." Rich smacked his hand on the table. "I need to shut up."

"Go ahead," Nita smiled more genuinely. "You're doing okay so far."

"I was just going to say, because you're so good looking. You know people assume that means something or that you'll act a certain way or..." he cocked his head sideways, "can we talk about something else, before I dig an even deeper hole?" His face reddened, even through his olive skin.

"I'm sorry, I didn't mean to be prying things out of you. I guess I didn't realize it was such a big deal. I just need to study. Things don't come real easy to me."

Rich smiled, "That's interesting, because that's not the impression people have. I mean, yeah, you put in as much library time as anyone else, but everybody has you pegged for a natural brain."

"Me? God, that is...I mean..."

Nita paused and considered what she had heard. "I guess I haven't given people much to go on."

"Guess not."

"It's just that all I ever wanted to be was a doctor. Ever since I was a little girl, I...." All of a sudden, tears were rolling down her face. She quickly tried to wipe them with her napkin. "I'm sorry. I don't know what..."

Rich looked stunned and perplexed. "Hey, I'm really sorry if I upset you. I didn't mean to say anything that..."

"No, it wasn't anything you said. In fact, I don't know where those came from," she wiped the last traces off her cheeks.

"Are you okay?"

"Yeah, yeah. I'm sorry. I don't know what happened," Nita said, looking down at the table.

"Guess you're sorry you invited me for pizza. Wait till you see what I do at the party," she attempted a joke.

"Listen, if you don't feel like going to…"

"On no," Nita said with mock emphasis, "I wouldn't dare not go." She paused and then added, "I mean I wouldn't want people to think I'm stuck-up or anything."

'Oh crap. That's not what I meant." Rich's face picked up a deeper shade of red.

"I'm just kidding." She reached over and tapped his hand, and then too late thought better of it.

She wondered about her decaying social skills. She wasn't that bad as an undergrad. She was not in a class with Janie, but at least she didn't bumble through a simple conversation over pizza. Maybe she had kept herself too cloistered.

As she drove to the party, she made herself nervous thinking about how she might mess things up even worse.

CHAPTER THIRTEEN

Nita and Rich parked near each other and walked to the house together. "Sure is warm out for March," she said. The street was a residential area with tree-lined sidewalks. "Look, some yellow crocuses are popping up."

"Last Friday was the first day of Spring."

Nita touched Rich's arm to stop him. "Listen, I'm sorry about what happened when we were eating. I never used to be awkward like this. In high school I was involved in things and knew lots of people. Maybe I am out of it. Even in college I was much more social. I went to lots of parties."

Before Rich could respond, a yell came from the front of a two-story stucco-coated house. Paul and some others were putting a tap on a beer keg on the front porch of the house. "Hey everybody, look at this–she really did come."

The others on the porch laughed and applauded. "Can I get you a beer?" Paul bowed toward Nita as she came up the three steps.

"I think I need one," she replied. "Medicinal purposes only."

Paul drew a beer and handed it to her, "Just what the doctor ordered. Sorry about the foam, though. New keg."

"Rich, you want one too?"

"Sure, if you're buying."

Although Paul attempted to corner her attention, Nita was soon chatting about dermatology with a small group of classmates, some of whom she wasn't sure she had ever talked to much. They all agreed that Dr. Speed was in an orbit all his own. Rich suggested that it was Reed's special way of preparing them for the pressures that would soon face. Others said he was just a coffee addict, end of discussion.

The party was crowded with med students and some other people she hadn't seen before. It was some time before she actually saw Sarah, the hostess. Sarah was wearing a tight-fitting low-cut top that accentuated her ample breasts. Her curly blond hair bounced as he came bounding down the stairs with the hint of marijuana smoke trailing her and the others who came behind. They were all giggling.

"Nita," Sarah shrieked when she spotted her. "I am so glad you came," Sarah stumbled and almost fell into Nita and just laughed at herself. "As you can tell," she slurred, "the party got started a little early. In fact, they just tapped the second keg. Good turn-out, huh? The people you don't know are mostly from my undergrad dorm here at UD. You went to Maryland, didn't you? Listen, make yourself at home. Need a beer? Oh, you got one. Well I need one." She started to head off to the porch, then turned back and said, "I really am glad you came, Nita." Nita was surprised when Sarah stepped toward her and gave her a hug.

"See, everything you heard about Sarah was true," Paul had come up to her again.

"I guess I haven't heard too much about her," Nita admitted, "but that's okay. She seems to be having a good time." As if on cue, music blared from a stereo in the living room. Cyndi Lauper was singing, "Girls Just Want to Have Fun" along with Sarah and others.

"Sarah always just wants to have fun," Paul said, singing along. "I don't know how she does it. She parties like a maniac and still manages to pass."

"I guess that beats just studying like a maniac like I do," Nita suggested, but then she set down her plastic cup and started clapping her hands and singing to the chorus.

"Whoa, where did that come from?"

"It was my friend Janie's theme song when we roomed together at Maryland."

"Well, that is a different side of Nita. All I can tell here is that you're something of a phantom. I figured you had some other interest, like maybe a guy squirreled away."

Nita could tell Paul was probing. She considered how much she wanted to disclose and then decided not to play games, too much. "Just me and my gardener."

"Your gardener? You're going to be a doctor and you're having an affair with your gardener?"

"Did I say that?" she tilted her head to the side. "Besides, what's wrong with gardeners?"

Paul looked confused. "Nothing. Nothing is wrong with gardeners. Hey, you already finished that beer." He picked up her cup from the table.

"It was mostly foam. They have a lousy bartender out there."

"It was a new keg," he defended himself.

"I'll do this one myself," Nita said heading out onto the packed front porch.

For much of the evening Nita circulated among the crowd, but often seemed to have Paul's shadow not far away. At one point she and Alvaro Menchaca, a student from Spain, spent time at the pretzel bowl together. She told him how impressed she was that he could do med school with English as a second language. He said he grew up in the north of Spain, but most Americans guessed that he was either Puerto Rican or Mexican. "They blur all Hispanics together, but that's okay. I understand." Alvaro said that his parents had focused on education from his earliest years, with fluent English being a foundation stone. He told Nita the irony was that although his parents sent him to the U.S. to learn American medicine, he was becoming particularly interested in ancient Chinese healing, which tended to be more holistic. Nita told him she would love to learn more about it too, if she only had the time.

Nita hadn't seen Rich since they had walked in. At one point she headed into the kitchen and heard his voice through the backdoor. It turned out there was a back porch with even more people out there, many smoking cigarettes. Rich held up his cigarette when he saw Nita. "Sorry, cancer sticks are one of my vices. I know, I know. You don't need to tell me how bad they are." He stepped down off the porch and stomped it out in the grass. When he got back, he pointed his empty cup at her and said, "Beer is another one of my bad habits, but only on weekends. You want one?" Nita finished what was left in her cup and said okay but that it would be her third and last.

For the next hour, Nita sipped her beer slowly and moved among the small talk. At one point, she got pulled into a conversation about AZT, which the FDA had just approved for treatment of AIDS. Nita had heard about it on the news while driving to the party. Megan Connelly was expounding about what an amazing development the new drug was. "Think how many patients there are who need this. This is a really big deal. The worry, though, is whether they will have the money to pay for it." Nita remembered Megan's comments on the elevator about how money and status were significant goals in medicine. She wondered if that was part of her thinking about her comments but decided not to ask.

By midnight many in the throng had slowed their flow of beer, although for some it appeared to be a little too late. It was interesting to see some of the students getting out of control. When she was coming down the stairs after a long wait to use the bathroom, she saw two guys standing at the window where the stairway turned at the halfway point. They were talking about looking at the stars. When Nita paused, Ted Dixon turned his head and said, "excuse me, this is the men's room." It was then that Nita realized that they were urinating out the window onto bushes below. She blushed and hurried down the stairs. Ted called after her, "Sorry but the line was too long up there." He and the other guy laughed.

When she came into the living room, the music had been turned up to the point that it was rattling the lamp on the end table. It was a hard-driving rock and roll song that she didn't recognize but that everyone else was singing the words to.

Sarah pushed a space open among the blue plastic beer cups on the coffee table and jumped up to dance. The crowd cheered in approval. Nita was impressed that she was actually a good dancer but worried that she was going to fall and get hurt, especially in her condition.

Sarah spotted Nita and yelled for her to come up too. The crowd roared their support, but Nita just shook her head. "Come on Nita, dance with me," Sarah yelled above the din. The jostling crowd called for Nita to jump up. A guy Nita didn't know used his foot to push open a space next to Sarah on the coffee table.

"Hey, Nita," someone called from behind her.

She turned to see it was Rich. "Come out here for a minute," he motioned toward the backdoor. He reached out to grab her hand and lead her out of the living room. The crowd momentarily moaned but then a girl Nita didn't know jumped up on the table with Sarah. Sarah gave her a hug and a kiss on the lips, which sent up thunderous approval from the audience, and Nita was quickly forgotten.

As Rich led her out the backdoor, he let go of her hand. The back porch was now empty. "Actually, I was just trying to find my way up to the bathroom," he said, "and then it looked like you might want an escape route."

"Much appreciated. This is even wilder than I thought it would be. I haven't been to anything like this since maybe junior year back in college."

"I guess everybody's letting off steam, as they say."

"Well I'm having a good time. It's nice to get to actually talk to some people I've seen the whole time, but never really got to know very well."

"Hey, I really do need to hit the bathroom. Do you want me to get you a refill on your beer on the way back?"

"No thanks. Oh, and be prepared for a very long wait upstairs."

Rich looked distressed. "I don't think my bladder can hold out for a very long wait."

Nita looked out into the backyard, which had an alley running behind it. "I don't suppose there's a men's room out in those bushes."

Rich said, "You really are smart, aren't you? Be right back." He set his cup on the porch railing.

In a couple minutes, Rich reappeared from the darkness. "That feels much better."

A crash came from the interior of the house. They both cringed, but then a roar of laughter erupted indicating that probably nobody got hurt.

"Is there a doctor in the house?" Rich joked.

"Not one that can still stand up," Nita replied.

"It is interesting to think that in the not-too-distant future about half those people in there will be physicians," Rich reflected.

"Speaking of that, I think I am going to try to slip out. I have a long drive home."

"Where do you live?"

Nita tried to explain where she lived and then tried to answer why she lived way out there, but had trouble coming up with a logical reason. She changed the subject to how she might get away without having to go back through the house.

Rich pointed to the side of the house. When Nita realized that that was where Ted and his friend had been urinating, she cautioned Rich that that area was known for "localized showers."

"What are you talking about?"

"Remember how you improvised back by the alley? Well others improvised out that stairway window."

"You are kidding me," Rich was genuinely perplexed. "Too much!"

"I couldn't make that up," Nita shrugged.

"It's one thing to slip out into some bushes in the back, but out a window...?"

"Yep, it surprised me too."

"For some of these folks, partying seems to be a way of life," Rich commented. "Makes you wonder about the people who hardly ever study but somehow still end up squeaking by. I think some of them really don't want to be here. It's like they're living their parents' dreams or something. You know, like Sophie, she's really smart but all she ever does is draw in her notebooks instead of taking notes. She told me she really wants to be an artist but she comes from three generations of prominent Massachusetts surgeons so she has to be one too."

"She'll graduate, I guess, but how will she know what she needs to know?" Nita asked. "It's scary. She must be super smart to pass with so little effort. I have to say, though, that some of her drawings are truly amazing.

I sat behind her last week and saw her flipping through her peds ortho notebook. Really amazing artwork of the bones and muscles. I imagine that level of detail would help you remember."

"I guess we're both being too serious for a party, huh?"

"Yeah, but you've got a point," Nita said. "I work my butt off, and I can't imagine how some of these people can make it through. I figure they're just a lot smarter than I am."

Rich said, "You know what they call the person who graduates at the bottom of the med school class?"

Nita smiled at the set up, "What?"

"Doctor!"

Nita had heard it before but laughed anyway.

"Hey, I'm sorry, you were trying to leave, weren't you," Rich said.

"I'm going to try the other side of the house. I think I will just thank Sarah on Monday."

When Nita came around the house, she surprised to find Paul and Sarah in the shadows beyond the front porch. Paul quickly withdrew his hand from inside the back of Sarah's jeans.

"Oh hi, I…I…," Nita stammered.

Sarah giggled and inched closer to Paul who was trying to pull away. "Hey Nita, I was wondering where you were," Paul slurred.

"Funny place to be searching," Nita laughed.

Sarah giggled again.

"No really, I wanted to talk with you."

"But he's got his hands full right now," Sarah laughed and moved up to him again, putting her left hand on the back of his jeans. "We both do."

"Enjoy," Nita said as she scurried past them. "Great party, Sarah. Thanks!"

Saturday morning, Nita put on her denim jacket and took her coffee outside. She shivered as she wandered out toward the garden. The sun was bright but the breeze was cool. She agreed to herself that she could visit the garden for a few minutes but not touch, since she had so much studying to do. Honking noises from the sky in the direction of the river drew her attention. Canada geese in a V-shaped formation were flying north up the river, encouraging each other as they traveled.

On Monday a small group stood outside the lecture hall as Nita walked up. The circle opened and invited her in. This expectation that she might join them was a marked difference from earlier when she was always on the outside. She hadn't thought too much about it, but now she recognized that she had been more on the outside than she realized.

"We were just talking about what a great party Sarah had. What did you think?" Brad Watson brought her into the conversation as she stepped up to the group.

"I thought it was lots of fun. I realized that I need to get out more."

"That's what we've been trying to tell you, girl," Shandra said. "You've been missing some good times."

"I should have listened," Nita agreed. All weekend she had felt a glow from having gone to the party. Her social isolation had become more apparent to her, and she now regretted not getting to know some of the people earlier.

"Hey, here comes Mr. Party, himself," Brad noted as Paul Alvarez came through the double doors from the stairway. "Great party, huh, Paul?"

"Yeah, it was good," Paul said in a monotone and proceeded past the group and into the lecture hall.

"Whoa," Shandra said after he zipped into the room. "Wonder what bee got up his bonnet today."

In a few short strides, Paul succeeded in putting a chill on the conversation. The group broke up and drifted into the lecture hall. A couple minutes later Dean Quinn arrived to provide details on the events that would occur to lead up to and qualify them for graduation. "Don't blow it. Don't slack off," he cautioned. "We have seen students think they can coast through the final stretch and get themselves into trouble. You still have much work to do."

After the dean, Dr. Hindal, who was the faculty sponsor for the senior class, talked about specialization coming out of med school. One aspect would be opportunities over the next weeks to experience areas they might be interested in. There would be numerous opportunities, but often they would be limited, especially the ones in the operating room so it would be first come, first served.

After the lectures ended, Nita went straight to the bulletin board to take a look at the options. Paul was standing next to her, but gave her a curt nod and grunt instead of his usual banter, which would be especially expected in light of her having attended the party. Nita wasn't sure if she had done something or if this was just a bee still in his bonnet in general.

Looking at the options Nita felt like she was a kid in a toy store. They could pick three items, anything from clinical counseling for potential psychiatrists to labor hall for those interested in obstetrics.

Over the years her interests had floated from one area of specialization to another. Currently her favorites were centered on pediatrics and neurology. She considered the possibility of combining the two. She had found that A. I. duPont Hospital right there in Delaware had residencies in pediatric neurology. She worried that it might be too narrow, though.

One of the options listed on the bulletin board was pediatric surgery. It fit her schedule and only had three openings so she grabbed one. Another was an experimental neurology clinic doing non-traditional techniques, so she decided to try that. Her final choice was a Parkinson's research program that linked genetics and nutrition to the treatment protocol.

She continued to look and think about the choices, but as she saw them rapidly fill up right before her eyes, she decided to be satisfied with the ones she had. She backed away from the board at the same time as Paul, and they stood together creating an awkward situation.

Paul busied himself putting on his jacket and throwing things in his backpack.

"Is something wrong?" Nita asked.

"No. Why would there be?" Paul turned and hurried past her and out the door.

Nita shrugged and headed to the cafeteria for a cup of coffee. As she paid the cashier, a waving hand against the far wall caught her eye. It was Doug, the neurophysiology grad student. She felt the ticking clock in her stomach and feared a long conversation, but she waved and headed over to him.

"Where you been?" he asked. "I've been reading up on dream symbolism, so I'm all ready to tell you everything you need to know."

Nita felt an encroachment as she sat down. There was no way she was going to tell him her dreams.

"Sorry," he said, "I was just joking. You don't need to look so worried."

"Oh, I'm sorry. I didn't mean to... I mean I..."

"It's okay," he held up his hands, "really."

"I'm just really distracted. Too much going on."

"Not another neuro test, I hope."

"No," Nita managed a weak smile, "just the...just the usual crap, you know. So, what does it mean if you dream that you're falling off a cliff?"

"Actually, I lied. I haven't really been reading about dream symbolism, although I did read one article that was pretty cool. It talked about how there are symbols in both your waking state and your dream state and that they can carry over from one side to the other."

"That's pretty weird."

"Well I read it in a magazine when I was getting my hair cut, so what do you want?"

"Oh, I thought you meant that you read it in a professional journal," Nita laughed.

"Nope. Sorry. But I do know that actually there are remarkable similarities in how the physiology of the brain works when we're awake and when we're dreaming. In fact, if you look at certain types of scans, they are exactly the same. For example, if you're afraid of snakes and you see one when you're awake and when you're dreaming, your reaction is essentially the same."

"Really? I guess that makes sense since it feels the same," she said as she considered the concept and what it meant for the strange dreams she was having. "I mean your emotional response is the same."

"Exactly."

"Well I saw an article in a laundromat magazine that had a list of dream symbols," Nita offered. "For example, it said that water in a dream was a cleansing or a transformation."

"Now not to doubt your laundromat journal, which is probably not as good as a barbershop journal," Doug smiled, "but my guess is that it's not that simple. I mean, what if you are an Olympic swimmer, but when I was five, I watched my mother drown. My guess is that water is going to have very different meanings."

"Did your mother drown?"

"No, that was just an example. Are you an Olympic swimmer?"

"Yes, as a matter of fact I am," Nita deadpanned.

"Liar."

"Maybe so, but do you realize that you talked about your mother the last time we met?"

"I did?"

"Yes, you did. As I recall you were distressed that she didn't appreciate the type of research you are doing."

"Jeez. Are you going into psychiatry?"

"Maybe I should."

"I could be your first patient," Doug paused then added, "but I'm not going to lie down on your couch."

"I don't have a couch, so there."

CHAPTER FOURTEEN

Nita was one of six students who signed up for the neurology option. The brief description said "non-traditional techniques," so she somehow assumed they might be talking about acupuncture or other techniques that had been largely lost in western medicine. When they were led into a conference room in the far reaches of the neurology department, she wasn't surprised to find a doctor of Asian descent standing in front of them. Everything from that point on, though, did surprise her.

"I am Dr. Philip Wang," the man said in an American accent, and the way he dropped his Rs from the ends of words made it sound like he had been raised in Boston. He appeared to be in his mid-thirties, small with a thin but muscular build.

"I want to congratulate you for choosing to expose yourself to these new techniques. What we have for you is a glimpse into a future that few people even know is coming," he paused for effect. "Nonetheless, this is a future that will revolutionize not only medicine – the medicine you will practice – but will actually revolutionize the human condition. I do not think it would be overstating the matter to say that these technologies have the potential to even change what it is to be human."

Nita looked at her classmates whose faces revealed that they were as amazed at his introduction as she was. Dr. Wang studied each of them with satisfaction. He nodded as he continued. "In a few minutes we will take you to see some experimental equipment. While we have not purposefully kept this secret, we have chosen not to make a big show of it. I suppose you could say that we talk about it on a need-to-know basis."

He looked at each of them, again satisfied at their wide-eyed attention. "It is not that what we are doing violates any laws or principles," he paused, "It is that human society doesn't have any laws or principles that guide or govern where we are going. Nonetheless, this is the world in which you will practice medicine. Some of it will start to be in place by the year 2000. And although that year sounds far off, it really is not. It's a shame med schools do not focus more on formal ethics training, because you are likely to need it before your medical career is too far along."

"You have all known people who take Ritalin or other medications that modify behavior. Perhaps some of you do. They have become so commonplace that we gloss over the societal implications of them and the moral decisions that parents make when they decide to put their child on such a drug to control ADHD for example."

"Basically, they as parents and we as a society are saying that you, child, are not okay the way you are. Your behavior is not acceptable. Therefore, we will give you a drug to make you more…" Dr. Wang held up two fingers on each hand and curled them downward to signify quotation marks, "…'normal' as we choose normal to be defined."

"This may seem to be a small thing to you, but I want you to hold that thought. To what extent will society go – should society go – to make people or even to force people to be normal."

"In a few minutes I will show you some work we are doing that will probe this very issue and many others like it. You will see equipment that can see inside the human mind. You will watch the mind work, and you will watch the brain think. I will show you what 'normal' brain functioning looks like and I will show you variations. When I show you brain activity of people who are prone toward depression or violence, you need to ask yourself, 'Should we as a society modify their brain function?' As you know, we already do, primarily through pharmacology. What happens as we do more and more in Deep Brain Stimulation and other non-pharmacological techniques? Powerful tools, to be sure. Who gets to decide how and when we should use these technologies?"

"In addition to overt problems of the brain, like Tourette's or epilepsy, I want to show you some subtleties, such as the brain function of a shy person and a person who is not musically inclined. Should we modify their behavior? We have those intervention therapies ready, and we are very close to having many more. What would you like?" he waved his arms like a magician, "A good sense of humor? Exceptional math capabilities? Ability to focus for a long period of time? I could create a catalogue, and you could go shopping."

"We already have parents designing their babies. Soon they will be able to modify almost anything they want," he waved his hands again. "How about some of each? An artist with a good sense of humor, who's a math whiz? Not a problem."

"And of course, you would not want any of those troublesome features like being prone to depression. Society simply needs to ignore the fact that so many of our greatest artists of all sorts did suffer from depression." He paused and asked, "Is that what we are willing to give up? For that matter, do we even know what we will be giving up? Do we know what we have already given up?"

Dr. Wang extended his arms wide in a welcoming gesture and said, "Eventually we can all be normal." He then moved his hands rapidly together until they were just two inches apart. "But normal could become a rather narrow band. Will society fix people who are too shy or who take too many risks? Will we fix people who don't behave conveniently for us? We are already doing it with Ritalin. How far do we want to go?"

By the time Nita emerged from Dr. Wang's lecture, her head was spinning. With Dr. Wang's technologies you could almost see inside the human soul. There was so much power to do so many things, but as he put it, where do you draw the lines and who should draw the lines? Should parents decide for their child or should doctors decide for their patients or should government decide for everyone?

That evening, back at home, Nita pulled her chicken pot pie from the oven, poked the crust with a fork and watched the steam rise. Her mind wandered back to Dr. Wang's comments. His remarks were exciting and frightening at the same time. There were no easy answers. Which of her behaviors would she like to modify to become more normal? For the last few years she was too reclusive. Did that need to be fixed? How about if she could learn more quickly without the excessive studying? That would help immensely. She forced herself to push aside his provocations. She needed to get going on her excessive studying. At midnight when Nita finally allowed herself to go to bed, she dropped swiftly and deeply.

"Did you hear something?" Rachel asked. She went over to the door of the cabin to check that the bar was secure. As she turned to walk away from it, a faint knock came from the other side.

Rachel peered between the thick planks of the door. "Who are you?" she shouted. Nita couldn't tell whether the volume came from a challenge or from the need to get her voice to travel through the door.

"My name is Sterling. Anna Sterling. Mrs. John Sterling. My child is sick. I...I thought maybe you could help."

"Who else is with you?" Rachel shouted.

"No one. Just the two of us."

Nita heard a baby cry. It was not a healthy cry but rather a weak and raspy moan.

As soon as Rachel heard it, she commanded Nita to help her with the bar. "Here, get this end. That baby needs help," she said with urgency.

She left Nita holding the heavy bar as she swung the door open. A pallid woman stood in the dark. Her trembling was visible in the dim light that wavered from a candle on the table.

"Come in," Rachel said gently.

"You won't..." the woman did not move to enter, "... you won't harm the baby, will you?"

"No," Rachel said firmly, "and I won't do any witchcraft or eat it or any of the other lies those church people like to tell. Please, bring in the baby. She's very sick."

As soon as they barred the door, Rachel turned to Nita, "Get that blanket from the bed and clear the table."

Nita moved a cup and saucer from a table in the middle of the room to a small table near the wall. Rachel lifted the candle as Nita went for the blanket.

"Spread it out on the table."

"There," she smoothed the blanket out, "now you can lay the child on the table."

"What is her name?"

"Elizabeth," the woman answered, hugging the baby tighter to her chest. "You won't tell anyone I brought her here, will you? I mean, I'm sorry.

I don't intend to be rude, but you know what they would say. I worry that they might..."

"Mrs. Sterling, I will not tell. Just as I have not told about the assorted others who periodically show up at the door of the Widow Rachel when the town physician has been unable to help."

Anna winced at Rachel's words.

"Oh yes, Mrs. Sterling, I know what they call me. And I know what they say about the Widow Rachel. And aye, I know that some change the word widow to witch."

Elizabeth struggled to cry and ended the effort in a weak cough. Anna hugged her to her chest.

Rachel put her arm around the shoulder of Anna. "Please now, let us put our little angel on the table so we can see how to help. Stay close and hold her hand."

Anna slowly placed the baby on the table and unwrapped the small gray blanket that surrounded her thin body. Rachel handed the candle to Nita.

Rachel placed her ear on the baby's chest and listened to her breathe. She tested her fingers for strength to grasp, which the baby clearly failed. Rachel looked into the baby's eyes and asked some questions of the mother about the baby's appetite and how long she had been ill.

Finally, she took the candle to the fireplace and used a metal cup to draw some water from a clay pot. She went to her shelf of containers and carefully selected three, then put small measures of the contents of them into the warm water. She stirred the brew with a wooden spoon and then tested it on her own lip.

She asked the mother to pick up the child and sit in a chair so they could feed it. With small sips the baby took some of the tea.

"Now speak to your child. She needs to hear your voice and know your love. Touch her face and her hands."

Rachel went back to the fire and drew some more water into another metal cup. She made a different brew and offered it to the mother. The mother looked warily at Rachel with the outstretched cup.

Rachel put the cup to her lips and took a sip.

Anna then took the cup in her free hand and sipped. Soon she had finished the tea and set the cup on the floor. "Thank you. I'm sorry. I don't mean to be rude. I don't know what to think."

"I understand," Rachel said, gently pulling a chair nearby and sitting. "People do not understand and that makes them afraid. But this knowledge of the healing herbs has been handed down through many generations of my family back in Ireland. These herbs and the relief they bring are simply gifts from God." Rachel pointed to the cross above her bed. "What was the mission of Jesus? He was first and foremost a healer—helping the lame to walk and the blind to see. And what was his message? Love. That is all I offer." She held her hands outright and open.

Rachel reached her hand slowly toward Anna and touched the forearm that held the child. "Your baby is very sick. She will need stronger tea, but I must go to search for the right roots. When can you bring her back?"

"I can try to come tomorrow late in the evening. Like I did today. Is that too soon?"

"I will leave early. I think I know where to find what I need. If I find it, I should be back by sunset."

Rachel gave the listless baby a few more sips of the medicinal tea, then said, "You should go. You will be missed."

Anna thanked her and apologized again as she slipped out the door.

Her footsteps quickly vanished in the close and threatening darkness. Rachel held the door slightly ajar. "Listen," she said. Nita strained to hear. Rachel placed her ear near the open space. "The river is talking. Hear and heed." She waited for a stretched moment. Nita could hear the surging sound of water. Rachel listened a bit longer. "Hark, hear and heed. It will take great *courage, and we will shoulder great distress." With a final, furtive glance out into the abyss of the night, she closed the door. Nita gripped the roughhewn wood as they slid the bar back in place.*

CHAPTER FIFTEEN

The following morning Nita was the first to arrive at the Nurses Station on the OR floor. She was told that two other students would be joining her. When the others arrived, she found that one was Paul. She greeted him normally and received a neutral "Hey" in reply. The third was a quiet, bookish, slender student with thinning hair named Martin Detwiler. He had been at Sarah's party, but like most times, he kept largely to himself, watching but not engaging. The three of them stood in an awkward silence.

After a few minutes, a doctor approached. "Hello, I am Dr. Thomas Schmidt. I am the lead surgeon today. I specialize in pediatric oncology." He was tall with neatly combed brown hair and blue eyes that somehow said he knew he was good looking. He was wearing the aqua-blue scrubs of a surgeon.

He shook each student's hand. He seemed to linger a moment longer on Nita's hand while looking into her eyes, but she dismissed the thought that it meant anything. Nonetheless, as soon as it was convenient, she checked to make sure that he was wearing a wedding ring and was relieved to see that he was.

Dr. Schmidt proceeded to explain that the operation would be on the right femur of a ten-year-old boy. He had developed a tumor in the thigh bone, and they hoped to remove it. "As with any surgery, there are risks. With this type of surgery in particular, much depends on what we find." He showed them X-rays and MRI images of the tumor and explained the complexity of the operation.

They were admonished that even though they would scrub and prep the same way as the surgeons, they were not to participate in any manner no matter what happened. Nita vowed to herself that she was going to stay away from even the slightest hint of any wrongdoing.

"Okay let's go meet Ben and his family."

In the brightly lit room, a young, nicely dressed couple stood on the far side of a sandy-haired boy in the hospital bed. The mother was touching the boy's foot, which was sticking out of the blankets.

"Good morning, Ben. How are you feeling today?"

"Thirsty."

"Yeah, well I'm sorry about that."

"And, I'm hungry."

"From what your mom told me, you're always hungry."

Ben smiled at his mother, "I'm a growing boy."

The boy's parents smiled, but their nervousness showed through. Dr. Schmidt said, "I'd like to introduce three colleagues of mine. They are sharp young people who are finishing up medical school and will be observing the procedure today. As I told you earlier, they will not be assisting in any manner but will just observe."

Then he pointed to Ben. "This is the famous Ben. Ben is a soccer player. He plays striker and by all accounts is quite good.

"Did I tell you, Ben, that I played soccer in college? Best sport in the world."

"I know, but my dad likes football. He thinks you should play football with your hands. How much sense does that make? Soccer is the real football."

Ben's dad picked up on the banter. "When I grew up in Cleveland, nobody'd ever heard of soccer. We played baseball and football."

"Sports of the past," Ben chided him.

A nurse came into the room to check Ben's blood pressure. Dr. Schmidt used the opportunity to tell Ben what to expect.

After giving him the details of the steps, he added, "And the final thing will be that they'll give you a mask to wear that will make you think you're an elephant because it will have something like a trunk. We'll all be wearing masks, but ours will be boring ones like this," he pulled a surgical mask out of his pocket and placed it across his face. "Yours will be the cool one."

"Do you have any questions?" he asked Ben.

Ben looked at his parents as if they had asked the question. "No," he replied simply.

"How about you, Mom and Dad?"

"No, I think you've covered it."

"Fine. The nurse will show you where to meet me when we're done."

When Nita, Paul and Martin entered the operating room, Dr. Schmidt told them that the anesthesia team had already started an initial dose to sedate the boy. "He'll be groggy, but I always make it a point to connect with him again."

Dr. Schmidt's manner impressed Nita. He showed caring as he checked in with the boy who was conscious but not fully aware of his surroundings. "Okay, pal," he said, "remember when I said that they'd give you a mask to wear when we got here? Well this nice woman, who is Dr. Reiger, is in charge of the masks. Actually, she is the anesthesiologist. Remember when you tried to say that in the room and we all laughed?"

"Are you ready, Dr. Reiger?"

"I am," she replied. Then she said to the boy, "Okay, my friend, this is when you start counting backwards from ten."

Ben only made it to eight before he was unconscious. Dr. Schmidt swung into action, checking equipment and telling people what to do. Periodically he would tell Nita and the others where to stand or what to observe as the staff prepared. When he spoke to them, he always made eye contact with Nita but not with Paul or Martin.

At one point, Dr. Schmidt motioned Nita a little apart from the others. He quietly said, "Listen, if you feel queasy or anything, that's okay. You can just step away. We'll understand."

"I'll be fine," she said firmly. "We've all seen surgeries before."

His eyes gave her an understanding look that further annoyed her.

Still in his quiet voice he whispered, "Having the surgical mask over your face accentuates your eyes."

Nita looked away from Dr. Schmidt only to have her eyes collide with Paul's. He had been watching their exchange. Nita matched his gaze and walked back toward him where he stood along the wall, a few feet from a table of gauze, sponges and other materials. Paul diverted his eyes, pretending to become interested in the way a nurse was scrubbing the patient's leg.

In surprisingly short order, everything was ready. Dr. Schmidt checked the X-rays one more time and then proceeded to the table where the boy's leg was exposed.

"Here," he said to Nita while motioning with his left hand to include the other two, "Take a step up just a little closer so you can see." His right hand, which was holding a scalpel, leaned on the boy's flesh.

"Everyone ready?"

The assembly of nurses and others nodded or gave some verbal assent.

"Dr. Reiger?"

"His vitals are good."

Dr. Schmidt looked up at Nita. "Here we go."

With a remarkably firm stroke, Dr. Schmidt cut deeply into the boy's thigh. Blood gushed from the incision, and nurses used suction and sponges to catch as much as possible.

Nita's stomach tightened as she saw the femur exposed. The meat of the child's leg was a sickly pink.

Nita looked away from the incision to a nurse preparing an electric saw. Watching a boy's leg be cut into with a power tool was going to be a new experience. She had seen surgery but not like this. Her stomach started to turn, and her head felt faint. She struggled to maintain her grip. She didn't want Dr. Schmidt to be right about her queasiness. She looked at Paul and Martin. Paul in particular looked like she felt. Martin on the other hand seemed intrigued and was leaning forward to get a better view.

"Blade B-1," Dr. Schmidt instructed the nurse with the power tool.

She inserted the blade and clamped it in place.

"Set it for 1.8 centimeters."

The nurse made an adjustment on the side of the instrument.

Dr. Schmidt took the saw and pressed on the trigger. The blade started moving with a noise that might come from a woodshop. He then released the trigger.

Dr. Schmidt looked up at Nita and spoke to the three students. "This is what we observed in the X-ray. You can see how the tumor inside has distorted the normal anatomy of the bone. This is where the tough part comes."

Nita could tell that he was elaborating for her benefit so that she was sure to appreciate how skilled he was. Dr. Schmidt looked again at the bone and then back up at Nita. She could see that he was pleased to have her as a spectator.

"Maximum retraction," he barked.

Two people in scrubs used metal tools to pull the muscle back to expose the bone.

Beginning slowly, Dr. Schmidt gently applied pressure to the trigger. The blade started a slow up and down motion. He pressed its tip into the bone above the bulge and let it bite into the hard surface. With increasing pressure, he moved the blade within the bone and started to slice along the edge of the bulge.

Nita's stomach calmed down, and she became engrossed in the procedure. This truly was an art. She had used power tools on wood, but this was clearly a much more difficult task.

"Rotate," Dr. Schmidt motioned with his left hand to roll the boy's leg.

"That's good. Right there." He continued the saw's motion smoothly along the near side. The bone started to open up and expose the angry red mass inside.

Paul bumped Nita as he stepped backward away from the table. She turned her head to watch him retreat away from the surgery. Dr. Schmidt slowed the saw and looked up briefly. He quickly shot his glance back down to the leg. The blade had moved farther in than he apparently intended. He tried to withdraw it slightly and turn it, but it caught on something inside and twisted his hand, pressing his finger harder on the trigger. This caused the leg to jerk in the grasp of the retractors. The leg lifted against the saw before he could release the trigger. It tore into more bone as well as skin. Bits of material splattered onto to Nita's gown as well as those around her.

"God dammit! Hold the fucking leg still," Dr. Schmidt shouted.

He withdrew the saw and shut it off. With only the slightest glance, he threw it at the scrub nurse who had handed it to him, but she was trying to readjust the drape that covered the lower leg. When she saw the tool coming, she managed to reach up with one hand, only to have the saw blade poke into her latex glove. The saw clattered onto the floor, and blood rose inside her glove.

No one attended to the saw or the nurse who rushed to the table by the wall. The next events were a blur. "Back out of here," Dr. Schmidt screamed at Nita and Martin. They moved quickly to a space against the wall where Paul was now standing. The staff whirled around shouting to each other and hovering over the wound. A nurse bolted to a phone on another wall and gave curt instructions, followed by a shout of "Stat!"

In a few minutes additional people in scrubs rushed into the room. Dr. Schmidt pushed aside space for the newcomers at the table to see the situation. One doctor poked around inside the leg.

Dr. Schmidt and the others then stepped back from the table and huddled in hushed voices on the side. When they broke the huddle, Dr. Schmidt looked at the three students and shouted, "Out of here—now!" and pointed toward the door. They quickly retreated to the room where they'd been given their scrubs. They looked wide-eyed at each other.

Martin said slowly, "Holy shit."

"What the hell happened?" Paul wanted to know.

"I think Dr. Schmidt must have screwed up or something," Martin said. "Seemed like the saw got away from him."

"How'd that happen? I mean he seemed to be doing fine," Nita offered.

Martin looked at Nita, shook his head and said, "Let's get changed."

When Nita came out from changing, the other two were already waiting. "Let's get out of here," Martin muttered. He led the way out the door and toward the elevator.

On the way down, Paul looked from Martin to Nita and back again.

Nita stared blankly. "What should we do?

Paul reflected her blank look. "Nothing we can do. I'm sure they will all handle it. They've seen stuff like this before."

Martin nodded.

Outside, they started to part ways, but first looked at each other knowing that some sort of a bond had been formed by the experience.

The next day, Nita saw Paul and Martin talking as she walked toward the lecture hall. Their faces were grim as they motioned for her to come over.

"They had to amputate Ben's leg," Martin told her, "mid-thigh, right above the tumor."

Nita thought immediately about the boy's love of soccer. "How is he?"

"Critical condition," Paul replied. "Standard for that sort of thing. He'll pull through, but…I mean Jesus…"

Martin said in a hushed tone, "We've been told not to talk to anyone about it. That includes you."

Nita's face drew a question mark.

"Don't know," Paul said to the unspoken question, "but the smart money says we better do what they say."

"Got it," Nita replied. She wondered if there would be some sort of investigation. It all happened so quickly, it was hard to say exactly what happened. She wondered how Dr. Schmidt felt. Was he devastated? How did a good physician recover after something like this?

Although she was in class all day, her mind could not stay off Ben and his parents. She wondered what Dr. Schmidt said when he went to talk to them. She wondered what Ben thought when he learned that he had lost his leg. How could a ten-year-old kid even begin to imagine what that meant for the rest of his life?

After class Nita tried to study, but quickly left the library and headed home. Her concern rose toward anger, but she wasn't sure who or what to blame. Was this Dr. Schmidt's fault or was this just one of the bad things that sometimes happen in difficult surgeries?

She tried to study at home but was getting nowhere and decided to just go to bed. Unfortunately, bed did not equate to sleep. Images of the OR kept coming back through her mind. When she faded off, she got splattered with bone and flesh again. She spent most of the night thinking about Ben. She wished she could talk to him to see how he was doing. But what could you say? Nothing was going to make it okay or make this nightmare go away. Maybe just being there, just holding his hand. Just listening.

What could you say to his parents? Would they sue? Probably. Would she be called as a witness? What would she say? She would just have to tell the truth, although she wasn't sure exactly what the truth was. She wasn't certain what had happened. She wondered if Dr. Burns would call her in. Did Dr. Burns even know about this? Why would she even be involved? How quiet could they keep something like this? Obviously, someone got to Martin and Paul very quickly and told them to talk to her. Would this just be quietly chalked up to the risks of surgery? Had they told Ben's parents that this was one of the possible outcomes? Maybe so. What would she say if they asked her what happened? Telling the truth was always the best way out of a problem. But what if you didn't know the truth? Tell what you think you know?

The following days were lost ground, lost spaces of time, lost sleep. She wanted to talk to someone but couldn't. At one point she and Martin and Paul all converged at the library entrance.

"Hear anything?"

"Nope."

"Nope."

They each shrugged.

CHAPTER SIXTEEN

On Saturday Henry showed up unannounced to help with her garden. She hadn't planned to do any gardening but decided it would be good for her mental health. They pulled the few small weeds that had popped up and planted some additional lettuce and spinach seeds that he brought.

When they were done, Henry took off his Orioles baseball hat and wiped his forehead with a red bandana that he pulled from his back pocket, "Hey, what did you think of my collection?"

"Oh, Henry, I'm sorry. I set the box in the corner and forgot all about it. It's been a bad week."

"Nita, Nita, no need to apologize. I know you have lots going on. Please don't worry about it."

"Can I keep it a little longer? I promise to look at it."

Henry opened the door to his pickup truck. "No problem at all. Take your time."

The remainder of the day, Nita struggled to study. Late in the evening, she gave up the effort. Remembering that Daylight Savings Time would start that night, she moved the time on her alarm clock an hour forward. She hated the time change. What she didn't need was one less hour of sleep.

When she finally fell deeply asleep, she tumbled back into the cabin with Rachel. They again sat staring at the fire.

"How is the baby?" Nita asked.

"Hmmm?"

"What was her name? Sterling? Elizabeth Sterling?"

Rachel stared at her with sadness. "The Lord took the baby."

Rachel went over and checked the bar on the door, then returned to her seat at the fire. She used a stick to poke at a log and roll it over exposing its glowing side. It crackled in response.

Nita stared into the fire for a long time, watching the embers pulse red, gold and gray. A scratching sound drew her attention to the hearth where Rachel used the charred end of her stick to draw three concentric circles on the large flat stone that was the center of the hearth. Rachel studied the circles but said nothing. Suddenly her head jerked to alert.

"Did you hear something outside?" Rachel asked.

Nita wasn't sure.

Rachel got up to check the bar on the door.

Before she returned, Nita heard a noise from up in the chimney.

As Rachel returned, Nita was about to say something when smoke started to pour out of the fireplace and into the cabin.

"Why do they hate me so?" Rachel cried.

"What's going on?"

"Ah Faith, they put something over the chimney again. Get low to the floor."

Smoke was rapidly filling the room, dropping the already low ceiling.

Crouching, they moved quickly to the door.

"Be cautious as you leave. I dah not know what they might do. The last time, they left a headless goat outside the door," Rachel shuddered.

Nita's heart started racing as Rachel lifted the bar to open the door. They could hear men laughing and calling. "Hey, witch. Fix this."

Something heavy hit the door.

They dropped to the floor where the smoke was now allowing them less than three feet of space. Rachel was coughing badly. Nita's heart was thumping in her chest. "We've got to get out of here. We've got to escape."

Nita's own voice woke her. Sweat was beaded on her temples as she stared at the ceiling of her bedroom.

She looked at the clock. It was 4:00 a.m. For a while she tried to get back to sleep and then finally gave up.

Over the next days, Nita returned to her old grind. The pressures of school displaced the worries about Ben. She also returned to her previous habits of not doing much socializing. Although she would sometimes sit with classmates in the cafeteria, mostly she kept to herself.

To complicate her life, Little Earl got sick. He developed a hole in his muffler that quickly moved from a minor noise to a deep-throated roar, not at all normal for her little friend. Henry recommended a service station where he had been taking his vehicles for almost forty years. The challenge was finding a time when Nita could give up her car for a few hours. Finally, she decided to just park herself there and study while they worked on him.

In her dreams Nita visited often with Rachel who grew more and more apprehensive. She checked the door constantly. Always they were in the cabin at night. Frequently Rachel jumped up in response to something she thought she heard. Other times she would ramble in a monologue that took the form of a dialogue with herself without the encouragement of a response from Nita.

"*Maybe I should move away. Farther west.*"

"*I am sore afraid to stay here.*"

"*But there are savage Indians in the Alleghenies. Should I fear them more than my own people? White people can be savages as well.*"

"*Where would I go?*"

"*The Cumberland trail runs deep into Indian country.*"

"*Why do the townspeople fear me? I came here to escape the sorts of people that live on bile and hate. Why do they hate me? Why do they fear me?*"

"*Did you hear something?*"

On Friday when she went to sleep Nita found herself with Rachel, but this time they were outside in the woods in the daylight. Rachel was collecting mushrooms, and she also inspected small plants that were sprouting everywhere.

"*See this one with the jagged leaves? Come back in the autumn for special seeds that will relieve the pain of rheumatism.*"

They wandered up and down hills on a beautiful day. "*Dahn ya just love the woodlands? So kind and generous.*"

"*I love the smells,*" *Nita nodded.*

"*Ah yes. The rich, fine earth,*" *Rachel held out her arms to take it all in. Suddenly, she pointed to a large moss-covered boulder.* "*Did you see her? Did you see that?*"

"*What? Where?*"

"*A fairy. She flew off the big rock and ran along the log.*" *Rachel chittered and giggled until she shook all over.*

147

"Really?" Nita looked at Rachel then at the log. "Really?"

Rachel raised her eyebrows and winked. "I won't tell." She giggled again and performed a little jig. "I'm not allowed to tell," she sang. "Aye, they can be mean if you cross them."

Nita laughed and clapped her hands.

Rachel was pleased with Nita's response. "You're as happy as you wish to be. Keep watch for the fairies for they are watching for you."

Finally, Rachel suggested that they should be heading back. "It's downing to dark."

From a cliff Nita saw a river that she recognized at the Susquehanna. Two strange looking boats were floating down it.

"More arks each year," Rachel commented, "going to the Port of Deposit as they call it."

They walked a trail that ran along the bluff over the river. The current appeared to be moving quicker than the arks, which were obviously heavily laden.

"They carry timber and coal from the Pennsylvania Colony."

"We'll go down here," Rachel pointed to a trail that ran along a tumbling stream.

At the top of the trail, over the water's noise they heard whooping and shouting. Rachel's face became alarmed. "Oh, God. Please no."

When they emerged in a gap in the thick woods, they saw smoke rising from near the river. They could hear shouting and breaking glass. "Please no," Rachel tried to hurry, but the trail was steep and treacherous.

When they finally reached the bottom, they saw three men wearing dark hoods running out of a cabin, which had flames shooting through its roof, they threw pottery as they ran. When they saw Rachel, they fled down a trail in the direction of the river's flow. "No please," Rachel pleaded to the sky, "My home, my home." She fell to her knees.

When they reached the cabin, the heat of the fire made it impossible to enter. Rachel's clay pots and china were scattered around the area. She crumbled to the ground and sobbed. Nita recognized the land where the cabin burned as a place near where her garden now sat.

The heat was too much. Nita kicked off the blankets, waking in a sweat.

Saturday morning Nita went to the shed and got the shoebox where she had put the artifacts she and Henry collected while gardening. She unwrapped the page of the Cecil Whig newspaper that held the pieces of the teacup. She felt like she was touching a nightmare. She expected the pieces to vaporize like the wisps of a dream upon waking. But they did not. The white and blue pattern on the cup matched what she had seen in Rachel's cabin, except that the blue had now faded considerably.

She walked to the pile of large hewn stones that Henry had found. She touched their burnt sides. She wandered the area, pushing her way through the brush and closely examining the ground. If anything remained of the cabin other than the rocks, she could not see it.

Nita sat for a while on a large block of stone. She estimated that Rachel must have lived there in the mid-1700s. There wasn't likely to be anything wooden left, especially if the fire in her dream had been real. She wondered if the town of Port Deposit had any historical records, maybe at the library or town hall. She wondered about Rachel. Did she really exist? What was her last name? What became of her?

On Tuesday when Nita finished a lab project, she headed to the cafeteria to grab some lunch while catching up on studying for an ophthalmology quiz on age-related eye diseases. She thought perhaps she would see Doug. She debated whether she'd tell him about her dreams. Maybe just part of one. Revealing what she thought about Rachel being real and the pieces of the teacup would be too much.

As she came through the cash register line with her tray, she heard someone yelling, "Hey, hey."

It took a moment for her to realize that she was the target of the shout but that it wasn't Doug. Dr. Schmidt, the surgeon from the OR, was waving his hand and motioning to her.

Nita nodded and tried to turn the other way to find a table.

"Hey, come on over and sit here. I just sat down." He pointed to the BLT sandwich on his plate.

Everything in her pulled her in the other direction, but her legs took her to his table.

"I was hoping I'd see someone I knew, but I'm sorry I don't recall your name. I don't usually get over here. I was giving a guest lecture to the first-year students."

"Nita."

"Right, Nita Thomas."

"I never got to say goodbye after that day in the OR," Dr. Schmidt continued. "Things got pretty hectic. Sorry I had to kick you and your friends out. I knew it was going to get crowded and busy."

"I understand."

"Do you think you're interested in pediatric oncology?"

"I'm not sure."

"Well I hope that incident didn't discourage you. In fact, if you need a mentor, I'd be willing to apply." The smile on his face told Nita he was applying for more than that.

Nita didn't reply. She looked down at her salad and twisted her fork in her hand.

"Well you know, in medicine you cannot always have everything go just the way you might like. Things happen. I hope you realize that. We will get past this."

Nita wanted to drop the subject. She was exhausted and had had too much coffee that morning just trying to stay alert. She kept her head down and proceeded to eat.

"You know, Nita, stuff happens. I mean things got a little rough in there. I'm sorry if I hurt your feelings."

Nita didn't finish chewing her bite, and when the words shot out of her mouth so did a piece of lettuce. "It's not about my feelings. That little boy lost his leg for the rest of his life! I am not worried about me being offended."

"Are you saying that I am to blame for him losing his leg?"

"No, I'm not saying anything. I'm just saying I feel badly for that little boy. I can't quit thinking about it. I just feel terrible."

"And I don't?" Dr. Schmidt's eyebrows scrunched closer to his nose, and he put his open hand on his chest.

"Dr. Schmidt, I am not criticizing you. I apologize if you took it that way." She saw that people at other tables were watching the interaction.

Even though she wasn't finished with her salad, Nita stood to leave. "I need to go study. Listen, I am sorry if I upset you. I didn't mean to imply anything…"

Dr. Schmidt glared at her from his seat and didn't comment.

Nita hurried to the library and found a seat at a table in the back. She stared at her ophthalmology text while reruns of her encounter with Dr. Schmidt played endlessly in her head. The replays drained her remaining bits of energy, and she nodded off, slumping onto her book.

A young woman in a black bonnet motioned for Nita to stop and move back against the brick wall. The rapid staccato of horses' hoofs thundered in their direction. Nita sensed the woman's panic, and they both pasted themselves against the rough red bricks as if they were part of the mural advertisement painted on the side of the store.

The ground shuddered as six horses with riders galloped past, never noticing the two women. "Them's Rebs," the woman said to Nita, the hate spit out with her words. "We's gettin' closer, so's no knowin'." Under the long prow of her black bonnet, the woman's green eyes shown like a cat's at dusk. "Best be skittish." She moved a couple steps forward in the side alley. Past the woman's shoulder Nita could see a sign on a store across the street that read "Sharpsburg Dry Goods." Bold streaks of gold hair snuck from under the back of the bonnet as the woman bent down to peak around the corner of the building. The woman was thin, and Nita guessed that she was still in her teens.

The woman darted back toward Nita. "Men's comin' on foot. Can't tell if they's soldiers or what. Best we skedaddle back out of town and into that brush ag'in." The woman swung past Nita and down to the end of the alley on fleet bare feet. Her gray dress rustled slightly as she ran. The hem at the bottom of the dress was frayed and ornamented with burrs and briars.

In a crouched sprint they dashed by an empty blacksmith's shop, past some vacant chicken coops, through the side yard of a yellow clapboard house and out into some brush that bordered a large clump of trees. The sun was dropping into a bloody horizon off to their left and a bright half-moon was rising to their right. What sounded like gunfire peppered far in front of them.

Once into the cover of the bushes, the girl squatted down. The gunfire continued. "Least it ain't like it was earlier today. Gads! Sounded like the whole world was crashing apart. My bettin' that least part of it was Snow's Battery givin' them Rebs down the road. Them boys from Port Deposit is tough ones. They'll show them Rebs not to come onto Maryland soil." She grew suddenly pensive. Cannon roared at a distance, and she hunched her shoulders down. The green cat eyes peered out and seemed to implore Nita, but only a statement came out, sounding like an affirmation supported simply by its own words, which were probably enough. "We'll find Johnny. Don't you question that. Ain't no Reb army can separate Jenny and Johnny. We been together since the day we was born, and ain't no war gonna change that." She nodded as if to agree with herself. The cannon roared louder and a bit closer, though still at a good distance. "I dint come all this way and risk the wrath of Mamma for nuthin'." The green eyes sparked until Nita thought she could see the fire of the mother reflected in the girl's defiance. "But after we's found Johnny and made sure he's okay, when we get back and tell Mamma, she'll say 'Jenny, I ought to take the switch to your backside...' but then she'll smile and say 'How is our Johnny? Are they treatin' him okay and is he bein' brave as the rest of them?' Oh, and then she may take the switch to my backside, but I don't care." Her back stiffened even in her squatting position, "No, I don't care...not if Johnny's okay. My hinny don't care if it gets another lickin'."

Jenny looked out from the bushes. "We best make use of the last light. Them trees out there must run along the creek. Think we can make it across that field?"

Nita looked at the farm field. The corn was mostly toppled and then she realized that lying among the stubble were motionless bodies of soldiers.

Jenny looked at Nita. "You quick? I'm quick. I'm quicker 'an most boys in Port Deposit. Only one I can never beat is Johnny. Now he is quick."

"You quick?" she repeated.

Nita nodded.

"Thought so."

With no further discussion, Jenny pushed the bushes wide and said, "Let's go. I'll race ya!" She shot out of the brush like a startled rabbit, and Nita jumped in hot pursuit. Soon they were into the farm field and sprinting full-out trying to hit the tops of the furrows to keep from stumbling. Nita heard a man's voice yelling, "Hey, hey," from back in the woods where they'd been hiding, but they hurtled on. Jenny called back over her shoulder to Nita, "Don't pay him no mind." Then she added, "If he was gonna shoot us, he'd already had."

About ten strides later, Jenny's foot caught on a musket that lay hidden among the cornstalks. She sprawled headlong and landed beside the blue-clad soldier who had once been its owner. His lifeless eyes were looking straight at her. Without a word Jenny bounced to her feet and was into her full sprint again, still ahead despite Nita's best efforts. Nita's lungs were burning from the sprint, and her eyes strained to see where her feet were landing as the fading light dimmed the details of the fast-moving field.

At the edge of the field was a long pile of gray stones about waist-high. Nita slowed as she reached it, although Jenny scampered across it like a chipmunk. On both sides of the stone wall lay soldiers, some with blue uniforms, some with gray. Some still clasped their rifles. One had his rifle in his right hand and a bayonet in his left. Blood had trickled and dried under a small round hole in the center of his forehead. A fly sat next to the little red river. The young man stared into the distance.

Nita was still gasping for air as she clambered over the wall at Jenny's urging. "I was right," Jenny said, pointing down a single-lane dirt road. "That's Antietam Creek down there." The road was cluttered with dead bodies of soldiers and horses. One horse kept moving its left hind leg and trying to raise its head. It would then rest its head on the ground. After a few seconds of rest, it would follow the sequence again. Over and over it repeated the motions until it suddenly shuddered and fell still.

Down the slope where the road turned to the left, Nita could see the end of a stone bridge. Only insects broke the silence as she and Jenny moved out of the woods. On the other side of the creek she could see a steep bank. From beyond the bank came a smattering of gunfire, which stopped as quickly as it started. Jenny paused to remove her bonnet, which had slid backwards on her head during the sprint across the field. When she popped it from the back of her head it unleashed a flood of blond hair. Jenny's round white face reflected the final rays of sunlight, and her cheeks glowed pink. She had just retied her bonnet on her head when her ears perked up. A second later, Nita heard the sound too. Behind them came a clatter of metal and wood interspersed with low voices of men.

Jenny and Nita retreated into some trees and lay behind a log. In a few minutes they saw a wooden wagon pulled by two brown horses appear on the dirt road up from where they had been. Two men in blue uniforms were on a seat at the front of the wagon with one holding the reins of the horses. Six other Union soldiers were walking behind the wagon with two carrying lanterns. The group continued slowly past Jenny and Nita. In the wagon's bed there were at least two other men. One was sitting with a bloodied left arm. With his right arm he was trying to give some water from a canteen to a man lying in the wagon. Three stretchers were stacked at the tailgate.

"Just leave the wagon here for a bit," a man with three yellow stripes on his arm instructed. "Jeb, you, Calvin and Willie go down and see if there's any alive among them on the road and the bridge. Sam, you and Thomas check over there to the left, and I'll look in these woods." The sergeant strode toward the trees where Jenny and Nita were hiding. He walked straight at them and aimed his musket exactly in their direction.

A scraping sound to her left startled Nita. It was another student pulling out a chair at her table. Nita looked quickly around the library to see whether the librarian had noticed her slumped onto a textbook again. Apparently, she had not. Nita tried to concentrate on the causes of macular degeneration, cataracts and other eye afflictions but with little success. The encounter with Dr. Schmidt continued to disturb her so she decided to head home.

At home she was equally unsuccessful at studying and soon went to bed where she drifted away. In no time she was back with Jenny, holding her breath and hoping the sergeant with the musket could not see them lying behind the log.

CHAPTER SEVENTEEN

*T*he sergeant stood ten feet from where Nita and Jenny were lying flat on the ground. He swung his rifle slowly over their heads, trying to discern any movement in the darkness. The other soldiers shuffled off in the distance, carrying stretchers and lanterns. Finally, the sergeant lowered his gun and leaned the butt on the ground. He cocked his head to the side listening. Nita felt something slithering from under her belly, but she held her ground despite the impulse to jump and scream. She didn't breathe as she felt its body diminish to a slender tail and move out from beneath her. Finally, the sergeant said in a low voice, "Anybody in there? Ambulance wagon's here." He paused and listened. "Yank or Reb, don't matter. Fight's over for today. If you're shot, come on out with your hands up or give a holler, and we'll come get you." He waited a minute longer, then said, "Last chance."

He turned and walked away as two soldiers who had gone off to the left, called to him. "Found one," one of them said. "Could use a hand, Sarge. He's a big un." They were struggling with a stretcher that held a husky man in a gray uniform. The sergeant hurried over to help as the man driving turned the back of the wagon in their direction. The other man from the front jumped down to help load the limp Confederate into the back.

Soon the men from the bridge came back up. "Sir, it is plum ugly down there. The bodies is so piled up you can't see what's what. I mean we could see somewhat with the lantern and the moonlight, but it's a real mess."

"You sure none's still alive?"

"As sure as we can be, sir. Nothing's moving, and nobody's talking. Must have been the devil to pay down there."

They turned the wagon around and headed back the way they had come. When the sound faded, Jenny and Nita stood to brush off their clothes and then cautiously moved out of the woods and down toward the bridge. The rising moon glinted off the smoke-colored water. Remnants of the battle were strewn along both banks, but the stream seemed not to mind. Even where bodies of soldiers and horses intruded into the water and disturbed its flow, it politely moved around them as if not wanting to disrupt their slumber.

On the arched stone bridge, the soldiers were tangled and strewn, in some cases three deep, making it look like God had played pick-up sticks with blue and red sticks. Jenny and Nita tried to avoid bothering the soft and shattered bodies, but they eventually realized that they had no choice if they were going to cross. They used their feet to nudge legs and arms out of the way, hoping they would not hear a groan or a scream. Silence fell heavily instead.

They fought through additional human litter on the climb up the opposite bank and encountered another silent army in another lane and another field. Jenny stalled and stared. "How can they do this?" She shook her head and shuddered as the cold and unflinching moonlight frowned down on the *untidy scraps distributed everywhere the eye wandered. Crickets and katydids added a hollow din to the scene.*

Gradually Jenny's mind returned to her quest. "How am I going to find Johnny? I just know he's not dead. He wouldn't do that to me." She turned to Nita and said, "We have a dream, him and me. We're gonna be a doctor and a nurse. Johnny's real smart and 'cause he's gonna be the man, he's gonna be the doctor. And me, I'll be the nurse, of course. And we'll get us an office right on Main Street, and we'll take care of the folks who are sick in Port Deposit—and of course other parts if they want to come. Johnny and me have been talking about this since we was five. We even drawed a picture of it. When this war started, Johnny even was thinking maybe he'd be a medic, but then Mr. Alonzo Snow and Mr. Theodore Vanneman got together in town and arranged for us to have a light artillery battery, and Johnny joined that with the other boys. I might do a little nursing whilst I'm here though." She scanned the field and moved backward into her thoughts. While she stared out into the dismal field, she suddenly cocked her head to the side. She pulled her bonnet away from her right ear and listened more intently. "You hear that?"

Nita wasn't sure. They both stood stalk still. All Nita could hear were insects. "Over there," Jenny pointed to the field in front of them and off to their right. From within the insect chatter, Nita heard a voice say, "Mam. Mam if you please."

Jenny was already moving in the direction of the sound.

"Over here," a hand raised from among the hundreds of unmoving forms.

They hurried up to a pale young man with a reddish beard lying on the ground. "I am so sorry to bother you, but if you please, could we get a drink of water?" Nita looked into the man's pained eyes, then saw that half of his stomach seemed to have been blown away, leaving a mangled mess in his torn gray shirt.

Jenny looked as if she was in shock. "Oh my, oh my," was all she could say.

"They ain't nothin' but Yankee bitches," came another voice about ten feet away. A man in a butternut shirt sat leaning against a sizable rock. "They ain't gonna help us, and I wouldn't take no water from them anyhow."

"Now, Byron, that is no way to talk to a lady. I don't care. It is just unacceptable to talk that way." The man turned his head back toward them and coughed. "You will have to forgive my friend, Byron, he is very angry right now."

Nita and Jenny looked at Byron and saw that the lower part of his left leg was twisted hideously to the side. The man with the meek drawl continued, "You see that Byron's sister, Miss Kate...well her fiancée was killed here this afternoon. And Byron had promised Miss Kate that he would look after Billy to make sure nothing happened to him," he coughed again.

"You don't need to explain nothing to them," Byron snarled. "Killed them stupid blue coats on the bridge like shooting squirrels on a fence and that's all the explanation I'm a' gonna give. Our Georgia boys was heroes today, and Billy with the best of 'em. "

The meek man coughed and said, "Well Byron, I will not dispute that our Georgia boys fought well and hard, but as the sun set on this day and I looked out over this field of wasted lives, I have to wonder about the cost of heroes. The price of war is too high, I have come to believe." The meek man coughed harder. "Could I trouble you, Mam, for a drink of water."

"We, we don't have any water," Jenny said.

When the next bout of coughing stopped, the meek man said, "I can tell you where there is some. That soldier right over there," he motioned feebly with his hand. "His canteen is full. I know it is because I guarded while he filled it just a short time before we was shot. He won't mind if I have some."

Jenny went over to the body, which lay face down. She turned to Nita and said, "I don't see a canteen."

Nita stepped over to her as the meek man said, "It might be underneath him. You can get it. He won't mind."

Together Jenny and Nita rolled the body over. The left arm flopped with a thud on the far side, and the canteen slid off in that direction too. When they looked at the man's face, they both gasped. His face was identical to that of the meek man.

Jenny slipped the canteen from the man's body, his arm offering no resistance, and brought it to the waiting man. As she opened it and held it out, she said, "He looks just like you." She knelt to hold up the man's head and put the canteen to his lips. He took a sip, but that just triggered another round of coughing.

The angry man answered Jenny by saying, "Well ain't you just the smart one. It's his goddam twin brother."

The meek man winced. Nita wasn't sure if it was from the recognition that his brother was dead or from the wracking cough that prevented him from drinking.

"Byron," came a weaker voice. "Please do not take the name of the Lord Our God in vain."

"You ain't no preacher yet."

"That may be true. And with today's turn of events, I may never be. But nonetheless, we must not violate His commandments. They are God's law, and we must obey." He coughed and blood trickled from the corner of his mouth.

"So, what about killing all them Yanks on the bridge?"

"I struggle with that, I do. I don't know how to reconcile that. I do ask the Lord to forgive me if it be a sin." He coughed and writhed as if he wanted to turn over.

When the fit passed, he smiled at Jenny and said, "My brother Walter and I vowed to our mother that we would never be separated in the war.

Wherever one went, the other would go. Well we did it, but now that's looking like it might not have been the best idea. Seems our family back in Georgia will have double the sorrow." He writhed and groaned.

Jenny gathered the man's head into her lap. "It hurts awful bad, Ma'am." He moved his hand toward the open side of his stomach but didn't touch it. "I am sorry to complain. And I thank you for your kind touches."

"Byron," he said as he stared straight up into the night sky, "would you tell our mother that we are sorry. Tell her Walter and William will wait for her at the gate."

Jenny stroked the beads of sweat from the man's forehead. "Your Lord and your brother are waiting. It's okay. Your mother will be along when she's called."

"Thank you," he whispered, "you are an angel." He closed his eyes and relaxed.

Jenny held him for a minute longer then gently placed his head back on the ground.

"Oh God, no! Not William too," shouted Byron. He squinted his eyes closed and let out a guttural moan. The moan evolved into a sentence, "Walter and William was better men than I could ever be."

Jenny turned toward him and said, "Then let that goodness live through you. You are the only thing stopping you." She handed him the canteen.

Byron looked at the canteen for a long moment then reached out and accepted it. "Thank you," he said quietly and took a sip from it. He looked down at his leg, which jutted out sideways. "Wanna hear something funny? I thought I would get through this war without an injury and nobody back home would believe I did any fighting. Well today when we was shootin' from behind a pile of rocks, a bullet must have hit the rocks and knocked a piece up that hit me in the mouth. Busted my tooth right off. I was kind of pleased," he grinned and pointed to the missing spot. "I figured now I had my proof, so I took the tooth out of my mouth and put it in this here pocket so's I could show people. You know, proof that I was in the war." He grinned again and then grimaced as he looked down at his leg. "Now I guess I won't have to tell them. They'll all know without asking."

He took a long drink from the canteen and asked, "What are y'all doing out here anyway?"

"I'm looking for my brother. My twin brother. He's with Maryland Battery B. It's a light artillery battery."

The man shook his head. "Good luck finding anybody in this mess. I wish you well in your search."

"Thank you, Byron," Jenny said.

"What's your name?"

"I'm Jenny. Jenny Nelson."

"Well I thank y'all for the help, and I apologize for my rudeness. I suspect they'll bring ambulance wagons along in the morning, lessen the fightin' starts up ag'in. They came around earlier, but William would not leave Walter so we just kept quiet and stayed."

When Jenny and Nita turned to go, he said, "Before you go, could you do one more thing, please? Could you move Walter and William together?"

They each grabbed a cold arm and struggled together to pull Walter over. The top of his pants kept catching on corn stubble. Every few steps they stopped to pull his pants back up. After they dragged Walter next to William, Jenny went to Byron and touched his head. "We got to go now, but you take care."

Throughout the night they wandered, looking for Johnny. Cotton clouds dabbed at the moon's half-closed eye. In areas where the ambulance wagons had not yet arrived, there was a constant moaning and calling. Quickly Jenny and Nita learned to ignore those sounds, along with the indistinguishable, inharmonious and irreconcilable clamor of the crickets and katydids. They pressed on looking for cannons, as the moon arced higher and then descended, like a slow-moving projectile.

When the first rays of daylight filtered into the nightmare, the world resurrected with activity from all parts of the low rolling hills. Jenny and Nita discovered they were in an area held largely by Union soldiers. They were warned numerous times that the fighting was likely to start up again at any minute, but it did not. A private with a Union artillery unit positioned on a small knoll told them where they could find Snow's Battery. "Just on the other side of that corn field that's filled with bodies. Go back a couple hundred yards on the other side from that little white church."

Their mental exhaustion exceeded the physical drain as they trudged past one hideous specter and on to another. They could barely stand by the time they got to the area where Snow's Battery was to be, but Jenny suddenly jumped with excitement when she recognized faces from Port Deposit. She rushed up to one boy whom she and Johnny had gone to school with. "James, where's Johnny?"

"Holy Jesus, Jenny. What are you doing here? How did you get here?"

"I come looking for Johnny. Where is he?"

James' head dropped a bit, and he paused before answering. "Johnny got hit," he looked at Jenny's eyes and then rushed to add, "but he's not gonna die or anything. It's his arm. Lieutenant Vanneman sent Ben Pepper to take Johnny over to a field hospital. That was about two hours ago."

"Where? Where is it?"

James pointed in the general direction. The rising light of day illuminated devastation that bled into the landscape. Everywhere there was destruction of men, horses and military equipment. Chaos followed the sun as riders, walkers and wagons hurried about in seeming circles. Some men, though, sat. They sat and stared beyond this place. One soldier in blue was curled under a tree that had had almost all its branches blown off. Although the man did not appear to be wounded, he shuddered and sobbed uncontrollably.

Jenny tugged at herself to go comfort him, but she pulled away to find Johnny. "I must come back here to help," she said in a voice noticeably higher pitched than before. "Someone must help that boy. Just as quick as I can, I will come back and place my hand on his shoulder. I'll remember that tree, and I'll find him and comfort him." Nita looked at Jenny, wondering what was happening with her. Jenny stared at the tree, which looked like a cross from which the crucified soldier had been dropped at its base.

James had instructed them on how to stay within the Union-held territory. As they did that, they became more comfortable with being out in the open. At a point where two dirt roads crossed, they had to yield to a column of blue uniformed soldiers with rifles who were escorting gray-shirted prisoners. Many of the rebels wore boots that flapped open at the soles or had no shoes on at all. As one particular man in gray approached, his blue eyes locked onto Jenny. "Help me, Miss. Can't y'all please help me. I don't want to be a prisoner. I don't even want to be a soldier. I just want to go back to Huntsville."

Jenny reached out her hand to the man, only to have a Union musket come between them and push her back. "Yous need to get back. Dees are prisoners. Dees are da enemy, and day's dangerous and crafty."

The gray prisoner turned his head toward Jenny as he moved past. He mouthed a pleading, "Help me please," as tears rolled down his cheeks.

"I must help him," Jenny's voice was shriller yet. She grabbed one of the Union soldiers marching alongside the prisoners by the arm. "Where are you taking them?"

"The train," he shrugged as he pulled his sleeve away from her.

"But where will the train take them?" she ran after him.

"Prison."

"But where?"

"I heared they was going to Fort Delaware," he shrugged again.

"Fort Delaware. That must be in Delaware. It is not so terrible far from Port Deposit. I'll just go there and help them. I'll find that young man and help him. I'll help him get back to Huntsville, wherever that is."

Jenny and Nita watched the long parade of hanging heads shuffle past. Jenny's hand seemed to reach out for each man, but not so far as to actually touch them. "I'll help you," she said to some, which only elicited confused looks from them.

Finally, one Union soldier, who stood guarding the intersection and had been observing them the whole time, walked over to Jenny and asked if she was a rebel sympathizer, "'cause if you are, you'll be arrested too."

"Oh no," Jenny replied in a squeak.

"Well then stay away from them."

"I'm looking for my brother. He's with the Maryland Battery B, but he's been wounded, and I'm goin' to the hospital to find him."

"Well Miss, one of these bastards is likely the one that shot him. You just might keep that in mind." Jenny withdrew the hand that had now been stuck in an extended position toward the prisoners.

At the rear of the walking prisoners came a dozen wagons, each filled with wounded Confederate soldiers. Many moaned and some shrieked as they jostled over the ruts at the intersection that ran perpendicular to their direction. From the back of one of the wagons that passed came a voice yelling, "Miss, Miss. Jenny. Jenny Nelson. Remember me. I was with William and you helped us."

Jenny waved back, but she seemed confused as to how she might know him.

The guard at the intersection looked with suspicion at Jenny. He walked over to a man on a horse, pointed to Jenny and said something. The man on the horse galloped off in the direction from which Jenny and Nita had come.

When the line of prisoners had passed, Jenny stood there still waiting. For long minutes she stood as if the way was still obstructed. Periodically her hand would extend toward no one who was there. Finally, a line of wagons approached from behind them, nudging them off the road and pushing Jenny into some level of motion.

Every twenty steps or so, Jenny told Nita that she and Johnny were going to be a doctor and a nurse. Her voice remained high-pitched, and she seemed to have detached from any involvement with the horrors around them. Eventually Nita saw a red-brick house in the distance that matched the description James had given them. Wagons, horses and much activity surrounded the place.

Nita guided Jenny in that direction, and they ended up in a line of soldiers in bloody blue swaying toward the building. Some were on make-shift crutches. Others were being carried along by soldiers who were less badly injured. Periodically a wagon with seriously wounded men would clatter past. At one point three wagons filled with dead soldiers wobbled past going in the opposite direction.

Jenny abruptly seemed to sense an urgency to get to the house. She began pushing past the soldiers in front of her, at one point even knocking over a soldier who was using a stick for a cane. Shouts of outrage and anger followed them as Nita chased Jenny down the lane that led to the house. Nita grabbed Jenny's flailing arm to try to control her, but Jenny whirled on her and slapped her across the face. "We must find Johnny before it's too late. He does not belong in this place with these ugly people. He cannot be here." Jenny then tore loose from Nita and ran zig-zagging through the crowded lane.

When they got to the house, its large front porch was jammed with wounded soldiers. Other soldiers were attempting to keep order. The crowd was clearly impenetrable, so Jenny lurched around to the left side of the house. There, outside an open window, was a pile of human limbs. As they attempted to walk past it, someone's lower leg was tossed from the window *with the brown leather shoe still attached. The shoe came to rest on someone's open palm as if he were trying on shoes in a cobbler's shop.*

A scream came from inside the room as a man begged them not to cut off his hand. The pleading voice was muffled and finally disappeared. Jenny stood mesmerized as a sawing sound began.

When the mangled hand landed near her foot, Jenny was jerked back to her mission. She ran to the rear of the house where three guards blocked access to the kitchen door. "I must get in," she cried, "my hand is in there."

The guards looked at her quizzically and shook their heads.

"But my shoe," Jenny pleaded.

All three of the guards looked at her bare feet. Finally, one of them said, "You don't want to go in there. It ain't no place for a girl." A scream from a different voice inside punctuated the man's comment.

Jenny's face became a demonic mask, and she stepped backwards from them. She continued to stride backwards until she bumped into a dappled horse tethered to a tree branch. She leaned against the horse and examined the house from the rear. To her right was the pile of limbs. At the back door the three guards watched her as a curiosity. To Jenny's left, on the side of the house not yet visited, was a large oak tree with branches touching the house and its roof.

Without a word, Jenny walked deliberately toward the tree, which put her out of view of the backdoor guards. When she reached the tree, she grabbed a low branch and deftly swung her right leg up and over it. Like a squirrel fleeing a dog she scurried up the tree and out on a limb that brought her within reach of an open window on the second floor. Nita struggled up the tree after her, but by the time she was to the level of the window, Jenny was already inside. Nita inched out on the limb, which bounced and jounced her as she neared the house. She wished she had observed how Jenny had success-fully maneuvered into the open window. Nita stepped her right foot onto the window ledge and then reached to grasp the sash of the upper window. As she pulled her body over, the foot on the ledge slipped but sailed into the house, crashing her thigh onto the ledge and leaving her left leg dangling. She heard a horse snort and looked down at a man with gold braids on his shoulders who was looking up at her. Nita swung her head through the window and pulled her left leg through.

The room was hot and carried a thick stench of sweat, blood and rotting flesh. Jenny was standing at the door arguing with a soldier who seemed baffled by her presence. "Lass, I got me orders not to let anyone but the wounded soldiers and medical folks in here."

"I'm a nurse," she shouted.

"Then can ya explain for the love of Pete why ya saw fit to enter by climbing through a window on the second floor?"

"Next," shouted a male voice from below.

When the Irish soldier bent to assist a wounded man, Jenny bolted past him with Nita close behind.

CHAPTER EIGHTEEN

*J*enny thrashed through the three bedrooms upstairs, startling the wounded soldiers who were lying in beds, sitting in chairs, some even sprawling on the floor, all waiting patiently for their turn with the surgeon.

She then tromped down the stairs toward the front door. In a long thin hallway that ran toward the rear of the house, wounded men sat on the floor and leaned against every available wall. Jenny and Nita stood at the base of the steps. From their right they heard a deep moan and a sawing sound. On what was apparently a dining room table lay a man who was biting a bullet between his teeth. A surgeon was sawing into his thigh as four large soldiers held him down. Blood covered everyone and everything in the room. Brass from the saw glowed yellow against the red.

From their left came a voice calling, "Jenny?"

Jenny spun toward it. In a parlor another group of men waited. By the window stood a thin soldier with blond hair, pale skin and green eyes. He looked a great deal like Jenny. Nita turned to comment, only to see Jenny rush forward and hug him. The embrace, though, was one-sided on the brother's part. His right arm hung limp in a shredded blue sleeve that was encrusted with blood and dirt. The round-faced boy winced as Jenny squeezed him, but she did not notice. "Oh Johnny, Johnny I found you. You're okay. Oh Johnny, it's us again, together. Now we can go back home to Mamma, and it will be just like it was before this stupid, mean war came."

Jenny pressed her head against the left side of Johnny's neck and nuzzled into his shoulder. Johnny's left hand touched her back. The other soldiers who crammed the room looked on with interest, this interruption having provided a distraction from the terror of what was likely to come for each of them, terror that was being given voice from across the hall on the surgeon's table. For a while they watched Jenny, but then they drifted off in their thoughts, one by one.

Nita examined the men who sat, stood and lay in the parlor. Some were remarkably young and some remarkably old. Each set of eyes was a theater of emotions, each playing out scenarios. A red-haired man pondered how he would farm with only one hand. A black-eyed boy wondered how his girlfriend would react to a beau with only one leg. A wild-eyed man had become mentally lost on his journey and simply gritted back the pain. A black man in the same blue uniform as the others periodically used his left hand to touch where his right ear had been. His right shoulder was distorted under his uniform, and his arm hung like it was barely attached.

Slowly Jenny released her death grip on Johnny. She shuffled back from him until she bumped a small wooden table that stood next to a rose-colored chair occupied by a man with a face of a similar shade of pink. His eyes were closed, and he gave the appearance of having nodded off while reading the Bible on a Sunday afternoon.

"Johnny," Jenny said with a scolding tone, "why are you here?"

A blue soldier with a blood-soaked uniform came to the entrance of the parlor and called, "Next."

"No," pleaded the man standing next to Johnny.

"Come on, soldier, we got no time to waste."

"No, please no. Someone else next."

The bloody man stepped over to the pleading soldier who said, "No, please, I can't."

But without further objection, the man let the bloody private escort him across the hall.

Johnny watched with intense interest. His green eyes gathered up each speck of information. His back stiffened, and his left hand involuntarily reached over to comfort his right arm.

"Johnny," Jenny repeated with her impatience rising, "why are you here? We must be getting home. Mamma will have our supper on the table, and she will be cross."

Johnny slid his green eyes over to the matching set in his sister. "Jenny," he said gently, "I been wounded."

"Oh no," she replied firmly, "we haven't time to waste. Supper will get cold, and Mamma will be cross. She'll take the switch to us both."

Johnny's left arm reached out to his sister's right arm. "Jenny, what has happened to you?"

From across the hall came a loud pleading, "No! No! Please no!" Then there was a muffling of the sound and the sickening sound of a saw. Jenny noticed none of it.

Johnny's left hand gripped Jenny's elbow until he sensed that he had her attention. "Jenny, I am next, and you got to listen to me. I been shot in my arm, and I'm feared they will have to cut it off." Jenny's wild eyes darted over to the window and left the room. "Listen to me Jenny" Johnny called. "They are going to have to cut off my arm. Look at it," he said as he pulled on her arm to swing her gaze back to him.

Jenny looked at her brother and whimpered. "But you're gonna be the doctor, and I'm gonna be the nurse. How you gonna be a doctor with only one arm? Johnny, we is both right-handed. Jes' tell me how you gonna be a doctor without your right arm. You see that is why I am trying to tell you that Mamma will be cross."

"Oh Jenny," Johnny drew her near, and she sagged limp against him. For a while they stood quietly.

"I am so tired of this war," Jenny whispered. "Why do they cut off everybody's arms and hands and legs and shoes?"

"Sometimes in medicine you have to do bad things. Sometimes there are only bad choices."

"Oh no," she pushed back from him, "that cannot be right. That just cannot be right. Medicine is for helping people. You're the doctor, and I'm the nurse, and we help people."

"Oh Jenny, it's true we had this dream since we was little ones. Medicine was our dream, but maybe our dream ain't gonna come out the way we thought it would. Maybe that's what happens to dreams when you grow up."

"Next."

Johnny and Jenny both looked toward the doorway where the same bloody soldier beckoned. Johnny shuddered back, and the eyes of the others in room watched as the incessant lottery took another from their midst.

"Come on soldier. No choice."

Johnny mustered his courage, and he straightened up. "Okay," he said as his left hand touched his right arm.

"Oh no," Jenny called as she hurried toward the bloody man. "You do not understand. Johnny is the doctor, and I am the nurse. We are helping people."

The man's tired eyes looked down at Jenny.

"He is the doctor," she nodded with conviction, "and I am the nurse. You have made some mistake, and Mamma will be cross." She put her hands on her hips and nodded her head in defiant confirmation.

The man tilted his head to one side to try to find sense in Jenny. Finding none, he reached out his left arm and brushed her to the side with the back of his hand. "Come on, soldier," he said to Johnny. "Doc's waiting."

Nita followed Jenny out the front door and into the crowd of soldiers on the front porch who were apparently less badly hurt than those in the parlor. Jenny pushed her way through them with Nita moving more slowly behind.

One of the soldiers who was leaning on the porch railing caught Nita's attention by tugging briefly on her sleeve. "Miss, would you mind terribly to fill my canteen at that pump around by the kitchen door? I did it once myself, but then I shared it around and barely got a drop. I just don't think my foot can make the trip again." He nodded toward his boot that had a bullet hole in the top. "Don't look like much compared to some of these boys, but it hurts like a dog's biting it. Would you mind terribly?" He held a round metal canteen by its strap and inched it slightly toward her. "We'd be much obliged."

Nita felt the eyes of those near them watching her. She reached out and took the canteen. "Sure. No problem. You say it's around back?"

"Yes, Miss. Thank you kindly."

When Nita got around back, she found a line of soldiers at the pump doing the same thing. Just as she filled hers, one of the soldiers from the back porch they'd encountered earlier walked up to her and said, "Hey, where's that friend of yours—the one with the black bonnet? They's some soldiers looking for her."

"She's around front I think."

"Then you tell her a sergeant and two privates is looking for her."

Nita walked back around the house past the tree she had climbed a little earlier and wound her way back up the porch steps to the owner of the canteen. She was accepting his eternal appreciation when a ruckus erupted on the left side of the house. She heard Jenny's shrill voice and a man shouting something in reply.

Nita rushed as quickly as she could down the steps and around in the direction of the noise. "I am the nurse," Jenny screamed.

Two privates held her arms, and a sergeant stood in front of her with a beet-red face. They were only a few steps from the pile of human limbs next to the house. "I heard you before," the sergeant said. "If you are a nurse, why doesn't the doctor verify that? You just saw him look at you out the window and say he had no idea who you are."

"I am going to be a nurse," Jenny squirmed in the soldiers' grips, but they held firm.

The sergeant stepped toward her so that his glowing face was at the entrance to the bonnet. "So first you said you were a nurse and now you say you're gonna be a nurse? Which is it?" He paused, but before she could reply he continued, "We heard you were a Reb sympathizer and maybe a spy. We have orders to bring you to the general for questioning."

"My Johnny will explain it to you," Jenny spit out the words in exasperation.

"And which Johnny Reb might that be? One of them prisoners you said you was gonna help?"

"Not Johnny Reb, you fool. Johnny Nelson. He'll tell you."

"Andrew," the sergeant addressed the bigger of the two privates restraining her. "She'll ride with you. Tie her hands in front of her, and cinch her to the horn."

Nita stepped over to the sergeant. "I think I can explain all this."

"And who might you be?" He turned from Jenny to look at Nita. He scanned down to her blue jeans and back up to her tan t-shirt.

"I know her, sort of."

"You know her, sort of? But you're gonna explain things?"

"Well yes, but I think I can explain."

"Why don't you begin by explaining why you are dressed like a man."

"I, ah, well…" Nita looked down at her blue jeans.

"I think you best just step back, or we'll take you in for questioning too."

"But I can explain…"

"Let me explain something to you," the man's veins in his temples bulged until Nita thought he was going to have a heart attack. "We ain't slept in over two days and ain't had a real meal in more than that. We spent all day yesterday watching Rebs kill our friends, and we ain't in no mood for dealing with lyin' Reb sympathizers. Now this is your last warning. You git out of here now or you're going with her." The stench of the man's breath caused Nita to step back.

The other two soldiers were already tying Jenny's hands. Nita watched as they wrestled the squirming and screaming woman up onto a black horse. The big soldier put a foot in a stirrup and shoved Jenny forward. He swung his leg over the horse and settled into the saddle behind her. He reached around and tied a loose end of the rope that held her hands onto the saddle horn.

The sergeant and the other private mounted quickly, and the three horses pounded past a gray, split-rail fence and down the lane away from the house.

Wednesday morning, Nita showered and dressed quickly then hopped into Little Earl and headed out her driveway. She feared she could be driving headlong into trouble. Her brain volleyed back and forth on what she had done wrong with Dr. Schmidt. Other than doing a better job keeping her mouth shut, she found little to criticize. Her anger rose until she

175

found herself tailgating a tractor trailer. She decided she better back off from the truck and from her impetuous pursuit of a problem she was not even sure existed. After all, what did Dr. Schmidt care with a mere med student? She may very well never see him again.

Nita moved into the slow lane on the highway and purposely shifted her mind to something more positive. She needed friends. Especially at a fretting time like this, she needed someone to talk with. She mentally scanned the women she knew in her class. They had all long-since clicked in with one or a few other women. Nita knew it would be a slow and difficult endeavor to make her way into a circle that had largely been set for at least a couple years. Women often looked askance at her, and though she deliberately tried not to be intimidating, clear down to finding drab clothing, she often failed. Women weren't comfortable with her. Searching back over the years, she realized with an ugly revelation that her last close friend had been Janie, her roommate during her freshman and sophomore years in college.

This left guys. Friendships with guys would kindle much quicker. Getting the fire started was seldom a problem, but keeping it under control often was. She had learned to be careful playing with matches.

Paul Alvarez was a likely candidate to help her. He made it his business to be friends with all the professors. Numerous times he had tried to connect with her, but she strongly suspected his interests went beyond casual friendship. Besides ever since Sarah's party, things had been strange between them.

Rich Arnone was more to her liking. Unfortunately, he tended to keep to himself, studying and getting good grades. In that regard they were similar. She enjoyed the time she spent with him at Sarah's party. She even liked his curly dark hair and thought it was cute how he would blush through his olive skin. She would look for an opportunity to talk with Rich.

As Nita neared campus, she gave herself a failing grade in being a friend. All she really had was Little Earl. She patted his steering wheel, then wondered how long it had been since she'd changed his oil. Even this relationship was faltering. Earl didn't ask much, but she gave even less.

That evening when she returned to her house, she found Henry coming out the front door. "I was over earlier to pick up some tools I left out back, and I heard a smoke detector beeping. Just a battery going dead, so I went and got new ones for both of them."

Nita thanked Henry, and as he drove away, she realized that he had become her closest friend. When she looked in the refrigerator for something to eat, she discovered she had half a jar of mayonnaise, a near-empty bottle of ketchup and a dozen eggs with an expiration date from a month earlier. She got back in her car and headed to D'Lorenzo's Pizza in Port Deposit. When she parked Little Earl, she happened to be facing a historical marker on Main Street. Nita was out of the car and halfway to the pizza shop's door when she spun around to recheck what the marker said. She gasped. "Snow's Battery" in large type. Below the heading were details about a light artillery battery, which was formed by Captain Alonzo Snow in Port Deposit during the Civil War. It went on to note the significant roles the battery played in the battles of Malvern Hill and Antietam. She stared at the sign as if it wasn't real.

While she waited for her pizza, Nita sat alone in a wooden booth, but Jenny and Johnny Nelson came rushing into view. Nita recalled the details of the search for Johnny after the battle near what Jenny termed Antietam Creek.

The man at the counter had to call to Nita three times before he could penetrate her trance. "Do you want anything to drink with that? It's to go, right?"

"Ah yeah, I mean no. I mean nothing to drink, and it's to go."

As she ate a piece of pizza at her kitchen table, Nita tried to sort the realities from the fantasies that her dreams clicked her in and out of. The distinctions were becoming less and less clear, but in some ways the dreams were becoming more starkly real. It felt as though Jenny was someone she actually knew, almost a friend. *Sad that someone who might not even exist might be one of her friends.*

Nita ate pieces of pepperoni off other pieces of pizza in the box. With most of the pizza uneaten, Nita put the box in the refrigerator. She made a grocery list, which consisted of her usual fare of food that was easy to prepare.

At her desk, she cranked open last year's obstetrics book to find the section on high-risk pregnancies. She had been told to be ready to attend a C-section the following morning. A young unwed mother was almost to her due date and the baby was beginning to show distress. The woman was a heavy user of alcohol and tobacco. Nita read in her book about fetal-alcohol syndrome and the potential for intrauterine growth retardation as two possible consequences of the mother's dependencies. Nita went to bed hoping that nothing bad would happen while she was watching the C-section.

CHAPTER NINETEEN

A shaft of sunlight shot down through a small window in the gray granite wall. Bars on the window cast a grid in the squared off light that illuminated a patch of the stone floor. Any light that tried to bounce off the floor was largely absorbed by the surrounding granite, which also seemed to absorb any warmth. In a dim corner of the tiny room, Nita saw Jenny curled on a wooden bunk. Her thin frame was now gaunt, and her gray dress had diminished to a flimsy shroud. The black bonnet sat on the floor next to her bunk. Jenny's blond hair was matted in clumps, but her green eyes flared from within the largely lifeless body. From the eyes came a mix of anger, pain and distress.

Jenny raised herself up on an elbow like Lazarus at the call. Her recognition of Nita's presence at first seemed to carry no surprise at all, then moved even further to a point where it seemed like she had already been talking to Nita. "...so, they don't even care what I say. But each day it seems that they bring another boat filled with Confederates. And they is all sick. Some coughs blood, most have terrible sores, and all of them got the Tennessee Trots—that's what the southern boys calls the runnin' shits."

Jenny swung her skinny legs around and sat on the edge of the bunk. She scratched at her thighs under her dress. "About each day a new boatload of 'em arrive, then each week or so they take a boatload over to New Jersey and bury 'em."

"Come on, I'll show you." She picked up her bonnet and rose from the bed. One of the ribbons that tied the bonnet was missing so she just pulled the hat down over her head and allowed the orphan string to dangle on her right shoulder.

Jenny lifted the latch and swung in the heavy wooden door. Warmer air drifted in along with a bit more light. "They don't lock me in no more. They know I'm too weak to swim across the Delaware River to try to escape, plus mostly I'm afeared of the haunts. Some boys tries their escapes at night, but I can see the haunts come out, plain as day I can see 'em. I'm no fool."

Nita followed Jenny down a corridor lined with other cells. The area smelled of urine. Each cell had a door of thick wooden planks with a small barred window. She could hear conversations among men in some of them. From one she heard vomiting.

At the end of the corridor they turned and descended a dozen steps into an open area in the middle of high stone walls. Men in Union uniforms carrying muskets walked a parapet above them. A small group of soldiers in blue drilled in the parade grounds. "Most of the prisoners are kept outside the fort in wood barracks," she explained. "We is on an island called 'Pea Patch' in the Delaware River. When I was healthy, I could have swum it, but not now." She mindlessly scratched at her thighs as she talked. "Most of the prisoners is outside in wood barracks," she repeated as her eyes drifted off. "They keep me in here 'cause I'm female but mostly 'cause I help the doctor. We don't really do much medicine, especially when you look at the thousands of sick boys...." Her voice trailed off, and she scratched her thighs.

Abruptly she turned toward to Nita and said, "But that's not it. That's not it at all. It ain't the wounds and the pus, it ain't the puking and the shits, and it ain't the coughing till their lungs come up." Jenny looked up past the high stone walls into the overcast sky. Nita waited, but Jenny was lost. Her hand reached out to lean on a pillar, but the closest one was some six feet away. She stood with her left arm out and her hand twitching in the air, but she seemed to have misplaced the original intent of raising her arm and so it remained suspended, pending further instructions, which were not forthcoming. With her left hand fidgeting out to her side, Jenny's right hand reached up and gently stroked the black ribbon hanging from her bonnet on her shoulder. "No, no, no," she said softly.

After a few minutes, the company of soldiers in the parade ground finished its exercise and was led by a sergeant off the field. They marched in formation toward Jenny and Nita where a space in the stone wall formed a sort of tunnel behind them. Nita stepped out of their way, but Jenny failed to notice the ranks moving directly toward her. The sergeant guided the troops to split around Jenny as if she were a stone pillar with one support stuck into nowhere. The soldiers reconnected past Jenny and resumed their march out through the tunnel.

"No, that ain't it," Jenny reconnected with her earlier line of thought. "The deeper hurts is in their souls. Their spirits is broken, and their hearts is crushed, and their minds is gone." Jenny turned her head toward Nita to make sure she grasped this important point. "Many of them is gone crazy. You can't believe. Many's crazy. They die of it. When you pull it up, you see the roots is all rotted." Jenny lowered her arm and stepped toward Nita. From within the bonnet came intense conviction, "If you cannot fix the soul, you cannot fix the body."

Jenny turned and wandered out in the direction the soldiers had marched. Nita followed her out of the fort and across a bridge that spanned a moat. She now saw that the fort was a massive granite fortress with a moat cut around it. The land outside the fort was lined as far as the eye could see with wooden barracks. Men in gray uniforms milled about as blue-uniformed soldiers with muskets patrolled the outer perimeter of the island. Beyond their perimeter the Delaware River moved along almost imperceptibly. Nita got the sense that time in this place moved in the same way. Like the river, although it moved, it always stayed in the same place with no apparent progress. The river and time seemed as if they were each about to coagulate. Everything was immersed in a fog of boredom and misery.

"I got a letter from Johnny about six weeks ago," Jenny said out of nowhere. "It was written real bad because his arm is gone. The letter said Momma died, but I don't believe it. I wrote back to Johnny with a plan of how to rescue me, but I ain't heard back. I figure he will just show up, maybe soon."

Past the end of the bridge that crossed the moat, Jenny stopped for no apparent reason. "I'm the nurse," she said, "but dreams don't always turn out the way you think they will when you're little and you draw a picture." Jenny moved on, drifting first to her left then meandering generally to the right. After a time, they arrived back at the bridge, where Jenny announced, "I'm the nurse. Dreams always does that sometimes." A light drizzle started to fall.

Jenny and Nita stood facing a corner of the oppressive fort until a soldier in a filthy gray uniform approached them. Two blue guards at the other end of the bridge observed with mild disinterest. "Pardon me, ma'am," said the gray soldier. Jenny seemed not to hear him. He waited a few moments and then said, "Jenny, we need you again."

Jenny turned unfocused eyes toward him.

Awkward moments floated past.

"Sorry to bother you, Jenny," the gray soldier moved his head back and forth in front of her face in hopes she would focus her murky stare. "It's a boy named Thomas. He's struggling, but it's time. He's talking about the farm."

Jenny nodded, a sadness rising and lapping at her eyes.

"Can you come?"

Jenny nodded. Jenny turned toward Nita and said, "I worry that I'm forgetting to feel. When you're a nurse for so long, you can forget."

The gray soldier took a few tentative steps and looked back to see whether Jenny was following. She was.

The wooden buildings they passed were in various fading shades of brown. The gray soldier motioned for them to follow him into a building that was half-way between brown and gray. Inside the long, dim barracks were more than fifty wooden bunks. The air reeked of urine, vomit and unwashed men. The low murmur from pockets of conversations stopped when Jenny and Nita entered. "Back here he is," the soldier pointed to a bunk toward the left rear. The only sound remaining was a wracking cough from a man lying alone on a bunk on the right.

The gray soldier stopped near the head of an emaciated form on the left, little more than a skeleton with gray gauze for skin. Dark brown eyes stared in a hollow trance, and breaths struggled to escape between blue crinkled lips. Nita could not see an obvious wound but imagined that malnutrition, dysentery and TB were all rampant in the barracks, probably cholera too.

The gray soldier knelt down next to the bunk. "She's here," he said. "She's the lady I told you about, Thomas." The gray soldier looked up at Jenny and said, "He doesn't know how to go. He's afraid, like the others."

Jenny nodded. She leaned over and picked up the bony hand that lay at the gaunt man's side. The gray soldier stood and stepped back. Jenny took his place kneeling next to the bunk. "Thomas," she said quietly. There was no response from the vacant eyes. "Thomas, Jesus is looking for you. Others are waiting too. They want you to cross over."

"It's bright," a voice scraped out, "and green."

"It sure is. It's a fine place to be."

Twig-like fingers wound around Jenny's left hand. She waited. Silence filled the room, punctuated only by coughing that seemed to echo from one place to another.

Jenny patted the man's hand with her right hand. "It's okay."

"There's a bright light." His eyes gazed up with increasing intensity and interest.

"You can go when you're ready, and I think you are."

The grip on Jenny's hand tightened until it left white halos at the tip of each twig.

A deep breath scraped in and stayed a while. When it left, it took the man with it. He closed his eyes, and his hand relaxed around Jenny's. She closed her eyes too. Even the coughing in the room went silent.

After a period, Jenny opened her eyes and placed the man's hand on his chest. As she stood, murmurs in the barracks began to buzz like flies on a window pane. Soon the coughing joined in the muffled chorus. The gray soldier thanked Jenny saying, "He was stuck. He'd hung on that way for almost three days. He needed your touch."

Jenny's face registered only weariness. "He was too young to die. Not like this."

The gray soldier nodded and led her toward the door. When they were almost out, a soldier standing in a group of three yelled at Jenny, "It ain't right. You ain't God. You're the devil. It ain't right."

Another soldier in the trio nodded and said, "She's the Death Angel. She's doing the devil's business."

Jenny stopped and looked at them with a confused grimace. Her mouth moved, but no words came out. The gray soldier stepped back to Jenny and said to the three, "Thomas needed her help. He was stuck in his suffering."

"It ain't right for her to decide. That's for God to decide."

The gray soldier said quietly, "Thomas is in a better place now." He turned to Jenny and said, "Let's go."

Outside, the drizzle had built to a steady rain. The gray soldier thanked her again and advised that she not pay those men any mind. Jenny's *mind seemed to have already wandered away. She was looking off to the river, which was visible through some trees, toward the dim light that was trying to flee this day. Jenny drifted past some blue guards on her way to the river. They seemed to barely notice her. She wandered along until she stopped on the bank. She and Nita stood and listened to the water slurping among sticks and other debris along the muddy edge of the island.*

"It's called Pea Patch Island," Jenny said. "Don't know exactly why." Jenny stepped up on a driftwood log and balanced on her bare feet. "But I can tell you this, time moves thick here—thicker than three-day-old pea soup. And the life jes' keeps oozing out. Their spirits is gone."

Judging from the buds on the tree branches and the cool breeze, Nita estimated it to be April. The rain retreated slowly back to a drizzle that barely pitted the surface of the river. Birds flitted about, but few sang. Jenny stood perfectly still on her perch on the worn, gray log facing the wide river. Nita stood next to a pool of brown water. A drop from a branch landed in the center of the pool. Concentric rings emanated.

Finally, Jenny stated, "In John 4:24, the Bible says, 'God is Spirit and those who worship Him must worship in Spirit and Truth.'" Slowly she extended her hands up and out over the water. "But the Bible don't tell you what to do if the spirits is in prison and truth is dying." With her hands extended, Jenny stepped down onto the muddy bank. "Oh, the river knows. It froths at its edges, but deep in its core moves the truth. Deep truth is where we be going. We may swim or we may drown, but we belong." She used her toe to draw three concentric circles in the mud.

Nita's dreams, which were feeling less and less like dreams, were draining her energy. Sleep had lost its regenerative power. To compound the problem, when she awoke, she faced the daytime nightmares of medical school.

CHAPTER TWENTY

As soon as she arrived on campus Thursday, she was told to go straight to the obstetrics unit. When she got to the Nurses Station, the chief OB resident told her to gown up quickly and go to Delivery Room One. When she arrived at the delivery room door, she looked through the small window and saw a pregnant woman sitting upright on the table with her naked back exposed through the hospital gown. The resident was scrubbing an orangish circle on her back with betadine. He then used a three-inch needle to give her a spinal. Nita had read how this would numb the mother from about her waist down.

Nita slipped through the door and found Sarah Mellis already standing near the wall. Minutes later, the patient was turned to lie flat on the table, and her distended belly was quickly exposed while an anesthesiologist adjusted her IV. After scrubbing and gloving, the attending physician and the OB resident draped the patient as the anesthesiologist monitored the woman's vitals. In short order, all was ready. The scrub nurse moved to the side of the resident as he drew a scalpel low across the woman, just above her pubic area.

Within ninety seconds with the mother still conscious, the OB resident was pulling the baby boy out. He suctioned the baby's mouth with a bulb syringe, clamped the cord and cut it. He handed the baby off to a female pediatric resident, who put the baby under the warming lights on a table near Nita and Sarah. Nita heard the pediatric resident then report to the obstetrician that the baby had a five Apgar at one minute. "Not surprising, considering," he replied.

After the placenta was delivered, the OB resident began suturing the incisions as a nurse showed the baby to the mother, before taking it to the NICU. Nita and Sarah watched the well-organized process as the team completed the procedure. Eventually the mother was taken to the recovery room. Nita whispered to Sarah as they left the OR, "Did you read in the book that the Apgar score was developed by a female physician who graduated from Columbia med school way back in 1933?"

"I saw that. Virginia Apgar. She was an obstetrical anesthesiologist. How cool is that?"

As they left the hospital, Nita felt a glow from seeing the successful C-section and got an extra boost knowing about the contribution of Dr. Apgar. Sarah seemed to have read her mind and said, "We are at an awesome place in our lives. I only hope we can contribute in a special way like Dr. Apgar did. Have you decided what you want to do next?"

"Actually, obstetrics does intrigue me."

"Me too. I have a cousin who is an OB/GYN nurse practitioner. She has delivered hundreds of babies. She said OB is either really happy or really sad."

Nita thought for a moment. "I can imagine that is quite true."

Sarah and Nita walked together to the large lecture hall. In addition to their regular coursework, the fourth-year students were required to attend seminars on various topics that would help them as they moved out of medical school. Today's was on the economics of medicine. A visiting professor from the University of Chicago described how by the end of the century economics would increasingly determine the manner in which medical care would be distributed. Her name was Dr. Susanne Sampson, and she presented a "cold, hard facts look at the business of medicine," as she put it. "Three inevitable facts must be acknowledged. First, medical care is expensive. As you students know, going to medical school is very costly. You expect to be compensated for your expenses and for your dedication. Paying doctors well is a basic requirement, lest we no longer attract the best and brightest to the field. Place on top of that the facilities, equipment, consumables like drugs, plus insurance and the cost of litigation, all of that and much more makes the practice of medicine very expensive. Moreover, all of these costs will rise sharply over the next ten to fifteen years. By the year 2000 there will be a big difference between those who can afford the best medical care in this country and those families who will have to settle for something less. She showed numerous slides with data that depicted healthcare costs vastly outpacing projected family income.

"The second and obvious fact is that someone must pay for medical care. My studies show that it cannot be government. Without going into all the calculations, I want to show some graphs of what this future will look like in the U.S." She flipped through a half dozen slides that predicted what the national debt would look like in best-case and worst-case scenarios, based on her assumptions about trade and GDP growth. "The bottom line is that our government will go bankrupt if it takes on all the costs for all the people. A conservative estimate is a national debt in excess of a trillion dollars in the early part of the next century." Irreverent laughs scoffed at her estimate. Dr. Sampson scowled back at the lecture hall. "You can laugh today, but denial will get you nowhere. This is the world in which you will be practicing medicine at the prime of your career. It is not yet fully the world you enter today, but economics will become the center of medicine. For any of you who would like to challenge the math and the assumptions, please see me at the end of the lecture. I brought copies of my work for the skeptics I always encounter.

"The third point is a bit more upbeat. That fact is that we have a good level of medical care in this country. Let me repeat that—we have a good level of medical care. The assumption in my study is that everyone in the U.S. will have access to that, and I think that is achievable. That is the good news," she paused for emphasis. "Ironically, the problem will become the rising quality of healthcare. While anyone will be able to get the good level of care that we see today, not everyone will have access to what is coming tomorrow. We have good medical imaging today, but in ten to fifteen years it will be amazing. The really good will be really costly. Only those with the financial means will be able to get that level of service. This gap will become politically problematic. But should it?" She let the question linger for a few moments.

"I would argue that it should not. We already differentiate between the rich and the poor in other ways. Not everyone drives a Cadillac. Some folks drive Volkswagens. That is accepted. Why shouldn't medicine be the same way?" She held out her arms with her palms upraised.

"The answer is that our baseline of expectations must change. When I was growing up in a modest suburb of Louisville, we had one telephone and one black and white television. We were satisfied. Now people expect to have multiple telephones, with one in the kitchen, one in the bedroom, even one in the basement. Plus, they expect to not only have a color TV but also a VCR. Of course, the VCR had not been invented so we didn't know that we needed one," she said with a smile. "Pretty soon everyone will either have one or feel like they need one. Then in ten to fifteen years when an even newer technology comes along, we'll all expect to get that. A black and white TV with no recorder was perfectly fine, but now it is no longer enough."

Dr. Sampson ended her lecture with some summary slides and an ominous prediction. "I have made only passing mention of what I believe will actually be the biggest economic problem of medicine in your futures. That will be litigation. The costs of lawsuits are skyrocketing. I predict that it will become impossible to afford to be in certain fields of medicine in the not-so-distant future." She pointed her finger at the students in the lecture hall and said, "I am talking about your future. I will go so far as to suggest that obstetrics will be the first to fall. That is because the cost of an error—or even an alleged error— while the mother is pregnant or during delivery will be astronomical to the point that obstetricians will not be able to get malpractice insurance or at least will not be able to pay for it."

With a grim face, Dr. Sampson said, "I know this is not the sunshine lecture you might have hoped for, but my research is very solid. My predictions are highly likely to come to pass, if not by the end of this century, certainly early in the start of the next.

"Will we find a way through it? I certainly hope so. Will it be easy? Certainly not. I encourage you to think about this topic. Stay aware of developments. Get involved. It's your future."

Although she had clearly ended, the stunned group was slow to provide the applause that was customary at the end of a guest lecture. Finally, the clapping started and spread.

Sarah and Nita went together to the reception for Dr. Sampson, which was down the hall in a faculty conference room. They each had a plate of fruit and some punch. They wanted to talk to Dr. Sampson, but the line to talk to the guest speaker was long, so they opted to slide out. When they were at the door, Nita's eye snagged on Dr. Burns who was in a cluster of doctors in a corner that included Dr. Schmidt.

As soon as they were out the door, Sarah said, "Wanna go get a burger and a beer?"

"I'm not sure about the beer, but I could go for a burger."

"Have you been to Iron Hill Pub yet? It's a new place on College Avenue. Not bad food, and the beer is cheap."

Before looking at the food menu, Nita read the back of the menu, which included a paragraph on the history of the real Iron Hill. It briefly mentioned that Native Americans were active there, and then more than a century later it was the site of a Revolutionary War battle. George Washington himself was there.

"I'm going to have a Miller Lite," Sarah announced. "What about you?"

"I should have an iced tea. I have to study, and a beer would just put me to sleep."

Sarah was on her second beer before their burgers arrived. "I heard you're having issues with Dr. Burns."

"I guess there are no secrets around here, are there?"

"She used to be my adviser, but I requested a change last year."

"Why?"

Sarah paused and considered her words. "I guess you could say I was starting to experience what other female med students had warned me about."

"What's that?"

Sarah paused again and lowered her voice. "Dr. Burns has a reputation for undermining female students."

"Why would she do that? I mean I heard her nickname is TD, but I don't know how all that connects."

"Of course, the Third Degree is a double entendre. She delights in putting students, especially female students in the hot seat. She loves to watch them squirm."

"Been there," Nita acknowledged.

"Me too. And if you really get on her bad side, well, that's what happened to Maggie Donahue."

"What? I don't know her."

"That's because she got kicked out of school. She was a year ahead of us."

"For what?"

"Mostly for getting on the wrong side of Dr. Burns as I heard it. She got the third-degree burns, as they call it. I never understood what she really did. It had to do with alcohol on school premises, like beer in her backpack. According to the handbook, yes, it was an infraction, but apparently, they have a good deal of flexibility. Unfortunately, your advisor holds lots of power. Don't piss her off."

"So, what's the other half of the TD double entendre?"

"I can only tell you what I heard from older students. Apparently, Dr. Burns fought her way into med school at Penn in the '60s by getting an M.S. first. But then when she started med school, she couldn't handle the pressure. She had some sort of breakdown and ended up switching over to a PhD program. That's why she teaches intro physiology and does urology research."

"What's that have to do with us?"

"She apparently resents female students, especially good-looking ones. Reportedly, she had two female classmates at Penn who did make it through, but she believes it was because they were pretty."

"Holy shit."

"Exactly. When I saw it happening to me, I did what I could to get out from under her."

"Damn."

"Just don't give her any ammo to use against you, and you'll be fine."

When they walked out of the pub, Nita told Sarah she had enjoyed the opportunity to get to know her better.

Sarah put her hand on Nita's arm. "Me too. And what I shared in there about TD is just between us, right?"

"Absolutely. I appreciate it."

CHAPTER TWENTY-ONE

*N*ita found herself sitting in a large lecture hall waiting for class to begin. Although the layout was familiar, with an amphitheater of wooden desks aiming down toward the front where the professor would stand, this was not one she had been in before. The chatter of students was increasing as they speculated on why the professor was late. Nita looked around but did not recognize any of the students from her class. Then she realized that all the students were male. Her stomach knotted as it might have if she had accidentally gone to the boys' gym class in high school. Scanning the room with rising panic for anyone she knew, she saw that the young men were all wearing starched white shirts and ties. Their hair was waxed formally into place.

Nita decided to rise quietly and leave, but before she could act, a door to the right front of the room opened. In walked two middle-aged men with similarly starched appearances. The first man sported a handle-bar *mustache. The students immediately silenced their conversations and rose. Nita rose with them.*

When the two new arrivals had positioned themselves in the center front of the room at a large wooden desk that stood waist-high, the man with the mustache nodded and said somberly, "Be seated, men."

With minimal clatter the class resumed its seated position and waited intently. The two men standing at the front had a brief sidebar conversation, and then the first man addressed the class again, "Good morning, gentlemen."

"Good morning, Dr. Stengel," the class said in unison.

"Gentlemen, a few mere months ago, the looming concern for your futures as medical practitioners was where you would serve in the Great War. We in the faculty are keenly aware that all but the Quakers among you have already enlisted, waiting only to be called up. Then as the war began to wind down of late, we cautiously let out a sigh of relief that you would be able to complete not only your third year of medical school, but move forward through your fourth and to graduation from the University of Pennsylvania School of Medicine."

"Unfortunately," Dr. Stengel paused as if it were almost impossible for him to go on.

A low murmur buzzed through the students.

The other man at the front stepped to Dr. Stengel's side, but he waved him off saying, "Thank you, Dean, but I shall conclude my part."

Dr. Stengel took a deep breath and looked into the faces in the lecture hall. The young men were leaning forward at their small wooden desks.

"Gentlemen, I apologize, and I will now regain my composure." He took a breath. "The faculty has come to a most difficult decision. You recall that last week, I provided a special lecture on influenza, with particular emphasis on what has come to be known as the Spanish Influenza. Even since that lecture only a few days ago, the conditions here in Philadelphia have worsened—considerably. The disease is spreading with alarming speed and with a

viciousness none of us has ever seen. Moreover, whereas the more common strains of influenza, as we discussed last week, are primarily a threat to the very young, the elderly and the infirm, the Spanish Influenza ravages more the young and healthy. It kills with alarming speed, in some cases within hours of the first evidence of symptoms. And it is a horrific death with victims hemorrhaging uncontrollably. I shared with you some of my experiences with the epidemic of 1888. The situation now, exactly thirty years later, I am sorry to say, is far worse."

"As you are aware, many of the medical practitioners of this city and other areas are away serving in the war. Philadelphia is desperate for trained medical people. The situation is grim, and if you read the newspapers, you see that some citizens are even wondering if this is the end of days."

The young man sitting to Nita's left gulped involuntarily. He was a handsome man with dark wavy hair, combed back and parted in the middle. His piercing blue eyes were attentive to all that was being said. He seemed to feel it deeply. Others in the auditorium commented softly to their neighbors.

Dr. Stengel held up his hands to silence the room. "With this background, Dean Williams has an announcement to make."

The other man at the front cleared his throat. "Gentlemen, as Dr. Stengel has indicated," he cleared his throat again and repeated, "As Dr. Stengel has indicated, the faculty, along with the administration of the Penn School of Medicine, have reached a difficult decision. Because of the extreme nature and urgency of the situation facing this city," the dean covered his mouth with a handkerchief and coughed. "Because of the situation articulated by Dr. Stengel, we are taking the drastic step of suspending all classes for third- and fourth-year medical students immediately."

More than a murmur rose from the room. The man to Nita's right said, "What? What does that mean?"

Dr. Stengel raised his hands, "Gentlemen, please."

The chatter dimmed but did not go out.

The dean continued after clearing his throat again, "Clearly we do not take this measure lightly. We recognize that this is a significant disruption of your dreams and your plans. We are sorry, but we are unanimous in believing that this is the right step, very difficult but correct."

A hand in the second row shot up. Dr. Stengel nodded to the young man, who had red hair and a flushed complexion.

The man rose and said, "Dr. Stengel, may I ask a question?"

Dr. Stengel looked at the dean, who in turned nodded to the student, "You may."

"Thank you. How long will this suspension of classes last?"

The dean answered, "We do not know. I should go on, if I may, to tell you of the rest of the plan."

The red-haired man sat down, and the dean continued, "You, the third-year students, along with the fourth-year students, will be assigned to staff an emergency hospital that is being set up. You will work there until further notice."

"What?" said a man sitting two rows in front of Nita. The man raised his hand, but Dr. Stengel shook his head and said, "Please let Dean Williams continue, and then we will entertain your questions."

"Thank you, Dr. Stengel," the dean said. Turning to the class, he said, "We recognize that this comes as a shock. Now here is the plan. In this emergency hospital, the fourth-year students will act as interns, and third-years will serve in a nursing capacity. The facility is the Medico-Chirurgical College, which I know some of you are quite familiar with having begun your medical training there before the recent merger with Penn."

A student off to the left raised his hand and spoke without standing, "Sir, that hospital has been torn down."

"Not entirely," said Dr. Stengel.

"That is correct," the dean said. "After church services yesterday, Dr. Stengel and I visited it. The demolition of the building has only gone halfway. It was ordered stopped last Wednesday, and workmen are now trying to rebuild some temporary walls and re-establish the plumbing, electricity and the boilers. Your first order of business will be to retrieve the beds that were moved out before the demolition and get them set up."

The student in front of Nita raised his hand again, and this time he stood. The dean nodded permission.

"With all due respect to you and the other faculty and administrators, this is neither fair nor appropriate. We are not qualified to serve in this manner. We have had merely one lecture on influenza. How can you expect us to serve as medical professionals?"

Another student raised his hand and rose. "Sir, with all due respect, my family paid my tuition intending that I would become a medical doctor—not to serve as a nurse. If they wanted a nurse, they would have sent my sister."

With that man still standing, another rose and said, "What is the risk to us? You said the disease is selectively hitting precisely people like us? This is not fair!"

Students in the room began to talk to each other, and some voiced questions without raising their hands or standing. Dr. Stengel and the dean were taken aback by the outbursts. Before they could react, the handsome man to Nita's left raised his hand and waited patiently to be recognized. Dr. Stengel clapped his hands and said, "Gentlemen, please. Come to order please." He clapped his hands again. Quickly the room quieted, and those standing retook their seats.

"We must have order," Dr. Stengel admonished. "We must maintain our decorum."

The final whispers were swept immediately from the room.

"*Thank you. Now, Mr. Wilson. Theodore Wilson, you had your hand raised,*

The man next to Nita rose slowly. He looked around the lecture hall at the other students, then in a rich, leathery voice he said, "*Gentlemen. Colleagues. Late yesterday, I received a message from my home in Maryland.*" All heads were turned toward him. They waited patiently for him to continue. Nita immediately got the sense that he was a leader in the class, one whose opinions and thoughts were respected.

The man bowed his head, and when he continued speaking, his voice was a little huskier than before. "*The message informed me that my sixteen-year-old brother died suddenly on Saturday from the Spanish Influenza.*"

A murmur of condolence moved around the room. "*My older brother, who just returned from serving in Europe, has it as well. They do not expect him to live. My father has been trying to phone me, but apparently there are few telephone operators reporting to work since they are all either sick or taking care of family members.*"

"*Friends,*" he continued, "*the world has changed. We are facing an enemy worse than the Hun. We are not fully prepared to fight, but fight we must.*" He turned to the man who asked about risks. "*Yes, there most certainly are risks. Some of us may not survive this war against an enemy we cannot even see, but if we think that we can hide here and that influenza will not find us, we are sadly mistaken. If it can find my brothers along the Susquehanna River in the backwater village of Port Deposit, Maryland, it will most assuredly find us here along the Schuylkill River in Philadelphia. I believe that the faculty have reached the right decision. We have something to offer, and we must go to the battlefront. God willing, we will live to return to this school, and when we do, we will be better doctors than we otherwise could have been.*" He turned and looked at the front of the room. "*For the brothers of others and for their sisters, I will do what I can in whatever small way I can to help.*"

A student on the other side of the lecture hall stood without speaking and nodded his agreement. As Nita looked around the room, most others seemed to nod as well.

The young man, who had announced his intention to serve, turned first to Nita then addressed the others, "A disruption of our dream is a problem only if we allow it to be. Even as this interruption is merely starting, we must begin working to rebuild. Pursuit of a dream is a journey, one with perils, detours and pitfalls. In reality, I believe this interruption is not a waylaying but rather is an essential part of the journey."

Nita felt herself being drawn into the man's strong eyes, a passionate blue. She leaned involuntarily in his direction. A calming sensation flowed over her like a warm and soothing bath.

The man's face seemed to respond by reflecting Nita's rising understanding. He nodded and smiled slightly, "God will meet our prayers and will help us, but God will not take the journey for us. The challenges along the way are meant to sharpen our resolve, not dull our passion. We must be careful that our dreams do not wither to become only a prayer. A dream is a prayer that needs your feet under it, else how can we move forward on the journey?"

Nita's heart surged with a feeling long lost, if even she had ever felt it. This man was what she needed. At a deep level she had waited for this connection. She swam slowly into his eyes and reached to feel his embrace.

The crash of the lamp from her night stand to the floor was minor compared to the shattering of her hope as the feeling fled from her. Nita ached for human contact. Her heart needed a personal relationship. She needed someone to touch and someone to share her dreams and fears with. She wrapped her pillow across her face and cried bitterly.

When her clock-radio came on, she smacked it off the nightstand, silencing the 1987 Taurus commercial. Eventually she pulled back the pillow from her face and looked over the edge of the bed to where her lamp lay in pieces on the floor with its decapitated shade a few feet away. The clock-radio dangled by its cord inches off the floor. Nita left everything there in spite when she rose to take a shower.

Friday evening as Nita and Little Earl pulled into the driveway another set of headlights followed them. Nita's brain quickly filled the void of information about who it could be with various negatives, including the biker from the laundromat, Paul Alvarez and even Dr. Burns. She stopped the car and locked Little Earl's doors. The headlights of the other car stayed on. Nita peered unmoving out the rearview mirror until finally the door-light of the other vehicle came on and the headlights went off. It was just Henry. Nita opened her car door and dragged her backpack out.

"Hope I didn't scare you," Henry waved to her. Jutting over the tailgate of his pickup truck was the end of a green canoe. Nita waved back and turned toward the house, hoping to signal that she did not have time or energy for more conversations about fossils or gardening. Her nerves were shot, and she just needed to be alone. Henry shuffled around to the back of truck and carefully lowered the tailgate. "You don't mind if I put this old canoe back by the shed, do you?" he called.

Nita stopped a short distance away. "No, that's fine," she said as she backed slowly toward the porch light that feebly lit the area where they had parked.

"It's a little faded but it's still good. Bessell and I used to like to paddle out on the river. I liked the quiet, and she liked to point out the hawks and turtles and everything else. Back then her yakking annoyed me," he paused as he pulled the paddles out of the back of the truck, "but, now I would give...," he interrupted himself. "Oh listen, that's just an old guy moaning. The thing I wished I'd learned sooner is to use the days I'd been given and see the pleasure in the little stuff. The days aren't as many as you think, and they sure aren't forever. Trick is that you never know when they'll be over."

"No, no problem leaving it here," Nita said as she turned away. When she glanced back, though, she saw him trying to drag the long craft out of the truck. She set her backpack down and said, "Here, let me give you a hand with that. I don't want you to hurt yourself, especially trying to do it in the dark."

"Well in case I do, I know where there's a good doctor," Henry smiled at her.

A grimace escaped Nita's face.

"Did I say the wrong thing?" he tilted his head slightly. "Anything wrong?"

"Nope. Everything's okay," Nita said as she lifted the front end of the canoe and led toward the shed.

While they walked, Henry talked about having gone to Opening Day for the Orioles two weeks earlier. He explained that it was the Ripken show, with Cal Ripken senior as the manager, Cal junior playing shortstop and Billy at second base.

When they got near the shed, Henry said, "We'll just set it behind the building so it's out of sight. When Nita backed around the corner, she tripped over an exposed root, which caused her to fall backward hard onto the grass with the canoe landing on her right shin. "Goddammit," she blurted out as she shoved the canoe off her leg. "Goddammit," she repeated as she lifted the pant leg of her blue jeans and rubbed her scuffed skin with its rapidly developing bruise. "I really don't need this!"

Henry quickly set down his end and pulled the canoe away from Nita, then rushed to her. "Oh my goodness, are you okay? Let me look at that. Geez, it's so dark back here, I can't see. Do you think you can walk? Here, let me help."

"I don't need any more help, thank you," Nita said as she pushed his hand away from her leg. "It's fine," she pulled her pant leg down and got to her feet. A sharp pain said it was not fine, but she refused to listen. Despite her denial, the injury forced her to hobble to the front of the cottage.

"I am so sorry," Henry said, following along beside her. He reached his hand out to support her but then withdrew it quickly when he saw her face send a "don't even think about touching me" message.

At the front door Nita picked up her backpack and yanked the door key from the side pocket. She shoved it in the lock and flung the door open.

Henry stayed outside as she gingerly stepped in, using the door frame for support. "Are you sure you're okay?" he asked cautiously. "How about if I get some ice to put on it?"

"Really. I'm fine. Thanks anyway," Nita leaned on the door as she started to swing it shut. "Good night."

Henry stood still on the front porch as the door began to close, his eyes telegraphing that he did not know what to do or how to help.

Nita said, "Really, I am fine. I just need to study. Good night."

As soon as the door closed Nita limped to the refrigerator and opened the freezer compartment. She pulled out a metal ice tray and took it to the sink where she fought with it to get a few cubes out. One cube clattered to the linoleum floor, where she looked at it with disdain and decided it could just stay there. She jerked a plastic sandwich bag from a box in the cabinet and put a few cubes in it. She sat on a kitchen chair and carefully slid her pant leg up. "Goddammit," she said as she saw the swelling was starting to turn purplish blue. "A fucking hematoma, thanks to a landlord who never seems to go away." She got an Advil out of her purse and poured a drink of water from the faucet.

She got her ophthalmology book and went to her bedroom where the broken lamp was still on the floor. She kicked the pieces of the lamp aside and pulled the clock-radio up by its cord and set it on the nightstand, relieved that she hadn't broken it.

She placed a pillow on the bed where she could elevate her leg. The ice bag kept sliding off her leg, so she used the blanket to try to secure it. Her head slumped forward, weighed down by all that was wrong in her life. After a while she lifted her head slightly and looked at her leg. The swelling seemed to have stopped getting worse, and the pain had lessened somewhat. Gradually the aching in her leg was replaced by remorse for how she had treated Henry. He felt terrible about what happened, and she had closed the door in his face. She set the ice bag on the nightstand and watched it slowly melt.

CHAPTER TWENTY-TWO

Sunday was Easter, but Nita blew off going to church in favor of studying. For the remainder of the day, though, she felt guilty, and then
the guilt evolved into worry that somehow, she would pay a price for
that decision.

The following week, as the bruise on her leg receded, her workload
seemed to mount despite the fact that in theory it was spring break. There
were no classes, but the extra activities the students were expected to participate in, like going on patient rounds and observing procedures, just kept
coming. They even scheduled an additional special lecture. The thought of
another talk on the future of medicine made Nita wonder if she was ready
for any more new ideas, based on her experience with Dr. Wang and his
lecture on the ability to modify what it means to be human and then Dr.
Sampson and her predictions about the economics of medicine. This one,
though, turned out to be interesting and not at all traumatic.

A man with pale skin and thinning grey hair glided into the small lecture room. His voice flowed softly, and he got straight to the point, "I am Dr. Harmon. I believe I have met most of you at some point during your time here. Today, I wish to share with you an eclectic mix of emerging concepts in preventive medicine.

Dr. Harmon began by discussing how genetic traits would be mapped for individuals and then interventions made through diets and medicines that are customized for the person's specific needs. He explained that this would create profound changes in medical care. "We will no longer be in the disease curing business; we will be in the disease prevention business. Beyond that we will move toward quality of life for our patients as whole people."

Nita wondered why he seemed to think disease prevention would be a major step. She assumed that was already a major goal. She started to raise her hand to ask the question but then thought better of it, lest she offend someone or create another conflict.

As if he had heard her thought, though, Dr. Harmon answered, "You may wonder about my statement that this is a significant shift when I talk about prevention. Certainly, there have been many words about preventive medicine, but if you take a close look at what has actually been practiced, you find that the overwhelming majority of efforts are simply reacting to conditions and symptoms not preventing the disease in the first place."

Dr. Harmon suggested that a more holistic approach to the person would someday include everything from their cells up to their souls. He watched their faces. "Does it not strike you as odd that we do so little with spirituality? Yet the spirit, whether it is the human spirit or a higher spirit is a most powerful force." He went on to say that dreams were perhaps a path to insights about the human spirit. "Each of us spends a considerable amount of our lives in a dream state, but we know essentially nothing about that world. Surely it has great relevance. It is sad, but things we do not readily understand, we dismiss as unimportant."

The more he talked, the more Nita became intensely interested in engaging Dr. Harmon. Perhaps this was someone who had some answers to her questions. From his comments, he clearly had done a great deal of thinking about the connections between dreams and the waking reality. Her mind churned over how to ask the question. How could she carefully mention her dreams and the fact that they more and more seemed to be entwined with her physical reality? She looked around the room at the others present and wondered what sort of trouble or concerns this might trigger. Maybe she could just ask a vague question and not mention her dreams.

While circling inwardly, Nita missed the fact that Dr. Harmon was ending his lecture. Suddenly he thanked them for their attention and departed. The session seemed to have raced by quickly, but his thoughts lingered. Nita found his ideas to be very encouraging and stimulating. She longed for ways to help patients in the bigger context of their lives. Too much of what she had seen so far was express-lane treatment. The doc took fifteen minutes to meet the patient, learn the symptoms and prescribe a fix. Most often that fix was to be purchased at a drug store, where they seemed more focused on selling greeting cards, seasonal decorations and toys than being part of the health system. Precious little time or space in the whole medical process dealt with root causes or non-chemical approaches.

Between the technologies and the insurance companies, the human part of medicine was being lost. Dr. Harmon was the first person she had heard spend much time discussing spirituality. As her mind wandered, she noted the irony that she was walking to the medical library to look up some pharmacology information regarding anesthesiology in emergency medicine. This underscored the idea that they focused on human chemistry much more than on the human spirit. She was willing to bet that the medical library didn't even have a book on spirituality. She decided that she would go talk with Dr. Harmon when she got the chance. Before she left the library, she looked up his office and phone number. On the drive home she debated on whether she should just drop in or call to make an appointment. By the time she pulled in the driveway her positive thoughts had been eroded by fear of doing something wrong again. She could not risk any further problems, especially none that could in any way link back to Dr. Burns, as Sarah had warned her.

When she went to bed, she was tormented by how paranoid she had become. It made her angry that she was so fearful that she would not even attempt to simply talk to Dr. Harmon. She tried to use her pillow to block out her anger and make room for sleep. For a long time and despite multiple repositioning, the approach failed. Eventually though, she drifted off.

Nita walked down the hall of a hospital. She was with a black doctor and nurse. They were in a hospital where all the patients and staff were black. The facility was spotlessly clean. Everything glistened white like a fresh snowfall.

Nita followed the doctor and nurse up metal stairs that clanged hollow as they stepped. Three flights they climbed. She could see the nurse's calves below the hemline of her white starched dress. The muscles under her dark skin bulged above her white socks and chalky shoes. The muscle definitions were so pronounced that she could actually distinguish the muscle groups, particularly the two sections of the gastrocnemius that made up her calf.

As they were about to exit onto the third floor, two orderlies wheeled a gurney through the doors to the stairway. The doctor and nurse held the doors open as the orderlies lifted the stretcher off the top of the gurney.

"Good day, Dr. Fred, Miss Eliza," said one of the orderlies. "We're taking Mr. Watkins down to the OR for his hernia operation."

Both the doctor and nurse stopped to speak to the patient. The doctor patted him on his shoulder. "Now listen here, Clay. We want you back on your feet real soon. I expect to see you in the stands when the Port Deposit Black Sox take the field for their first game of the season. In fact, you better be ready in case they need you to suit up again," he smiled.

Nita looked down at the broad-shouldered man who appeared to be about forty. His huge right hand, which rested on the white sheet, looked almost like a baseball glove. He smiled back at the doctor, "I'll be ready Dr. Fred. You, too. They might need you in at shortstop again."

"Oh, I'm much too old for that now. But I will say that I do miss those days. We had some mighty good players and some good times."

Eliza gripped the man's hand. "Dr. Fred, you got to let them get on their way. The OR is waiting. Good luck, Mr. Watkins. We'll see you this afternoon."

Nita found herself in the backseat of a large black car with a high roof. The shiny black metal dashboard rolled down to a thin assortment of small round gauges in front of Dr. Fred, where his hands gripped the amber Bakelite steering wheel. White ivory-looking knobs were perched on metal shafts in the middle of the dash.

Eliza sat in the passenger seat. She was obviously upset about something. "Fred, you got to stay focused. You are spending too much time at each patient's house. That is why we don't get home till midnight most nights. I need to see my baby. Besides, my breasts hurt something awful if she doesn't get to suck."

"I am focused, Eliza."

"You are not. You sit and talk about the weather, and then you eat, and then you drink coffee."

"Eliza, you know that the Richardsons do not have the money to pay us. They feel bad about that. We need to visit with them and let them feed us."

Eliza let out an exasperated sigh. "Well, there needs to be a balance."

"Maybe Momma should have sent you to medical school instead of me."

"You know darn well she would have if they'd just let girls in. But no, you men are the only ones who can do the doctoring. Women can only be nurses." Her sarcasm left a bitter scent in the air.

"Yes, Eliza, I know. And I am still angry that I had to go all the way to Washington to go to medical school because I had the wrong skin color for the white school. But I refuse to let that consume me. It doesn't hurt them in the least—just me."

Nita recognized the road they were on. It was just north of her house. The river was on their left, and the old abandoned grain mill was coming up on their right. The mill's roof had not yet rotted through, though. Just past the mill, Dr. Fred swung the lumbering car onto a road on their right. Nita knew it as Rock Run Road, which climbed up to the section where about twenty black families lived.

The car roared as Dr. Fred slammed down the gas pedal and shifted into a lower gear to clamber up the craggy road. After about a half-mile of bouncing and swerving, they came to some small houses. Because of the steep grade, Nita didn't see the little road off to the right until the car swung onto it. The car jerked in and out of ruts as they found their way down to the end of the lane. On the left the houses were up some stairs, and on the right they were down the embankment so she could just see their roofs.

When they got out of the car, two skinny brown dogs raced up, barking and wagging their tails. The last house on the left, which was partially hidden among trees, appeared to be their destination. It was small and covered with red shingle-like material with black lines, designed to make it look like brick.

Dr. Fred got his black bag from the back seat, and Eliza lifted a white canvas bag from the front. Nita followed Fred and Eliza as they climbed the dozen wooden steps to the narrow front porch. The front door creaked when a heavy-set black woman opened it. "Thank you so much for coming Dr. Fred, Miss Eliza."

"Mmmm, mmm. Can you smell those greens cooking, Eliza?" The tangy scent stung Nita's nostrils as she followed them into the living room, one end of which was the kitchen. Nita heard Eliza emit a muffled groan, but her voice said, "Sure does smell delicious, Mrs. Harris."

"Well I know how you two like to eat when you come to check on George."

"You sure got that right, didn't she, Eliza," Nita saw Dr. Fred wink at Eliza and grin.

Eliza rolled her black eyes. "Mmmm, mmm," she replied ambiguously.

They walked over to a young black man who sat in the corner with his leg propped up.

"How you doing, George?"

"'Bout the same, Dr. Fred." He hiked up his left pant leg and exposed his calf. On the front left was a round hole, which had healed over with a scar. On the back side, half the calf muscle was missing. He turned it so the doctor could see it. The wound hadn't closed, and it oozed blood. Dr. Fred bent over and probed it gently with his finger.

George winced but just said "Guess that German bullet did some damage."

"Guess it did, George," he examined it again.

"He can't put no weight on it," said the woman who let them in. "Can they do something to operate on it? It ain't getting' no better."

Dr. Fred stood and faced the woman as she continued, "He can't work like this. What's he supposed to do?"

"Well, an operation is possible, but it is far beyond anything we can do at our hospital. They could do it at City Hospital, but...well... you know how that is." Dr. Fred shook his head. "I will send another letter to the Veteran's Hospital, but they are so overloaded there with all the men coming back now, they're likely to just tell me they've done all they can, just like last time." He shook his head again.

"I understand," the woman said.

Eliza knelt down next to George. "Let me clean that up some for you and put some new medicine on it," she said as she pulled some gauze and a white tube of ointment out of her canvas bag.

When she was done, she stood and said, "And I brought you something else." She reached into the bag and pulled out a book. I know how much you like to read, so I picked this up for you at the used book store in town."

"Oh, Miss Eliza," Mrs. Harris said, "you shouldn't have."

When they got into the car, Fred looked at his sister. "That book was good medicine, Eliza."

"You're not the only healer in this family, Fred Boykin, just 'cause you got the M.D. after your name."

"I am well aware of that, and I appreciate it. I couldn't do this without you."

"Hmmpf," Eliza replied, but Nita could tell that she valued the recognition. "I think we should stop and see Marsha Taylor and her new baby while we are up here."

On the way back down the hill, they pulled over and parked at a wide spot on the right side of the road. Again, Fred and Eliza retrieved their bags. This time they crossed the road and knocked at the door of a small wooden house. There was no answer. Fred and Eliza looked at each other. He raised an eyebrow, and she shrugged and shook her head in response.

Fred knocked harder. They heard a baby cry.

He tried the door knob, and the door opened.

"Anybody home?"

The baby's cry was the only answer.

"Marsha? Sonny? Anybody home?" He stepped into the house slowly at first, then he rushed in.

"Marsha, Marsha." A young black woman lay on a bed in the corner of the room. She was tiny and thin. A crying baby lay next to her.

Eliza scooped up the baby as Dr. Fred knelt to tend to the woman. "She has a weak pulse." He slung the blankets back from her, to reveal blood-soaked sheets from her waist down.

"She's hemorrhaging. She's lost a lot of blood. Sonny must be at the quarry. We need to get her to the hospital immediately."

Nita was in the backseat with the woman's limp head on her leg. Eliza held the baby, who was still crying. Nita saw Eliza open the top of her white dress. Soon the baby quieted.

The car bounded down the hill and careened left onto River Road. "She's going to need a transfusion," Dr. Fred said to Eliza.

"But we don't have any A positive blood. We used it all in the delivery."

"Then we need to take her into town."

"Fred, you can't do that!"

"Watch me."

"Fred, they won't take her."

"They'll have to. We can't let her die, which is what will happen if she doesn't get a transfusion." He drove like a wild man down River Road toward Port Deposit.

"Fred, you know what happened last time."

He didn't answer.

In a few minutes he swung the car around to the back of a square red brick building. A large red sign announced the Emergency Entrance. Eliza buttoned up her dress and hefted the sleeping baby in one arm and her canvas bag in the other. After Fred lifted the frail woman out of the back seat and Nita got out, Eliza handed the baby to Nita. Fred hurried to the ER door and backed through it.

The baby snuggled toward Nita's chest as they followed into the ER. By the time Nita got inside, turmoil had ensued. Two white doctors in white coats were confronting Dr. Fred, who was still holding the woman. One of them said, "Look Fred, you know as well as I do..."

"Yes, John," he interrupted, "and you know as well as I do that this woman will die if she doesn't get a transfusion immediately."

"There are strict rules, Fred," the other doctor said, "colored people cannot be given white blood."

"Well we do not have the right blood type, and she will die without it. We used all the A-positive we had delivering her baby."

The first doctor replied, "Look, Fred, I am sorry. There is nothing we can do."

Suddenly Eliza appeared from an inner door of the hospital. She was still carrying her white canvas bag. "Come on, Fred," she motioned to him. "I told you we shouldn't have come here. Let's get her to the colored hospital." She winked at Fred in an odd way.

At first Fred began to object, then his eyes narrowed. He turned to the doctors. "You're right. I'm sorry we bothered you."

Outside, Eliza took the baby, and Dr. Fred carried Marsha's sagging body back to the car where he placed her in the back seat with Nita.

He got in the front seat, closed the door and looked at Eliza.

"Drive!" she commanded.

When they arrived at the emergency entrance of the other hospital, Eliza produced a glass jar of blood from her canvas bag. It was labeled A-positive. Dr. Fred yelled for a gurney and placed Marsha on it. As Fred and Eliza ran ahead, the two men with the gurney raced to the rear hallway of the ER. The doors slammed open, and Nita's alarm clock went off, jerking her to her other life.

A few nights later, Nita drove home from campus listening to National Public Radio as "All Things Considered" aired a special interview with a professor from Harvard who was writing a book on the future of healthcare and what the ideal system would look like. He spoke about the need to focus on wellness rather than illness. He also emphasized the need to make medicine universally accessible and affordable. "Whether a child is born into poverty or wealth should not be the determining factor in whether that child gets good healthcare," he said. He offered that there are creative new approaches that could bridge between the high costs of good care and the limitations of paying for it. One new element he predicted would be the rising role of nurse practitioners, positions that were a combination of nursing and some of the traditional roles that had been set aside for physicians, such as seeing patients and writing prescriptions. He noted that nurse practitioners were being used with great success in a number of places around the country.

Nita sat in her driveway to listen to the end of the story. She wondered if maybe being a nurse practitioner would have been a better route for her. They seemed to have it best in many regards. They could spend time with patients, bonding and getting to know them, yet they could do procedures and see patients without a doctor being present. As she opened Little Earl's door to get out, she told him, "Everybody seems to acknowledge that healing has to involve more than just a quick conversation followed by a prescription, but not much is moving very quickly in that direction."

CHAPTER TWENTY-THREE

Nita couldn't wait for the semester to end. Just a few more weeks and she would be done, but those weeks promised to be hell. The workload was ungodly. All of her classmates looked terrible. Many were sick, yet there was no option but to press on.

Nita tried to take care of herself by eating properly and getting at least some sleep each night. But most nights when she slept, she was back with Dr. Fred and Eliza, often listening to them heatedly debate some point. They had a relationship that seemed to be built on tension, like a bridge over a river that needs both sides pulling just to stay up.

They were driving up Rock Run Road. Again, Eliza was complaining about how long Fred took with everything. "Why must you talk with each child in the family at length when only one is sick?"

"We minister to the whole family."

"Ministers are we now?"

Fred looked at her in surprise. "We are very much ministers," he said with conviction.

"Well excuse me, but I was not aware that I was in the presence of Reverend Boykin."

"Eliza, healing was the first ministry of Jesus. Much of what he did was heal people. We are carrying on his work, just as Reverend Holloway carries on the spiritual work of the Lord through the church."

"Oh, now you're up there with the Lord, are you?"

"You know, Eliza, this sarcasm is not very becoming."

"Well excuse me for that, too. Maybe if I had a few minutes off to rest and be with my own family I would be more pleasant, Reverend Boykin."

When they returned to the hospital, there was a white man in a navy-blue suit waiting in the parking lot. Nita saw both Fred and Eliza tense up. "What do you suppose the mayor wants?" Eliza asked.

"Can't be good," Fred answered. "He only comes out here when he's looking for trouble."

Fred drove slowly past the man and parked about twenty feet way.

He got out of the car and greeted the man cheerfully, "Good afternoon, Mayor. How are you this fine day?"

"I'm here on business, Fred."

Eliza got out of her side and started to walk toward the door to the hospital.

"Eliza, don't you go sneaking off. This involves you, too."

Eliza looked surprised and came around near where the man was standing. Nita had observed that when Eliza wanted to hide her emotions, her mouth and eyes set narrow. When she was relaxed, her eyes were wider and the ends of her mouth turned up. Now her lips were in a straight line. She didn't speak as she faced the mayor.

"Last week the two of you came into the white hospital with a colored girl."

"That's right," Fred said.

"You demanded blood for her, but they wouldn't give it to you."

Fred's eyes narrowed.

"When you left, there was a jar of blood missing. Exactly the type you were looking for."

Eliza and Fred stood stone-faced.

"I don't suppose you know where that blood went."

Eliza and Fred stood quietly with no expression.

"The boys tell me that Taylor girl is back home now."

He got no response.

"Kind of funny that she was about to die and then suddenly recovered."

Fred shrugged slightly but said nothing. He stood in front of the mayor staring straight into his face.

"Listen, Boykin, you know the rules. This is the last time you're gonna pull this sort of stunt, you and your fat-ass sister here."

Fred's face flinched slightly. Nita saw his right fist start to curl, but he said nothing.

"You know there are some boys in town that don't like coloreds much. I sure hope they don't hear that you put white blood into some colored bitch."

Fred's black eyes stared coldly into the mayor's red face.

"You best be careful, Boykin. One of these days you're gonna go too far."

The mayor crunched through the gravel to his shiny black car and shot stones at them as he sped out of the parking lot.

"White bastard," Eliza spit the words out.

She stepped over to Fred and put her hand on his shoulder. "You did right not to let him bait you. He knows about you and your fists from your *boxing days, and he just wanted you to take a swing at him. Lookee over there behind the market. The sheriff's been sitting there watching the whole thing. It was a set-up."*

Nita looked at Fred's clenched hands, which were vibrating. His voice quivered when he finally spoke. "I should have flattened his nose on his fat face. I could have busted him up good before the sheriff even got over here."

"That's just what they wanted you to do, and you'd a regretted it." She put her arm across his shoulder.

"I know, Sister, I know." Fred squatted down and drew three concentric circles in the gravel. He stood back up and stared in the direction of the sheriff, and then used his foot to erase the circles. "I know, but I might have done it just the same."

Nita's anger woke her. She looked at the clock and found it was only 5:00 a.m. She decided to go ahead and get up. She had a comprehensive test on diseases of the eye at 10:00, and additional cram time would help.

She took a shower and then studied while she ate a bowl of Cheerios. By 7:00 a.m. she was feeling the effects of the short night, but she had to get to campus so she had another cup of coffee and headed in.

When she got to the lecture hall, only one other person had arrived. Martin waved her over to where he was sitting. "Did you talk to anyone about that incident in orthopedic surgery last week?"

"No. Why?"

"Keep this to yourself, but people are asking questions. Paul and I each got called into the dean's office. They didn't talk to you yet?"

"No," Nita's brain started to race ahead. She wondered if this had anything to do with her lunch with Dr. Schmidt, where he misunderstood her remark about what happened to the boy during surgery.

"What did they ask you, Martin?"

"I guess it was more telling than asking. They asked what I thought happened, and then they explained to me what happened and how I needed to realize that because I was new to surgery, I could be mistaken about what I thought I witnessed," Martin paused. "I don't know. It just seemed weird. I wonder if there is a lawsuit or something."

"What did Paul say?"

"Paul just told them he was turned the other way and didn't see anything. He said they seemed satisfied with that."

Others were starting to come into the room so Martin and Nita cut off the conversation.

The ophthalmology exam went well, but when Nita walked out of the room, she was handed a note saying that she should report to the dean's office immediately.

When Nita got to the open door of the dean's office, Dr. Burns was sitting with him. Their conversation stopped when they saw her. "Come in," the dean stated. Dr. Burns had her sternest look fixed to her face.

Nita walked toward the dark desk in the center of the room. Dr. Burns, who had been seated at the near side of the desk, stood and walked past Nita to close the door. Nita watched her stiff and deliberate stride. The office was large with thick wooden furniture. Shelves full of books lined one wall. Dogwood trees showed some white flowers outside the window behind the dean. The broad desk with neat stacks of papers dwarfed him. He had a rather small head on a bony body, and his perch behind the desk made him look almost like a child at his father's desk, trying to appear important.

Dr. Burns returned to her red leather chair and sat erect. "Sit down, Miss Thomas," she pointed to the matching chair in front of the desk.

Nita lowered herself into the chair and looked back and forth between the two inquisitors, unsure who would speak.

"Miss Thomas," Dr. Burns's voice began with a squeak much like the way the first notes of a violin strain forth, "I thought we had an agreement."

Nita nodded involuntarily, then wasn't quite sure what she had agreed to. She was off-balance and shifted in her chair as if to compensate. Her blue jeans squeaked on the leather.

"I thought you agreed to behave yourself for the remainder of your time here." Dr. Burns tilted her head to the side in a non-verbal version of "Didn't you?" She stared out from under raised eyebrows.

The word "behave" had a jagged edge to it. Dr. Burns was speaking down to a recalcitrant child. Nita felt heat rise from her chest up her neck and into her cheeks. She purposefully did not nod this time. She stared back without expression.

Silence grew in the room. Words clamored, wanting to jump from Nita's throat, but her clenched teeth kept them contained. She wasn't even sure what they might be if they were released. She had not yet been accused of anything, yet her muscles surged to self-defense.

Dr. Burns seemed to luxuriate in the silence. She swam like a graceful swimmer while watching another person struggle for air. Dean Wherle squirmed and shifted his hands on the desk. He adjusted some papers in a small stack centered in front of him and cleared his throat. Dr. Burns and Nita looked over at him, assuming he was about to speak, but he had merely been fidgeting in the tension. Nita suspected that Dr. Burns was a little peeved at the disruption of her carefully crafted silence.

When the dean saw that they both expected him to speak, he cleared his throat again, and more deliberately adjusted the papers while looking down at them. He raised his head in authority, but the words that came out were carried by a voice smaller than a man should have. "Ms. Thomas, are you aware of the significance of the accusation Dr. Schmidt has brought against you?"

Nita wasn't sure how to answer. Either a yes or no was wrong, especially since she didn't know there had been an accusation. She stared for too long at the dean. Her lack of a response made room for Dr. Burns to regain control by jumping to the dean's defense.

"Miss Thomas, when Dean Wherle asks you a question, at least show enough respect to answer him."

Nita's dark eyes flashed at Dr. Burns before she could stop them. In that moment they told Dr. Burns that Nita viewed her as a damaged, undermining bitch. Dr. Burns's head recoiled slightly from the sting. Nita quickly corrected her gaze, but she had already validated Dr. Burns's perception of her as an arrogant young woman who did not know her place— someone who had already ridden too far on her good looks. Others, like herself, had had to fight their way every step and settle for second place, while the pretty ladies were coddled by the men in power. Dr. Burns's eyes sharpened into daggers, and her neck turned blood red.

The dean missed the non-verbal exchange, but he sensed that the pressure had risen even higher, although he was unable to put his finger on it. He fidgeted more and cleared his throat causing the two women to again look at him.

Nita struggled to control her voice and the words it would carry. "What exactly is the accusa…," she halted and rephrased her question. "What did Dr. Schmidt say?"

Dean Wherle cleared his throat again and moved his papers. "He said that you…"

Dr. Burns interrupted the dean in mid-sentence. "He said that you accused him of medical incompetence in the situation with the boy's leg, and that furthermore if you had not been distracting him with your flirting it might never have happened."

"He what!!!?" Nita's hands slammed onto the arms of the chair, pushing her body halfway up and out before she could regain control. Dr.

Burns's eyes widened to saucers as the anger exploded on Nita's face. Nita forced herself back down to the edge of the chair's cushion. In the instant of retreat, Dr. Burns charged. "Miss Thomas, please control yourself." She looked over at the dean to make sure he appreciated the full effect of the move and counter-move.

Nita's heart slammed in her chest, and rage shoved her to where she knew she must not go. "That's a l…," she caught herself at the last second. "That is not correct. I was not flirting with him. When we had lunch…" Nita clipped her sentence and planted her lips firmly together, knowing that anything that emerged could only do more damage.

Dr. Burns moved in for the kill. She leaned forward in her chair with her fingers curled over the ends of the chair's red leather arms. Her gaze locked onto Nita like a fighter pilot's radar holding a defenseless enemy in its cross hairs. Slowly she shook her head. "I think," she paused for emphasis, "your impertinence speaks for itself." She looked over at Dean Wherle and nodded, prodding him to nod in agreement, which he did. She then looked back at Nita, whose chin had risen slightly and was pointing toward her in defiance.

Dr. Burns shook her head again in weary dismay. "Miss Thomas, you are my advisee, and for that I hold myself accountable. Until recently, you had good grades and no major incidents to consider. To think now that you would have the audacity to slander someone of the stature and standing of Dr. Schmidt is just beyond…" she looked back toward the dean and shook her head in high-minded amazement, a motion which he promptly mimicked with his head. Dr. Burns allowed the sentiment to hang in the room. Nita felt as though she was dangling by a rope cinched around her wrists. She twisted in the air, powerless to defend herself. Dr. Burns looked at the dean with tired eyes, "I know this is my problem to handle as Miss Thomas's advisor, and I do apologize for this regrettable situation."

When Dr. Burns spoke again, it was with contentment, like a smoker who lights a new cigarette and takes the first puff, watching with satisfaction as smoke rises and curls. "I have tried to help you, Nita," she said softly, obviously delighted that she had played this hand so masterfully. "I tried to guide you," she puckered her lips and looked at the dean with resignation. "I'm afraid there is little more I can do."

Dr. Burns shifted in her chair to face the dean head-on. With her lips still pursed, she asked, "What sort of investigation and hearing will happen next, Dean Wherle?"

"Well...ah...there...let's see...I suppose you are suggesting a formal hearing in front of the Judiciary Panel, which..." the dean said, but Nita sensed that he did not appreciate having been moved into a corner. "We can investigate further before deciding on a formal hearing." he said, patting the stack of papers with his small white hand.

"And until then, what restrictions will there be on Miss Thomas?"

The dean answered Dr. Burns without looking at Nita. "Well in a case like this with potentially serious accusations, the policy manual says she will not be permitted to attend classes, take tests or participate in the functions of the school until the investigation has been completed and the panel has ruled." He concluded the sentence with a rising intonation, almost as if it was a question. Nita suspected he merely parroted the words Dr. Burns gave him before she arrived. She sensed that the dean had been through this game before, and that Dr. Burns had mastered him and whole scheme.

Dr. Burns looked at the dean with quiet eyes, nodded, then smugly turned her head toward Nita. She gave a half-smile and cocked her head slightly to the right. Nita quickly realized that her ability to graduate was now on the line. "How long does an investigation take, and then when does the panel meet?" Nita asked the dean.

"The panel meets in two weeks," Dr. Burns accidentally answered for him. She then recovered and said, "I believe that's correct, isn't it, Dean Wherle?"

"That's correct."

"What is the procedure? How does this work?"

"As your faculty advisor, Dr. Burns will send you a letter and will help you prepare. In short, you will have a chance to state your case and there will of course be other fact-finding."

"Who is on the panel?"

Dr. Burns rose to signal that the discussion was finished. "Yes, Nita, I will be in touch with all the specifics and to help guide you. I will follow up with you so we do not waste any more of the dean's time." Outside the office, Dr. Burns hurried away without further comment to Nita.

CHAPTER TWENTY-FOUR

Friday morning Nita went to Dr. Burns's office. When her administrative assistant looked up, Nita said, "I'd like to talk to Dr. Burns?"

"Do you have an appointment?"

"Well, no, but we have an important matter to discuss. My name is Nita Thomas."

"I know. I'm sorry, but you'll need to make an appointment."

"Okay, when can I see her."

The woman opened a black desk calendar. Before she could hide the pages, Nita saw that it was almost empty for the day.

The woman lifted the calendar to block Nita's view. "Hmmm," she mumbled, obviously intending to signal that finding a time for an appointment was going to be difficult. "Dr. Burns is very busy at this time of the term, with finals coming up the week after next. Hmmm," she repeated as she flipped the pages of the calendar. "Let's see, she can probably see you on Tuesday."

"But I really would like to find out..."

The woman looked over at the closed door to Dr. Burns's office and leaned forward toward Nita. In a hushed tone she said, "I will do what I can. I'll talk to her, but...," she looked toward the door again..." well she, you see, I really need this job, and...I'll do what I can. For now, though, I will put you in on Tuesday."

"Thank you. What time on Tuesday?"

"How about early? Can you make 8:00?"

"I will make it."

"And I will get a message to you if I can get it moved up, but..."

"Thank you. I appreciate your help." On the woman's desk, Nita saw an array of framed school pictures of the woman's three children.

As Nita started to leave, she turned back and asked, "Can you please tell me the date when the Judiciary Panel meets the week after next?"

"Dr. Burns will need to give you any information on that."

"I understand."

The woman then pointed to the black calendar. She quietly opened it and flipped the pages to the week after next. She pointed to Tuesday and then quickly closed the book. She looked up at Nita with apologetic eyes.

Nita nodded and turned away.

On the ride home, Nita fumed about Dr. Burns. How was it that she managed to intimidate all these people? She even had the dean on a leash. How did she become so vindictive? She recalled what Sarah had told her about Penn. Something bad had happened. Sarah said she had some sort of breakdown and had to leave the med school. Now others were paying the price. Unfortunately, Dr. Burns's job at UD put her in the middle of her recurring nightmare. She was surrounded by MDs and med students, constant reminders of what she perceived as her failure. Her daily surroundings were irritants of a deep wound, continually reopening it and preventing it from healing.

Little Earl navigated the drive toward their home while Nita fretted. What would happen if she had to miss some of her finals? How would that impact graduation? For that matter, could the Judiciary Panel do even more than that? Could they really expel her? Would they really kick her out of school? From what Sarah said, it happened to that other female student, Maggie something. Nita wondered if she should try to get an attorney. She recounted the alleged offenses in her mind. The piece with Dr. Schmidt and the boy's leg seemed to be what capped everything. There must be more to that situation, probably a lawsuit. Then there was the situation with Elmer and Dr. Warner. How was it that simply showing caring for the patients was against the rules? But it was. The handbook was clear that she had overstepped. Even at that, mostly what she seemed to have done was step on the egos of powerful doctors. She strongly suspected the root cause was more related to that. Unfortunately, that was the ammunition that Sarah had warned her not to give to Dr. Burns.

Dean Wherle said that during her hearing she would have an opportunity to tell her side. Maybe what she should say is that this was all about the egos of a couple of docs and that any bruising of their tender feelings seemed to be more important than the fact that a vibrant elderly gentleman had died and an athletic boy would go through life without a leg. What if she hit them with that? Little Earl pulled up to her house. "What do you think, Earl, should I just tell them what's really going on?" Earl seemed to agree, so Nita went inside, determined to put them on the defensive in the hearing.

She found three cans of Rolling Rock beer hiding in the back of her refrigerator. She drank two of them, ate a bag of pretzels and fell asleep. When she woke, it was morning and she realized that she had not had any more of her strange visitations.

It was Saturday morning, and the following week was termed Reading Week, which historically was the designated period for studying for finals. While eating a bowl of oatmeal, Nita pondered her situation and what she should do. She decided she would contact an attorney but wasn't even sure where to begin looking for one who had any knowledge or experience in dealing with a med school investigation and a Judiciary Panel hearing. Then she thought about starting to write up her statement of the facts, but wasn't sure of the format or parameters. She really needed to talk to Dr. Burns. The bitch was turning this bad situation into a nightmare. Actually, Burns was the witch who was concocting the brew and stirring the cauldron. While the coffee pot brewed, Nita stewed over the situation, and her frustration grew. She stared at the prospect of not getting her degree. All that work and now it might be for nothing. Could that really happen?

Lacking any clear direction on how to address the Judiciary Panel hearing, assuming there would be one, which seemed likely, Nita decided that the one thing she could do was study. She had to maintain hope that somehow, she would be able to take her finals and graduate. She would study her butt off so that if and when she took the tests, she'd prove at least that she was no slouch. But she wasn't a slouch. Her grades already showed that. She sat down at the kitchen table, put her face in her hands and cried. She used a napkin to wipe the tears, then needed another to blow her nose. She needed a friend.

"Janie, this is Nita."

"I know. I knew you were going to call. I told Frank. What's wrong?"

"I don't even know how to start."

"Try."

"Well, the bottom line is that I may get kicked out of med school."

"Holy shit, Nita. What happened? You're about to graduate."

"Yeah, well we'll see."

"What kind of trouble are you in? What happened?"

"Okay, but please do not tell anyone about this. I'm not supposed to discuss it." Nita explained what happened in the OR with the boy's leg and then the situation with the surgeon in the cafeteria. "I mean, I was frazzled and I guess I was not diplomatic. But I mean, Dr. Schmidt was trying to hit on me. I know it. Then he got pissed off, and well, it got ugly."

"Okay, but that doesn't sound like enough to get you kicked out of school."

"I agree, but you don't know Dr. Burns."

"Who's he?"

"She. She is my advisor. Apparently, she doesn't like female med students, and she has a lot of power in this situation."

"Oh, lovely."

"I've been warned that she even looks for ways to get women expelled. She has done it before."

"Oh my God. What can you do?"

"Well, right now I have to wait to see what they will do. There is some sort of investigation, then there may be a judicial hearing of some sort."

"At what point do you get to defend yourself?"

"I'm not sure. I guess maybe in both parts. It's a royal mess, Janie. Have you ever been through anything like this?"

"Which part? I've never been through an investigation or hearing, but I sure as hell have had to deal with guys hitting on me and then the consequences of not playing along."

"Really? I mean I've had guys hitting on me, but I was always able to deal with it, I guess."

"Well good for you." Janie almost sounded a miffed. "Guess I wasn't that lucky. I got fired from my first job after two days. How's that for consequences? In high school, I got a job at the Dairy Queen near my house. I really needed the job, because my dad had just lost his. Well, the manager of the DQ started right away calling me his little pixie. By the end of my first shift, his comments got worse and worse. He told me my breasts were cute and I had a nice ass. The next night, after the place closed, I was counting the money from the register and he came up behind me and patted me on my butt. I whirled around and told him that if he ever did that again I was going to kick him in the balls."

"Good for you, girl!"

"Not good. He fired me right there."

"Yeah, but you didn't want to work for him anyway."

"No, and as you can probably tell, I'm still pissed. I really needed that job. I needed to work. It took me a long time to find another job. Plus, I couldn't tell my parents. My dad would have gone down there and beat the shit out of him."

"Good."

"No, Nita. We didn't need any more problems. Plus, I realized I had to learn to deal with this crap on my own. Hell, I still put up with it right now at the Pittsburgh Aviary where I work."

"Really?"

"Hell yeah. I guess it goes with being pretty, and you certainly qualify for that. Guys are going to hit on you. You've got to learn to deal with it."

"Bull shit. It's not right."

"I absolutely agree. But it happens. I read an article that said it goes all the way up the ladder everywhere—in companies, colleges, politics, everywhere."

"So, what do you do? Kick them all in the balls?" Nita chuckled.

"Some of them need it. They are just assholes. And some of them are just old guys who don't know any better. They don't get it that it is not okay and that we aren't flattered when they comment on our looks and start flirting. There is one old guy at the aviary who is constantly touching my shoulder. I tried to tell him, but he still does it."

They each shared stories of guys who got aggressive and how they dealt with it. Finally, Nita asked, "So, what am supposed to do now with this mess I'm in, Janie?"

"I doubt that kicking your Dr. Schmidt in the balls is a good tactic, but you could try it," she laughed.

"Okay," Nita laughed with her. "I will look for an opportunity."

"In all seriousness, though, as far as he's concerned you already kinda did that."

"Plus, I think my advisor is a big part of the problem."

"I read another article that talked about something called Horizontal Violence. Sounds like that's what you're dealing with too."

"What the hell is Horizontal Violence?"

"The article said it can take many forms, but in the workplace, it often shows up as either overt or covert aggression, especially between women or between members of the same minority."

"That doesn't make any sense."

"Well, they are just starting to really study it, and it turns out it is a big deal, especially in healthcare."

"I can't believe this."

"Well, what you are describing with Dr. Burns sounds exactly like what I read. It said to fix it you need someone higher up to deal with it, or it will only get worse. I hate to tell you, kid, but this is one big pile of shit you're dealing with."

"At least I understand it better, even if I don't know what to do about it. There is no way I can try to go above Dr. Burns or Dr. Schmidt. That would just nail my coffin shut."

Nita asked about Frank, and she and Janie chatted for a little while longer. As soon as they hung up and she was putting her coffee cup in the sink, there was a knock on the door. "Anybody here?" came Henry's voice.

"Come in," she called. "Oh wait, it's locked, I'll get it." She cinched her bathrobe and hurried to the door.

"I wanted to check on how your leg was healing. I hadn't heard from you, but I didn't want to bother you. I sure felt bad about you getting hurt."

"Oh, it's fine – just a little bruise." Nita stuck her leg out to show him. "Not much left of it. Listen, I'm sorry I was in such a bad mood. Lots of stress from school."

"No need to apologize to me. I felt bad that you got hurt trying to help me."

Henry was holding a cardboard box that rattled a little as he walked to the table. "Hey, I was straightening up my basement, and I came across something I thought you'd like to see. It's old medicine bottles. I know you don't have time now, but maybe on a day when things lighten up a bit you can look at them." He set the box on the kitchen table, then looked at Nita. "Hey, you okay?"

"Yeah, why?"

"Your eyes are kind of red and puffy. You sick?"

"No," she wiped her eyes. "Must be allergies."

"Yeah, could be. My Bessell had allergies. They can be a real pain. I could recommend some medicine if you want, 'cause Bessell tried just about everything." Henry abruptly smacked himself in the side of the head with his right palm. "Listen to me. You're the one's about to become a doctor, and I'm giving you medical advice. You're graduating soon, aren't you?

"Hope so," Nita said with a faint smile.

"Is there a problem?" Henry sensed there was something behind the comment.

"Oh no," Nita tried to cover for it. "Just have to pass the finals first."

"Oh well, I know you're busy. I just wanted to drop this off. You can look at them whenever you get a minute."

"No, that's fine," Nita took a deep breath. "Let's see what you have in the box."

"Well my Bessell wanted to plant some roses alongside the old shed near where we put the canoe, so I dug up all along the side. Well she wanted it deep so her roses would have plenty of room for their roots. Anyway, when I was digging, I started finding a bunch of old stuff. Whoever built the shed must have used his old junk for backfill next to the foundation. Most of what we found was old bottles. 'Course you know me, I had to keep them. And Bessell, too. We got 'em cleaned up as best we could. Seems they're old medicine bottles and the like." Henry started pulling out bottles wrapped in old newspaper.

The first bottle he unwrapped was about four inches tall and was a narrow rectangular shape. He examined the front to read the raised lettering on it. "Looks like some sort of iron supplement for women," Henry handed the pale blue bottle to Nita.

The next bottle was green-colored glass with gold lettering. It still had a cap on it. "This one was for Absinthe, whatever that was," he said, setting it on the table.

Nita picked up the bottle. "Absinthe was mostly alcohol, but it had some other botanicals in it that made it dangerous. It was also called the green fairy. It was green and very potent, anise-flavored." Nita paused and explained, "I had to do some reading on the history of pharmacology. Interesting stuff."

She handed the bottle to Henry, who shook it. "It's empty. Guess that's good." He picked up another one. "This one's a pretty color, but it doesn't say what it was." He handed Nita a cobalt blue round bottle with a glass stopper.

Nita looked at each bottle without thinking too much about them. When Henry had emptied the box, he had the kitchen table filled with old newspapers and about fifteen bottles. "Anyway, I thought you might get a kick out of seeing them. Bessell and I had fun with them. Like I told you, you never know what kinds of treasures you'll find here."

"Listen, I better get going," he said with an apologetic tone. As Henry started rewrapping the bottles in the newspapers, he paused and looked at Nita. "Are you okay? Seems like something is wrong."

Nita took a breath before answering. "No, I'm fine."

"Well I'm just an old man, and you can feel free to tell me to mind my own business, but I'm sensing something is wrong."

Nita looked at him and scrunched her mouth. A tear escaped from her right eye.

Henry's eyes softened. "Anything I can do?"

"No, I don't think so." Then Nita added with a faint smile, "Unless, you perform miracles."

"No, I'm afraid not. But, now my Bessell.... I still talk to her all the time, even though she's been gone so long. I suppose you think that's crazy, but we still talk. I'll get her on it," he nodded as if that was a significant move in the right direction. He then covered for it by saying, "Seriously, if there is any I can do, you just ask."

"Thanks very much, Henry. You always make me feel a little better."

He quickly finished repacking the bottles and moved to the front door.

"Could you show me where you found the bottles?" Nita didn't want Henry feeling like he had intruded.

"Sure, it's just out by the shed." He set the box on the front fender of his old red Ford pickup. "You okay in that bathrobe? It's still pretty chilly."

"Oh, I'll be okay for a minute."

Henry waved his arm as they walked around the side of the house and said, "Your garden's looking good,"

"Yeah, but the weeds sure do like this weather. I just don't have the time right now to keep up with them."

"I may stop by next week and take a whack at them if that's okay."

"Oh, you don't need to bother."

"I don't mind. Brings back lots of fond memories. Funny, but you don't realize it at the time, but these were some of our happiest times out here, fussing about what to plant where and trying to remember what we did the previous year. As I look back, even the weeding was a joy." He chuckled and stared at the garden that was sprouting onions, peas, lettuce and spinach. "Funny, but this little patch here is sure filled full of memories." He paused and looked at Nita then added, "If you dig, you will find some amazing things here – maybe even some answers." Henry shrugged, turned and took a couple steps toward the shed, then said over his shoulder, "Sorry. You don't need to hear an old coot like me jabbering on."

"No, I like to talk with you. And I think I'd have liked Bessell."

Henry turned abruptly to face Nita. He looked like he was going to cry. "Oh, you would have. And she'd have liked you. She'd have bothered you even more than I do, though" he laughed.

"You don't bother me, Henry. You help keep me anchored to what's important."

Henry tried to soak in the comment, then shook his head. "Hey," he said, distracted by the end of the canoe protruding out from behind the shred, "when the weather warms up, feel free to take that canoe out on the river. The paddles are under it, and you sure earned it," he nodded toward her leg. "Well anyway, here's where we planted the roses. You can actually see a couple of them trying to hang on." The side of the gray wooden shed was a tangle of weeds and grass. Straggling out from among the brown and green jumble were some long-legged stems with thorns. "Roses are high maintenance. Got to prune them and dust 'em and make sure they get enough water. But they're worth it. The good things aren't usually easy, and roses are a good example." Henry pushed some weeds back from around one of the roses. "Ouch," he jerked his hand back.

"You okay?"

"Yeah, but these things sure will bite you. I was just looking to see if its tag was still on it." He licked at the blood that appeared on his finger. "They have me on blood-thinners, so my blood is slow to clot. They say I need to lose some weight, and I guess they're right. I weigh 180 now, which is too much for an old guy five-foot-eight. I eat at the diner too often is the problem."

Henry fished around down near the base of one of the rose stems and located a metal tag on a wire. "Yep, here it is." He scraped away some dirt and read the name. "This here is the Peace rose. We both loved that one. Has yellow blooms with a kind of a peach-colored edge to the petals. It was probably our favorite."

While walking back to his truck, Nita noticed Henry was limping more than his usual shuffle. "Your knee hurting you?"

"Just old age. Comes with being seventy-two, I guess." He stopped to look at the side of Nita's cottage. "The house is older and in better shape," he chuckled. "That is one of the original windows," he pointed to the window to her bedroom. "You can tell by the wavy lines in the glass. The house was built a little before the Civil War, so it's about 130 years old. I think it's a great little place."

"How long have you owned it?"

"We bought it in 1960. Bought it from a black family. They'd done work on it to bring it up-to-date. It was in good shape when we got it. Needs some more work now, though."

When Henry left, Nita went back inside. Since Emergency Medicine was to be her first final, she got that book out. It was a thick and complicated text. The volume of material made her wonder how ER docs did it with everything that came at them from heart attacks, to obscure diseases, to gunshot wounds. She spent the day buried in notes and texts, trying to get all the key elements embedded in her brain.

About 11:00 that night she was saturated and exhausted. She decided that a good night's sleep, hopefully without crazy visitations, would put her in a good position to pick it up again Sunday morning. She took a shower and crawled into bed, expecting sleep to arrive quickly as it generally did. She waited, but it did not come. She felt like she was waiting at a bus stop, but the bus never appeared.

CHAPTER TWENTY-FIVE

Instead of sleep, cold streams of fog slipped down from the cliffs of her worries. The dismal fog crept from the bluffs and into her bed, wrestling the blankets of warmth away as if they owned them. Anxiety shared her bed like an unwanted lover, the clock ticking his heartbeats. Soon dreads of many shapes swooned over her, vying for her attention. The final exams loomed large on the ceiling but were soon eclipsed by the glare of the situation with Dr. Burns. Gradually Nita came to challenge even her dream of becoming a doctor. She wondered if she was deluded in thinking that this was the way she could help people. Maybe the whole thing was a delusion. Her desire had been trodden under the demands, politics and jerks of the school. What a contrast to the naïve preconception she held four years ago when her acceptance letter arrived at long last in the mail. March 1, 1983 seemed liked more than four years ago. On that day she felt as if she was finally on the path she had dreamed of for so long, and she wished her parents were alive to share in the moment. Her father had died from an aneurism three years before the car wreck that killed Carly, and her mother never fully recovered from her injuries. She declined for years, finally dying right after Christmas the year Nita graduated high school. Nita ended up being her caregiver in many ways. Her mother's orthopedic issues were the most obvious problems, as she never really regained her mobility, but her depression was the millstone that truly pulled her under. Nita sometimes wondered if the accident had actually planted the seeds of her dream to be a doctor. Unfortunately, the dream now had devolved into struggles on many fronts, none of which she anticipated.

An owl hooted somewhere in the distance. Nita turned in her bed, and her unease over the school worries yielded to deep-seated apprehension over the recurrent clicks, the tormenting snaps into other worlds. She knew they were not random and certainly not normal. More and more she was convinced that that they were some sort of psychotic hallucinations. The fact that she seemed to be gathering lessons from them made them even more troubling. Their roots were tangling in her mind, sprouting into realities. She thought of Chee-na-wan and Kanianguas when she studied orthopedics and anesthesia. Rachel was with her in pediatrics, and Jenny wandered with her on the entire ill-fated quest to become a healer. Nita felt like she and Jenny were imprisoned together on an island of the dying. Like Jenny, she was going insane. Maybe the whole dream of becoming a doctor was insane.

Nita looked at the clock and was distressed to see that it was past 3:00. Her fond hopes of a good rest had been supplanted by a cluster of fears that sprouted like mushrooms on a damp night. Panic grew as she thought of all she needed to do and the debilitating effects that a lack of sleep would impose. She needed to shift her mind away from all the worries and calm her angst. Nita reached back into her past for a sleep-inducing tactic. She decided to pray, just like she had in the terrible days after the car accident. She brought her hands together into a knitted ball and begged for help, not just for sleep this night but for understanding and guidance. Slowly she slipped away.

A tapping at the door of her bedroom preceded a gradual opening. First, a stark yellow light cut into the room, then a long cane penetrated. The door slid silently agape. With gentle tapping on the floor, a man entered, initially as a silhouette until he flipped up the light switch on the wall, revealing a well-dressed figure with dark glasses, which were staring at her. His right hand held a white cane with a red tip. His left hand groped the air. Suddenly he lurched to his left knocking into the dresser that sat against the wall at the end of Nita's bed. His hand swept wildly, knocking her hairbrush and other belongings to the floor. A seldom used bottle of Muguet De Bois perfume clattered onto the hardwood but did not break.

The man poked at the air with his cane. His left hand swept coins from the dresser, sending them scattering and rolling. He careened from the dresser toward the end of the bed but bounced away without touching it. He staggered left, then used his cane to navigate around the far side of the bed. Nita jumped from the opposite side and ran to the wall. His thrashing and tapping stopped. He opened her closet door and pulled the string that hung from the light socket inside the closet. The bare bulb blinked on, spilling an extra slice of light into the bedroom and illuminating the white cane that lay on her bed pointing in her direction.

The man slowly bent to pick up a stack of shoe boxes that Nita did not remember being there. He set the four boxes on the bed near her pillow and placed his hands gently on the top box. Lifting the black lid from the box, he took out a pair of small white shoes that Nita recognized as the shoes she wore for her First Communion. He put the shoes back in the box and replaced the lid. He pushed the blankets and his cane back from the side of the bed, then placed the box that held the First Communion shoes on the bed near him.

The man reached again to the stack of boxes and lifted the next lid. From the tan box he took a green suede platform shoe that Nita had worn in high school. She smiled when she saw how silly it looked with its four-inch thick sole and brass tacks. The man smiled too. He replaced the shoe, closed that box and set it on top of the first.

When he opened the third box from the stack, he flinched slightly. From it he gingerly lifted a worn running shoe. He waved his hand beneath his nose to avert the odor and quickly returned it to the box, closing the lid. Nita would have liked to have taken a longer look, because that pair of Reeboks had been her favorites. She remembered saving enough money from waiting tables at IHOP during college to finally buy a pair of decent running shoes. But the man set that box on the first two.

He turned to the final box from the original stack. It sat stark, white and alone on the bed. Instead of opening it, he reverently placed both his hands on the lid and bowed his head. He stayed in this position for quite some time, apparently praying. As if mustering his courage, he slipped his hands to the ends of the lid and slowly raised it, like a priest preparing for Communion. He carefully set the lid next to the box and peered into it as if gazing into the abyss. Nita craned her neck to see what was in the box, but at the same time with intuitive reluctance her body leaned back toward the wall where she still stood.

The man lifted his head so that his dark glasses faced Nita. She bent toward him. His mouth quivered, and a tear rolled from under his left eye. His head slowly bent down again toward the open box. Carefully he reached in and withdrew a small blue canvas shoe. Nita gasped and staggered backward against the wall. The man held one of the shoes her sister Carly was wearing the day of the car crash. Nita had been taken by a neighbor to the hospital, arriving minutes before her six-year-old sister died. When they were going to take Carly away, a crying doctor gave Nita the shoes and Carly's Partridge Family lunchbox, which she was still clutching when they brought her into the Emergency Room.

When sunlight hit Nita's face, she saw that it was almost 9:00 Sunday morning. The night's worries and the troubling dream lingered as she ate some oatmeal. She decided to go to Mass at St. Teresa's in Port Deposit, a humble gray-stone structure with a small white cross out front. Nita felt hypocritical only showing up when in great need, like before last year's finals. Now here she was again. She sat in the back pew. The bible reading, however, made her presence feel oddly appropriate. The Gospel was about Jesus healing the blind man. The priest pointed out that we are all blind. "This isn't just Father Roger saying this. Jesus is showing us that we are all of us blind. We are blind in so many ways. Our world has miracles everywhere, but we are blind to them. Jesus helps us see. He shows us the way, but we have to open our eyes."

When Father Roger announced that he had a joke to illustrate the point, the congregation groaned in a good-natured manner.

"There was a flood coming into a town that floods periodically, sort of like Port Deposit. The radio warned people to evacuate. But one man was very religious, and he told his neighbor that he didn't need to evacuate because God would save him. A while later a police car came through town, and with a bullhorn the officer warned everyone to get out. But the man knew that God would save him. After a period, water from the flooding river was lapping at his porch. A fire truck came sloshing down the street with firefighters in boots knocking on every door. The man greeted the fireman who came to his house and thanked him for the offer to help, but said that his God was going to save him. The fireman argued that the man needed to go with him, but he politely declined.

"Soon the water was flowing into his front door and then into the windows on the first floor, and so the man went to the second floor of his house. Some emergency workers came by in a small motor boat and urged the man to climb out the bedroom window and get in the boat. The man declined, saying God would protect him.

"Eventually the man was on the roof of his house, and the waters were still rising. A rescue helicopter flew over and lowered a ladder near him. The man waved it off, and yelled that God would save him.

"Finally, the house was completely immersed, and the man drowned. When he got to heaven and saw Jesus, he said with distress, 'Hey, what happened? I trusted you to save me, but you let me drown.' Jesus looked at the man and replied, I sent you multiple warnings, then I sent a firetruck, then a boat and finally a helicopter. What more did you want me to do?'"

The congregation laughed and some applauded. Nita wondered what rescues she might be blind to.

After church, Nita felt a little better. She focused on her studying and made good progress, but also felt the rising panic of how much she would have to do just to pass the Emergency Medicine final. While she tried to concentrate, her mind periodically veered off onto the Judiciary Panel. What if preparing for that turned out to be more than just getting her thoughts together and showing up?

Monday morning as she was finishing her coffee, she saw movement out the side window and spotted Henry, wearing his usual worn-out Dickies khakis and armed with a hoe and a large white bucket. He limped to the edge of her garden and set down the bucket. He took off his black and orange Orioles cap and leaned on his hoe. For long minutes, Nita watched Henry stare at the garden. She would have liked to go talk to him, but she had so much work to do that she didn't want to risk getting caught in one of his extended visits. Pleasant as they were, she could not afford one right now. She sat down at her books, and when she stood up again to get some more coffee, Henry was gone and so were the weeds from her garden.

That evening she decided she'd better get her clothes cleaned so that she'd be ready for whatever happened after her meeting with Dr. Burns the following day. The Port Deposit Laundry Basket was almost empty when she went in. Nita quickly recognized the large woman with blond curly hair who had intervened between her and the biker in an earlier trip to the laundromat. The woman had the same little girl clinging to her sweat pants, which this time were green instead of gray. The little girl tugged on her mother's pants and pointed to Nita. The woman smiled and waved.

Nita smiled and wiggled the fingers of her right hand, which were holding her plastic laundry basket.

Nita was pushing blue jeans and t-shirts into a washer when the woman and little girl came over. "Hey," said the woman, and "hey" echoed the little girl.

"Well hey," Nita replied. "I remember you two from being here before. How are you doing?"

"Oh, we're hanging in there."

"But Mommy don't have so much work now."

"Now you hush, Kitten," the mother said as she tussled with her daughter's hair. The woman smiled at Nita, "It's funny, she won't hardly never talk to strangers. Seems to have taken a liking to you, though."

Nita squatted down to the little girl's level, "Well I like her too. I was glad to see her in here this evening. Can I call you, Kitten, the way your mommy does?"

"Ah-huh," the girl nodded. "What's your name?"

"Now, Kitten..." the mother cautioned.

"My name is Nita,"

Kitten reached out and touched Nita's hand that rested on her knee. "My mommy's a waitress, but they don't have enough work for her."

Nita turned her hand over and held Kitten's, then stood up. "Tough job. I worked at an IHOP for a while in college."

"Yeah, it's tough, but it's a job. I just wish they could give me more hours. Might be the sound of a window opening, though. For too long I been stuck in a rut waitressing up at the Pilot truck stop by the interstate. Maybe I just need a kick in the butt to go do something else. Sometimes a problem is just what you need in life." The woman punctuated the statement with a pained smile, then whispered, "But it's a good bit easier without a little one. Of course, I wouldn't trade her for the world, though."

Nita nodded and finished putting her clothes in the washer. "Is the change machine working today? Last time I was here it was empty."

"Yeah, he was filling it when we got here."

"Hey Kitten, could you help me go get my change?"

The girl leaned back her curly locks and looked up at her mother. "Can I?"

"Well sure."

When they got back, Kitten and Nita had their hands full of quarters. "Need to borrow any detergent?" the mother laughed.

Nita laughed with her. "You saved my butt last time. Every time I come in here, I think of that, and I look around to make sure my biker buddy isn't around."

"I hear he's in jail."

"Really?"

"Yeah, apparently waiting trial for knifing somebody. Killed the guy."

"Geez, I guess I better watch who I pick fights with."

"Well, sometimes you do have to fight to do what's right. You just got to be ready for the consequences."

"Or I need to hope there's a friend who will step in to get me out of what my mouth got me into."

The woman looked across the room. "Kitten, it looks like our washers is done."

"Can I stay over here?"

"Well sure."

Nita said, "Hey I think I got too many quarters. Would it be okay if Kitten and I went over to the candy machine?"

"Really? Can I, Mommy?" Kitten jumped up and down.

"Well sure." The woman looked at Nita and said, "But nothin' with peanuts. She's real allergic."

Nita said to the woman, "You want something? I've got lots of change."

"One thing I don't need is to gain any more weight. Even my sweat pants won't fit."

The woman had beautiful green eyes and curly blond hair like Kitten, but she was seriously overweight.

While Kitten ate her Skittles, her mother and Nita sat and chatted. The woman looked at the text book in Nita's empty basket. "Anesthesiology? You were studying when you were in here before, too."

"Yeah, I'm in med school."

"Wow, you must be real smart."

"At least I think I'm still in med school."

"Whadaya mean?"

"Seems my mouth picked some fights there, too. And it was with the wrong people."

"You're not too bright for being so smart," the large woman chuckled. "My kind of girl. I been causing trouble for myself and getting in my own way pretty much all my life."

"Mommy can I go over and watch the TV?"

"Okay, Kitten," she rubbed her hair, then turned back to Nita. "Of course, sometimes you need to stand up and fight. Frankly, it took me too long to stand up to her father. He'd been abusing me, calling me names and treating me bad. But when he started in on her...well, that was it. It was ugly, and it was difficult, and it sure did set me in a bad place, but it was absolutely the right thing to do. I guess sometimes you have to take an ugly road to get to a good place. Of course, what do I know, I'm still on the road. All I can say is it's a better place than I would have been in, and I feel better with myself for fighting the fight."

The woman's mind seemed to have shifted to an extended cycle. Although she looked in the direction of Kitten, she was obviously processing information well beyond the laundromat. Finally, she looked back at Nita and asked, "What kind of fight did you pick?"

"Oh, I guess it's just too much politics. I'm not very diplomatic, as you noticed. That's what got me in trouble. Plus, I really resent that there is not enough focus on the patient. Not enough caring and human touch."

"Well I'm not anywhere near as smart as you, but it does seem that we have things pretty screwed up. The way I look at it, if I took my car to the mechanic and he recommended some tests for diagnosing the problem but before I could let him do anything I had to call the insurance company and ask some stranger's permission and she might just say 'no,' even though she's never even seen my car, well that would just seem all messed up. But that is exactly what I had to go through to take Kitten to the doctor a couple years ago when she was having headaches. It was a major battle just to get permission to find out what the problem was, let alone fix it. The insurance company seemed more interested in giving me headaches than helping get rid of hers. How did we end up with a system that says some lady on a phone who's not a doctor and who has never even seen Kitten gets to decide what should and should not be done?" The woman's face had become enflamed as she talked, and she now had her hands on her hips defying Nita to answer the question.

Nita smiled and held up her hands. "You aren't going to hit me, are you?" she said with a chuckle.

"Oh, I am sorry. Was I shouting? It just upsets me so."

"All I can say is that I agree with you. I don't have any answers, though."

"Well someone needs to find some answers and fix some things, because there are real people out here who is suffering. It's just not right."

Kitten appeared between them and tugged on her mother's pant leg. "Are you okay, Momma?"

"Oh, there I go again." The woman looked at Nita, "I'm sorry. I just get worked up."

CHAPTER TWENTY-SIX

When she got home, Nita's mind swam in turbulent currents of agony and anger in anticipation of her meeting the following day with Dr. Burns. For much of the night she debated whether she should just play by their rules. She could say that she did not know what happened in the operating room, which was mostly true, and she could offer an apology for the misunderstanding in the cafeteria. After all nothing she did now was going to change what happened to the boy. But what about Dr. Schmidt's allegation that she was a distraction and, in some way, responsible for the error? Nita spun and thrashed through the dark hours until she found herself preferring to deal with one of her odd visitations rather than the present reality.

Dr. Burns's administrative assistant looked up when Nita entered at 7:45. Nita stepped to the woman's desk and said, "Excuse me, I'm Nita. I have an appointment with..."

"She told me to tell you she will see you when she is ready. She doesn't want to be disturbed." the woman said, widening her eyes.

Nita went to a chair by an end table near the closed door to Dr. Burns's office and sat. She could hear Dr. Burns's voice, apparently talking on the phone. The more animated parts of the conversation made it through. "I do not know what to do with some of these young women. They seem set on making trouble for themselves. They don't know how good they have it, yet they constantly sabotage themselves." The other person on the call was clearly in agreement. "Exactly, exactly. It's pure arrogance." Dr. Burns said. Eventually the call ended with Dr. Burns suggesting they meet for lunch soon.

When the office door finally opened at 8:15, Dr. Burns glared at her. "You're late."

Nita said, "I was here early. I have been waiting. I understood that you did not want to be disturbed so I didn't knock."

Dr. Burns glared as if she did not believe her. "Come in."

Nita sat in a chair facing the desk. Dr. Burns opened the file in front of her. "Perhaps you have been through judiciary hearings at other times in your academic career or your personal life." She said it not as a question but more as an accusation or a logical assumption.

"I have not," Nita immediately chided herself for her clipped response.

She received a doubting gaze from Dr. Burns. "Well assuming that is true, let me explain some basics. I will be your advocate, your defender as it were, during the hearing."

Nita interrupted her, "Excuse me but I did not hear any results from the investigation. Dean Wherle said that a hearing may or may not happen, based on the investigation."

"Oh, there will be a hearing, make no mistake about that. In a case this serious," she patted the file in front of her, "there most certainly will be a hearing. Now if you will allow me to proceed without interrupting," she looked coldly at Nita. "Your case will be heard by the Judiciary Panel. They are seven people who are on a two-year rotating assignment from the faculty and senior staff. Dr. Jason Kent, who is Vice President of Student Affairs, will oversee the process. It will be his job to assure, among other things, that order and proper decorum are maintained at all times." Dr. Burns glowered at Nita, "There will be no outbursts or other inappropriate or disrespectful behavior." She stopped and waited for a response by Nita.

Nita fought off her tongue by clenching her teeth.

"Did you hear me Miss Thomas?"

"Yes."

"Then at least be respectful enough to acknowledge that you did."

Nita nodded, straining to keep any sort of expression from her face.

"The official charge will be read by Dr. Kent at the start of the hearing."

Nita interrupted her and asked, "When will I get to see the actual charge? Not until that point?"

"My secretary sent it to you."

"I have not received anything."

The doubting look reappeared. Dr. Burns held the look in place for an extended time. Nita's face held a voided expression. Finally, Dr. Burns pressed a button on her phone and picked up the receiver. "Elizabeth, you sent that package to Miss Thomas, did you not?"

"Umm-hmm. And when did it go out?"

"Okay. Thank you."

Dr. Burns hung up the phone and said, "It went out in the mail yesterday. It was sent to your residence." She waited for a reaction from Nita but received none.

"As I was saying before you interrupted, the charge will be read by Dr. Kent. You and I will then have an opportunity to speak, followed by the others who are interested parties."

"Who are they?"

"Others who have an interest in this situation."

"Can you give me their names?"

"Why?"

"I... well I...," Nita sighed and took a breath. "It seems, Dr. Burns," Nita attempted to measure out her words in careful doses, "I feel like I am not able to prepare. Can I meet with Dr. Kent in advance?"

"Why? What is there to prepare?"

"That is what I am asking. Without knowing the charge or even who else is involved I don't know..."

"Come now, Miss Thomas, don't try that cute, coy crap with me. Maybe your pretty face gets you places with others, but not here, not with me. You know damn well what this is about. Your behavior in the OR was highly inappropriate and then you went so far as to implicate one of our leading surgeons as the cause."

"So, this hearing relates solely to the situation involving Dr. Schmidt?"

Dr. Burns smiled, "Are there other situations we should be considering as well?"

"No."

"Well we both know that there are. Perhaps you know of more than I do."

"No."

"Then perhaps you should quit interrupting and allow me to go on," she tilted her head to the side and raised her eyebrows.

Nita nodded.

"Thank you." Dr. Burns seemed pleased with her ability to tie Nita in knots. She relished each sparring match. She was keeping score, and by her own estimation she had won every round.

"So, you and I will present our case and then the others will speak. Normally Dr. Schmidt..." Dr. Burns abruptly halted and attempted to backtrack. "I mean normally at this point...I mean at this point the other parties speak, as I said before you disrupted my train of thought." She seemed suddenly flustered. "Yes, as I was trying to say, then the members of the Judicial Panel will have the opportunity to ask questions. There are two hearings that day, the other being a student who has been caught cheating. The time allotted for both hearings is two hours. You need to be there on time."

"I have not been told when or where the hearing will be held."

Dr. Burns was clearly annoyed. "Next Tuesday, 9:00. In the faculty conference room down the hall."

"Thank you."

"Do you have any other questions?" The tone of voice made it clear that no more questions were welcome.

"I don't think so. Perhaps after I have had a chance to read the material you sent..."

Dr. Burns stared coldly at Nita.

Nita received the packet at home just before noon the following day. A formal and legalistic letter detailed the charge as "inappropriate behavior in a medical setting so severe as to distract the surgeon, Dr. Thomas Schmidt, from the operation, causing a serious and irreversible consequence to the patient, specifically the loss of his leg." It went on to say that the behavior in question was flirtatious in nature. In addition, it alleged that there was "an attempt to transfer the blame to the surgeon."

As she read the letter, her heart pounded its way into a full-blown rage that they would have the audacity to charge her with culpability for the loss of the boy's leg. Her rage boiled over to the point that she could not continue reading the material in packet. She slammed out the front door and into the rain-soaked yard. She ended up standing in the rain facing her garden. For a long time, she stood with tears washing down her cheeks in the steady rain. Gradually something peaceful from the garden reached out to her. She realized that Henry's weeding had made it look beautiful and fresh. The lettuce leaves nodded with the arrival of rain drops. An earthworm emerged from the wet soil and began a journey down one of the garden rows in a quest known only to it.

Nita's mind snapped back to the impending doom. Her rage had been cooled a bit by the rain. Her t-shirt was soaked, and she was chilled. By the time she reached the porch she was convinced that if anyone had seen her standing in the rain staring at a worm in the garden, they would think she was losing her mind.

While she made a cup of tea, she glared from a distance at the contents of the package, which were still strewn on the kitchen table next to the envelope. Her fury flamed up again but not to the point of earlier. She worked to convince herself that this was nothing she did not already expect. Seeing it in writing felt like she was reading her own tombstone, but it simply validated what she had anticipated.

Nita opened a can of tomato soup and poured it in a sauce pan. As the soup was heating, she sat at the kitchen table, mindlessly dunking her teabag up and down in the cup. She slid the small pile of papers together and stacked them onto the envelope. She resolved to read all the material slowly after she had eaten. Halfway through her soup, however, she found herself reading the cover note and then the details of the judiciary process. Finally, she re-read the charge. "Okay," she said aloud, "so there it is. Nothing unexpected." Beyond the charge, the other particularly irritating piece was seeing that "Dr. Barbara Burns will be your advocate and advisor in the process." Again, nothing new, but aggravating nonetheless. The Judiciary Panel would consist of seven faculty and senior administrative people from the university who serve on a rotating assignment. An appended page listed their names and titles. Nita recognized two of the names, but did not actually know any of the people. Dr. Jason Kent, Vice President of Student Affairs, would conduct the proceedings. The sheet on the process stated that he would read the enclosed charge. Nita and Dr. Burns would have an opportunity to speak, followed by Dr. Schmidt and any others who had direct involvement with the situation. Nita, the guidance said, was welcome to submit any names for consideration. She began thinking of who she might ask until she noticed that the deadline for submissions was yesterday. The lack of fairness of the entire process was appalling, and her anger rose. She managed to salve it by telling herself that there were no names to call anyway. Martin was the only possible witness who might know the truth, and she was quite certain that they had already gotten to him. No doubt all her classmates knew about the hearing by now, and all of them knew better than to get involved.

The description of the proceedings stated that the Judiciary Panel would then vote in closed session on what actions to take. The normal process was that this occurred immediately and that if the person wished to wait, they could be informed promptly. Only if added information was needed would there be a delay.

Nita sat at the table and stared at the papers. Periodically, she would pull one to review a detail. The key decision for her was whether to accept some level of blame and then apologize, thus hoping for some chance to finish her degree. She was already going to miss her Emergency Medicine final in this process, but that might be salvageable. Would accepting blame give space for lenience or might it set her up for further legal action as well as expulsion. She wished she had an adviser other than Dr. Burns with whom to discuss the options. The only other alternative she could think of was to contradict the version of events as offered by Dr. Schmidt, to tell the truth about what had actually happened. She had not been flirting and had nothing to do with outcome of the surgery. Clearly this was not the version Dr. Schmidt would be giving. Perhaps there would be others from the OR. She had no idea who else was now aligned against her. The second option placed in stark opposition her word against that of the powerful doctor.

While trying to study for her impending finals, her mind drifted incessantly to the judiciary hearing. Her body and her brain begged for sleep, but when she finally allowed herself to go to bed, sleep fled before the anguish of her predicament.

When the day of the hearing finally arrived, she drove to campus well ahead of the appointed time of 9:00. As had been instructed in the packet, she waited outside the faculty conference room. Shortly before 9:00 a young man with long stringy hair and a sport coat and tie arrived. He plopped down in a chair near Nita and said, "This sucks. All I did was help my room-mate with a research paper."

Nita shrugged.

"What did you do?"

"Nothing."

"So why are you here?"

The door to the conference room opened. A middle-aged, portly and balding man emerged. He identified himself as Dr. Kent. "Miss Thomas, we have you scheduled to go first. The young man jumped up and said, "Hey, is it okay if I go first? I have to get to work by 11:00."

"Well, we…Miss Thomas?" Dr. Kent looked at Nita.

"Please," the young man pleaded. "If I'm late, they'll fire me."

Nita reluctantly agreed and for a half-hour sat waiting, still debat-ing whether to apologize or tell the truth. The door opened again, and the young man facing the cheating charge came out and sat in a chair farther away from Nita. He hung his head and stared at the floor between his feet. Finally, he looked up and said, "They take this shit real seriously. I mean fuck, I wasn't expecting this sort of shit. I figured if I just showed up wearing a tie and said I was sorry, that's all it would take. I mean fuck."

Nita looked at him but her thoughts were deep within her own circumstance, and she had no words for him.

After about ten minutes, the young man was called back into the room. When he emerged, his face was streaked with tears, and he said nothing as he hurried past her. The door closed behind him.

In about five minutes the door reopened, and Dr. Kent called her in. As she entered, all conversations stopped. Seated on one side of a long, oblong conference table were the people who obviously made up the panel. The table was heavy dark wood with a glass top. No one sat on the side of the table opposite the panel. The large brown leather chairs were pushed neatly in place. On the wood-paneled walls of the room were oil portraits of men who must have been notable in the school's history. Brass plaques, too small to read at this distance, were attached to the bottom of each frame. Wooden chairs stood at attention along the walls below the portraits. All were empty. Nita scanned the room and noted the absence of Dr. Burns and Dr. Schmidt.

Dr. Kent said to Nita, "I would like to ask each of the panel members to introduce themselves." Dr. Kent's cheeks were flushed red, and Nita wondered if he suffered from high blood pressure. "Panel, this is Miss Nita Thomas. You have read in your briefing materials the circumstance involving Miss Thomas. Dr. Gravely, as chair of today's panel can we start with you?"

A woman with dark eyes, high cheek bones and short dark hair at the far-left end nodded. "Good morning, Miss Thomas. I am Irene Gravely. I am a professor of pharmacology." Next to Dr. Gravely sat an African American woman who nodded slightly to Nita. "I am Dr. Sheryl Washington. I teach in the School of Nursing." A black man sitting next to her smiled solemnly and said "Dr. Edmund Adamson. School of Dentistry."

A thin, pale woman was next. She introduced herself as Dr. Susan Annis, an administrator in the School of Nursing.

"Good morning, Miss Thomas," said the man beside Dr. Annis. "I am Dr. Nicholas Roesller. I am new to the Department of Orthopedics."

The next man had a ruddy complexion with an abundance of unruly gray hair. "I am Dr. Jeffrey Geer. I do research in biomechanics."

The final panel member was an Asian man whom Nita recalled seeing before. "My name is Yu Jian. I am an administrator in the medical school."

Nita wondered where the other people were—Dr. Burns, Dr. Schmidt and any others. Dr. Kent answered the unasked question by saying that he would now bring them in. He went to a door in the opposite corner from where Nita entered and summoned people in. Dr. Burns was the first to enter. She was followed by Martin, Nita's classmate who had been in the OR with her and Paul. Another man and woman entered, each wearing a white lab coat. They were followed by one additional woman wearing scrubs. Nita assumed they had all been in the room when the incident happened, but she did not recognize them because they would have been wearing surgical masks. The door closed after they entered. Where was Dr. Schmidt? Nita wasn't sure what to make of his absence. Perhaps he would arrive later.

CHAPTER TWENTY-SEVEN

Dr. Burns hurried over to Nita and extended her hand. "How are you, Nita?" she greeted her in a loud and cordial voice. "It's nice to see you again. We've certainly seen a great deal of each other lately, haven't we?"

Nita's stomach developed a nauseous knot. "It's nice to see you again, Dr. Burns. Thank you for your help."

Dr. Kent instructed Dr. Burns to sit with Nita at the table opposite the panel. The other newcomers were asked to sit in chairs at the perimeter of the room. He then went to the side of the table with the panel and sat next to Dr. Gravely on the left end.

"Thank you all for coming this morning," he said in a somber tone. "We will now begin the hearing. First, I will read the charge involving Miss Thomas. Miss Thomas and Dr. Burns will then have an opportunity to make some comments. Dr. Schmidt will not be able to be here today. He has been detained by another matter, but he has submitted his comments in written form, which I will read. We will then ask for any comments from those here who were present on the day in question. The Judiciary Panel may ask questions at any time for clarification, and in addition after all remarks have been made, they may ask any additional questions of Miss Thomas, Dr. Burns or any of the witnesses."

He paused and asked, "Does anyone have any questions at this time about the process?"

A few heads shook slightly. He turned to Nita and asked, "Miss Thomas, do you understand the nature of the proceedings? I know from talking with Dr. Burns that she has spent considerable time with you in preparation."

"I understand," Nita responded.

"Good," said Dr. Kent, "then we will begin."

He cleared his throat and picked up a piece of paper from a small stack in front of him. "We are assembled here for a hearing before the Judiciary Panel of the College of Medicine and Related Arts. The case involves an allegation of inappropriate behavior by Miss Nita Thomas, while she and two other fourth-year medical students were observing an operation being performed by Thomas Schmidt, M.D. Dr. Schmidt alleges that due to a distraction by Miss Thomas, an accident occurred during the surgery that resulted in irreparable harm to the leg of the patient. The operation was on the right femur of a ten-year-old boy. The boy had developed a tumor in the thigh bone, and the operation was intended to remove the mass. Unfortunately, due to the accident, the leg had to be amputated from the mid-femur area. Dr. Schmidt states that the root cause of this tragic accident was flirtatious behavior of a sexual nature initiated and sustained by Miss Thomas. This caused him to lose concentration while excising the tumor. Dr. Schmidt indicates that during a later encounter, Miss Thomas accused him of purposefully harming the boy, while attempting to absolve herself of any culpability."

Dr. Kent looked up from the paper and turned toward Nita. "Miss Thomas, are the charge and its seriousness clear to you?"

"Yes."

You may now respond to the charge by addressing the panel.

Nita looked at the faces assembled opposite her. They showed somber attentiveness. Despite her heart pounding in her chest, a certain calm came over her, and she felt comfortable speaking, although even at this point, she wasn't sure what she would say.

"Thank you, Dr. Kent and panel. First, I want to say that I am intensely saddened that this entire situation has occurred. The result of the situation will be borne by the young patient for the rest of his life, and I know that all of us, including Dr. Schmidt, are profoundly troubled by this. We all enter the medical field fully intending to help and heal people, and of course first to do no harm. In my heart I know for certain that I had no intention of creating a distraction or of perpetrating any inappropriate behavior. I felt honored to be able to observe the operation and was thankful for the opportunity. If Dr. Schmidt feels that I did something wrong, I cannot attest to that. All I can say is that I am certain that I had no intention of doing so. Therefore, while I firmly believe that I have no culpability for what occurred, I would nonetheless offer an apology for any inadvertent role my presence may have played." Nita stopped, thought about saying more but decided against it.

Dr. Kent asked Nita if that concluded her formal response, and she acknowledged that it did. He then asked Dr. Burns if she had any comments.

Nita looked over at Dr. Burns seated next to her. She was wearing a crimson business suit with black trim. It had an upright collar whose stiffness seemed a perfect fit for the wearer. She turned and looked at Nita with a bloodless expression then turned back toward the panel. "Not," she paused ominously, "at this time."

Dr. Kent continued, "Then at this point I shall read the written comments of Dr. Schmidt in his absence. He picked up another piece of paper from his stack and cleared his throat. "This is from Dr. Schmidt: 'First I would like to send my apologies to the Judiciary Panel for not attending the hearing in person. As you may know, I chair the board of our county's Boys and Girls Club and an urgent matter has demanded my attention there. I hope you will understand.

"'I would like to stress my sorrow related to this situation. If there was anything I could have done to prevent it, I certainly would have. Quite frankly I was not prepared for the behavior of Miss Thomas, having never seen the like in my entire medical career. You are all now aware of the flirtatious behavior that occurred in the operating room, but I feel I must also inform you of what happened after the accident in the interest of a full understanding.'"

Dr. Kent paused in his reading and looked up at Nita and then over at Dr. Burns. Nita glanced at Dr. Burns and was puzzled to see a smug smirk edging its way to her face. She got the feeling that Dr. Burns knew what was about to come next and that it would be decidedly not in Nita's favor.

Dr. Kent cleared his throat and continued reading from Dr. Schmidt's statement. "'The day following the accident, Miss Thomas contacted me and asked to have lunch with me. She suggested a restaurant off campus. Because I was uncertain of her purpose and being a married man, I wanted no opportunity for any furtherance of her advances or even any chance of impropriety. The pretense of the lunch, she said, was to discuss a possible career in surgery. Now I will tell you that I always make myself available to the medical students who seek my advice and counsel. In this case, however, I was a bit wary. Something just did not feel right. Therefore, I suggested that we meet in the cafeteria at the medical center. Although Miss Thomas attempted to disagree, I held to my position, and she eventually relented.'"

Nita squirmed in her chair, and her eyes bulged. She could feel the heat of her temper crawling up her neck. What Dr. Kent was reading was a total fabrication. Nita had been prepared for an ordeal, but she had no notion that Dr. Schmidt would go so far as to manufacture something so absurd.

With his head down, Dr. Kent continued, "'As it turned out, my suspicions were well founded, if incomplete. Miss Thomas arrived at the lunch wearing a suggestive outfit and immediately attempted to initiate some comments that I will choose not to disclose at this time, but suffice it to say that they were clearly sexual in nature. I changed the topic to what I believed to be the more appropriate and pressing topic. I began by trying to gently explain why the accident in the OR was so tragic. To my surprise, Miss Thomas seemed remarkably dismissive of it. When I persisted in wanting to make sure she understood the gravity, she suggested that perhaps if we could meet for dinner, we could resolve the little misunderstanding, as she put it. Miss Thomas continued to make sexual advances at the lunch table, and quite frankly I became more and more distressed by her behavior and attitude. When I rejected her advances and suggested that she should show some remorse for what she caused, she abruptly reversed course and attempted to blame the entire accident on me. At his point I lost my composure, as you can probably imagine if you can think of yourself in my place. In closing I want you to know that I have thought long and hard about sharing the details of this encounter. I finally decided that in fairness the panel needed to have the full picture. Thank you for considering my comments.' That concludes Dr. Schmidt's written statement," Dr. Kent said.

"That is a lie!" Nita blurted out.

"Miss Thomas," Dr. Burns shouted, "control yourself. Dr. Kent, my apologies. This is the behavior I warned you about. Even though I specifically cautioned Miss Thomas about maintaining appropriate decorum, she clearly has difficulty controlling these outbursts."

"I am sorry," Nita said to the panel. "I simply cannot let that statement go unchallenged. It was Dr. Schmidt who made advances toward me."

"Miss Thomas," Dr. Burns repeated, "please control yourself."

Dr. Gravely, whom Dr. Kent had indicated was chair of the panel, held up her hand in the direction of Dr. Burns. In a calm and firm voice, she said, "I will handle this. Miss Thomas, you will have every opportunity to express your position. Let me first ask whether there are additional comments from the witnesses here at this time." Dr. Gravely looked at the people sitting along the wall. No one moved or signaled an intention to speak. Their faces had taken on the motionless stature of the portraits that hung above them. Dr. Gravely waited patiently. Dr. Kent cleared his throat, but before he could speak, Dr. Gravely held up her hand again. Her dark eyes moved deliberately from one witness to the next.

Nita turned and looked at them as well. She wondered why they had come if they were not going to comment. She, on the other hand, most assuredly had some additional comments that were begging to explode into the room. She felt as though she was in a death-struggle with her own mouth.

After long moments, Dr. Gravely said, "It seems a bit curious to me, that you put forth the effort to come here, yet you choose not to speak." She waited, but no one responded. "Okay then, we shall ask some questions. Martin Detwiler," she said as she looked at the other medical student who had been with Nita near the operating when the accident occurred. "I believe that is you," Dr. Gravely nodded toward him.

"Yes."

"Can you tell us what you saw?"

"I... ahh...I, well, the whole thing was confusing. I had never been in an OR for this type of surgery before and I wasn't sure..." Martin stopped talking, apparently having finished what he wanted to say.

Another panel member, the black man, raised his hand slightly.

"Dr. Adamson," Dr. Gravely called on him.

"Martin," he said in a strong, deep voice, "can you tell us, then, what you think happened. What was your impression?"

"I... ahh...I, well, I'm sorry. I really don't know for sure."

"I see. Do you have an opinion? Was Miss Thomas flirting with Dr. Schmidt, or was Dr. Schmidt flirting with Miss Thomas or was nothing of the sort happening?"

Martin looked toward Dr. Burns as if seeking guidance or relief.

"Why do you look toward Dr. Burns, Martin? Have you been coached?"

Martin's face turned red, and his eyes darted back and forth between Dr. Burns and Dr. Adamson.

"I see," said Dr. Adamson without waiting for a further comment.

The thin woman to Dr. Adamson's left raised her hand.

"Dr. Annis," said Dr. Gravely.

Dr. Annis seemed to have tissue paper for skin, and on her head stood wisps of hair that were faded from red, like grass in a meadow in late autumn. She looked at the witnesses and said, "We are all here for a singular purpose, which revolves around fairness and truth. We have one young man who will deal with the consequence of what happened for the rest of his life. We all hope and pray that he will, in time, find a way to turn this into a positive. There is little more we can do for him than pray. The opportunity, though, before us is to try to treat this situation fairly and honestly. Honesty and fairness are our opportunity and our obligation, each of us, with no abstainers. The only reason for anyone to remain silent is for that person to have nothing to say that will shine an honest light on what happened and why. With that burden firmly pressed upon you, we are asking each of you to tell us what you believe happened." She stopped, and her gray eyes looked at them.

One woman seated against the wall shifted slightly in her chair, but no one indicated any intention to speak. Finally, the woman who shifted raised her hand timidly from her lap and said, "If it helps, I did not see Miss Thomas do anything inappropriate."

"Thank you," said Dr. Annis. "And your role in the OR that day?"

"I'm an OR nurse. I was assisting."

"Thank you. And did you see any other behavior worth mentioning?"

The woman looked like she had much to say but was struggling. "No. I mean, it was busy, and well... you know."

"No, I'm not sure what you imagine I know."

"Well, I mean there was a great deal going on, and well, you know how..."

"Know what?"

"Well it's just Dr. Schmidt. That's the way he is. I don't think anyone meant any..."

"Go on, please."

The woman's neck retracted like startled turtle. It seemed as though she had heard footsteps in the forest and immediately withdrew.

"Go on, please."

"That's all."

Dr. Annis' gentle gray eyes probed the woman's face. She seemed to be extracting more information from the woman's eyes, and the woman seemed ready to give up that information as long as she did not have to speak anymore. A clock ticked on the wall, punctuating the silence. Nita could hear her own heart beating as she looked from Dr. Annis to the OR nurse and back again.

From the right end of the panel, a pencil tapped on the table. The man with the unruly gray hair who was second from the end was not aware that this minor percussion was drawing attention. One by one the panel members and witnesses looked over at him. He, however, was staring down at a blank yellow tablet in front of him. He was mindlessly tapping the eraser of a yellow pencil on the table. By the time he looked up, only Nita was still looking at him. Without raising his hand, he said, "Dr. Gravely I think this is becoming a waste of time. If there is no further information to be obtained, then we need to move on."

Dr. Annis answered before Dr. Gravely could. "Dr. Geer, with all due respect, we are, in fact, obtaining information. We must listen to both the silence and the words."

The man resumed the pencil drumming and shrugged. When Dr. Annis turned away, he leaned over to the Asian man next to him and in a disgusted whisper said, "This is a waste of time. Dr. Schmidt did not even show up this time."

"Excuse me?" Nita said.

Dr. Geer looked up, surprised that she'd heard him. "I'm sorry, I just made a comment to my colleague. I beg your pardon."

"Did you say something about Dr. Schmidt not showing up this time?"

Dr. Burns reached over and grasped Nita's wrist. "Nita, please control yourself. It is not your place to challenge the panel."

Nita snapped her wrist away from Dr. Burns. "I want to know what Dr. Geer said about..."

Dr. Burns rose partially from her chair. "Dr. Kent, we have a point of order here. Clearly Miss Thomas cannot abide by the requisite decorum, and I believe that since there are no more comments forthcoming from the witnesses, this hearing can be moved to a close as Dr. Geer suggests."

Dr. Gravely held up her hand. "Dr. Burns, I am the chair of this panel and will control it as I see fit. I will decide when this phase is to be brought to a close. I suggest you abide by your role as Miss Thomas' advisor. Thank you." She stared firmly at Dr. Burns.

Dr. Burns locked onto the gaze with defiance. Slowly she resumed her seat.

Dr. Gravely leaned over and discussed something briefly with Dr. Kent. She then leaned forward and looked down the table to her left and said, "Since the issue of Dr. Schmidt's previous appearances has been surfaced here by a panel member, I will entertain the question from Miss Thomas. Now, to all panel members, we will need to be careful that we do not go beyond the surface so as to avoid introducing confidential information from other proceedings."

Dr. Burns leapt from her chair. "This is an outrage. This hearing is about Miss Thomas and not about Dr. Schmidt. Dr. Kent, this is highly unusual and inappropriate."

Dr. Kent raised his hands palms up to indicate his helplessness. Dr. Gravely interceded in a voice that was soft, which gave it more power than if it had been raised to the tenor of Dr. Burns's. "Dr. Burns, take your seat," she instructed in a manner that had the firm overtones of a third-grade teacher guiding a student for out-of-line behavior.

Dr. Burns complied, but with the look of a recalcitrant teenager.

"Thank you," said Dr. Gravely without a trace of politeness or appreciation. Her gaze lingered on Dr. Burns.

When Dr. Gravely turned to Nita, she said, "Miss Thomas, one of the panel has introduced a topic of potential relevance. You had a follow-up question for clarification. I must advise you, though, that there will be limits on what can be further disclosed. Do you understand?"

"Yes, I think so."

"Fine, then you may ask your follow-up question."

Without addressing Dr. Geer specifically, Nita said, "I just wanted to know whether there have been other situations—other hearings—that involved Dr. Schmidt."

Dr. Gravely held up her hand before anyone else could speak. She turned to the witnesses along the wall and said, "Before we get into this area,

I want to ask one more time, do any of you have any additional comments to add that will shed light on this hearing?"

They all shook their heads, apparently recognizing that they were about to be released from an uncomfortable situation.

The ends of Dr. Gravely's mouth turned down. She made no attempt to hide her disappointment in their lack of cooperation. "Thank you for your time. You may go now."

They all rose quickly and exited by the door where they had entered. When the door closed, Dr. Gravely resumed answering Nita's question. "Yes, Miss Thomas, there have been two other hearings that involved Dr. Schmidt," she then added, "in my eighteen months on the panel."

"Did they," Nita chose her words carefully, "did they involve anything related to or like my situation. I mean did they...not did they involve an accident in surgery, but did they relate to, I guess you could call it sexual harassment or things of the nature? Harassment, I believe, is at the core of this hearing."

Dr. Burns slammed her hands on the glass top of the conference room table. "None of that is your business. You are impugning the reputation of a respected surgeon."

"Dr. Burns," said Dr. Gravely, "please."

"This is a blatant attempt to distract the panel from the point of this hearing."

Dr. Annis raised her hand and spoke. "Frankly, Dr. Burns, I think this is a central point of the hearing."

Dr. Gravely took control of the proceedings again. "Miss Thomas, while we cannot divulge any details, I believe you..."

Dr. Kent touched Dr. Gravely on the arm and then whispered something to her. Dr. Gravely replied with a firm, "No." Dr. Kent looked at Dr. Burns as if to say, "I tried."

"As I was saying, Miss Thomas, while we cannot divulge any details, I believe your question merits a response. The answer is yes."

"Both of them?"

"Yes."

"Thank you, I..." Nita thought of driving the point home but decided against it. "Thank you", she repeated.

Dr. Gravely said politely, "You are welcome."

Nita heard a barely audible growl emanate from within Dr. Burns.

Dr. Gravely looked down the table and asked, "Are there any additional questions or comments for Miss Thomas that the panel has?"

"They shook their heads."

"Then we will ask Miss Thomas and Dr. Burns to go out into the hallway while the panel deliberates."

Nita rose from her chair, but Dr. Burns did not. "Normally," Dr. Burns said, "the faculty advisor remains in the room."

Dr. Gravely said, "That is at the discretion of the chair. I am asking you and Miss Thomas to wait outside. Thank you."

Dr. Burns remained a moment longer in her chair staring at Dr. Gravely, then rose abruptly and exited, allowing the door to close before Nita got to it.

CHAPTER TWENTY-EIGHT

When Nita got outside the room, Dr. Burns was gone. Nita paced for a while and then sat in the same chair she had occupied while waiting for her hearing. The minutes moved sluggishly. She replayed the tape of the meeting in her head, wondering what had just happened and what it all meant.

After about forty-five minutes, the door to the conference room opened, and Dr. Kent summoned her in. When Nita walked in alone, Dr. Gravely asked, "Where is Dr. Burns?"

"I don't know. She was gone when I got out there, and she didn't return."

"Fine," Dr. Gravely said, continuing her disgusted attitude toward the advisor. "Please be seated, and Dr. Kent will inform you of our finding.

Nita took her same seat and the panel members who were standing took theirs. Dr. Kent cleared his throat and read from a hand-written sheet of paper. "The finding of the Judiciary Panel, having reviewed the available information is that Miss Nita Thomas is exonerated of the charge. Her record will be expunged. She will be allowed to continue with her studies and exams, and upon successful completion of all requirements will be graduated with her degree."

A tear found its way to Nita's right eye. Dr. Gravely smiled graciously. "Miss Thomas, we are sorry that you have been put through this ordeal, and we wish you the best."

"Could I ask one detail?"

"Certainly."

"I missed one of my final exams due to the timing of the hearing."

"Dr. Kent will arrange for you to be able to make up that test." Dr. Gravely looked at Dr. Kent, who nodded but did not smile.

Dr. Nicholas Roessler, who had not spoken during the hearing, said, "Dr. Gravely is the hearing now formally adjourned? If it is, I have something I would like to say to Miss Thomas.

"Yes. This hearing is now complete."

"Thank you," Dr. Roessler said. "Miss Thomas, I think you deserve to know that we have determined to not let your ordeal just drop. Quite frankly it is not right that you have been put through this. In advance of this hearing I did some research on my own to more fully understand this situation. As it turns out there appears to be a pattern of indiscretions, which are routinely covered up by Dr. Schmidt's pedigree. Moreover, there appears to be a pattern of retaliation to any who step forward to address the situation. Without going into any additional detail, which I think would not be appropriate here, I believe you deserve to know that this panel has resolved to investigate the situation further."

"Thank you, Dr. Roessler," Dr. Gravely said. "We would, of course, ask you to keep that confidential, Ms. Thomas."

"I understand," Nita said.

"Now," Dr. Gravely said, "Dr. Kent you may go, and Dr. Geer, I know that you have a commitment you are late for. Miss Thomas, the rest of us would like to ask you to stay for a few minutes if you possibly can."

"Ahh, sure," Nita said, uncertain of why or if there was yet another matter she should be concerned about.

"If you could wait outside the room for a few minutes, we shouldn't be long."

Nita went back out and took the same seat as before. She put her head in her hands, relieved, exhausted and a bit confused.

The door to the conference room opened and an odd sensation flowed out. Dr. Gravely held the door for Nita to enter. Dr. Kent and Dr. Geer had departed, but the remaining people all had their same seats. Nita returned to her seat, and a feeling of familiarity filled the room as the panel members looked gently at her. No one said anything for a long while. Although not uncomfortable, the peculiar atmosphere grew rather than subsided. The longer Nita looked at the panel, the more she felt she recognized them all, but at the same time she knew that she didn't.

The Asian man spoke first. "Do you drink tea, Miss Thomas?"

"Sometimes."

"Let this feeling steep. Allow it to brew for a few more minutes."

Nita nodded, not knowing exactly what he meant, but understanding nonetheless. The room developed an unstable quality where things were both real and surreal at the same time.

The next person to speak was Dr. Gravely. "Nita, we have something very special to tell you. You have been selected to be asked to carry forth the difficult journey of healing. We will explain what that means and what many other things mean that you have been experiencing. The people you see sitting here are those who have guided you for a long time. We are all united with you. We are bound together to carry forward healing for the human condition. We are connected through the land currently called Port Deposit, specifically the place where you live. When I first met you there, of course, the land belonged to the Susquehannocks. Our climb was steep like our trek up the Octoraro. And it was full of perils. Lessons are learned through our trials and perils. By sharing lessons, we guide each other, and we support each other. The journey thus continues."

The black woman, who had not yet spoken, picked up the line of thought. "You have had guides along your way, some obvious and some not so obvious. Some guides teach you the wisdom gained over ages of healing. Our spirits have connected with you in what you perceive as your dreams. Certain guides also work with you in what you perceive as your waking life. We all need guides. Certainly, my brother in our earlier existence was particularly high maintenance," she said as she looked at the black man seated next to her at the table and smiled.

"You, too, have presented some challenges," she smiled at Nita. "There were a number of times when your tendency to talk without thinking created its challenges, but we managed to keep you from the worst of the consequences."

Dr. Annis chimed in, "Of course this particular situation today was especially challenging. We were not at all sure how we were going to deal with this," she shook her head. "But you are young now and are still planting the seeds of your wisdom, sort of like the seeds you and Henry have planted in your garden," she winked, and Nita felt a bit dizzy. How did she know about her garden? Was Henry...?

"Yes," Dr. Annis answered, "Henry is one of your guides. He is currently the keeper of the land. In a previous time, you knew him as Tong-quas. He has learned a much more mellow approach but is still desperately defending that land along the Susquehannah. There are many of us who step in from time to time—for example to keep you out of a fight in a laundromat," she nodded.

Nita's eyes bulged in disbelief. "Like we said," Dr. Annis smiled, "you have pre-sented your share of challenges, but you are important to what we are trying to accomplish. And of course, then we took the opportunity for you to meet Kitten, the woman's little girl with the curly hair. You have already started to mentor her, even though you scarcely realize it." Dr. Annis' eyes showed a deep concern as if she could see the future.

The Asian man picked up on the expression and spoke to Nita. "We work together to try to assure each other's safety and to encourage and bol-ster each other. Sometimes the courage to do what is right is hard to come by. For that matter, sometimes it is hard just to know what is right, let alone do it. We help each other to find the truth and encourage each other to trust their instincts. Instincts are breaths from a greater spirit, but they can be faint signals, difficult to discern. It helps to have validation of the way to a truth and then support in the courage to pursue it. Ours is a dream that is ever evolving. We are building a road through a wilderness. There are no maps, so we strive to blaze a trail for others to follow. They, in turn, will chart a course for those that join later to further the dream.

"You will hear us speak of the dream. Let me comment that it is not a coincidence that the word dream carries two significant connotations. The word that is used for what our minds do in the sleep state is the same word we use to describe our highest aspirations. When we go to sleep our minds conjure up strange worlds seemingly totally from within ourselves, worlds that can be wonderful or terrifying or both. In the waking state, though, we sometimes talk of dreams in what we may assume is an entirely separate use of the word. When I was a child, I dreamed of being a firefighter. Newlywed couples dream of having children. People in a cramped apartment dream of having a larger home. A woman in a dead-end job dreams of having her own business. Most of us give at best a fleeting pause to what appears to be disconnected uses of the same word—dream. I would posit—you might say deposit in your port of a mind," he winked to assure that the others got the clever connection, "I might posit that this is no coincidence because the

dreams of our sleep in fact project out into our waking life, and there are many elements that leak through, one to the other and back again. Our sleep state and our waking state are thoroughly connected, and our dreams are one of the bridges. The Buddhists go further to suggest that all of life is illusory, which is not to say it is not real. On the contrary, all is real—all of it is real. Part of the magic of living is learning and allowing ourselves to explore the many hidden dimensions. Just as in a dream of your sleep state an experience can be heart-poundingly real as well as strange and fantastic, your waking world is exactly the same. To say that one set of experiences is real and the other is not, well that is an artificial distinction and one that denies some remarkable dimensions of the human experience. These dimensions are interwoven to the degree that as Carl Jung said, 'Who looks outside, dreams; who looks inside, awakes.'"

"Excuse me, Yu Jian," Dr. Gravely interrupted him. "We do find this helpful and enlightening, but I think we should focus for a moment on the substance of our dream. Sheryl, do you want to start? You certainly have a passion for the topic."

"That's her polite way of saying I, too, get carried away," the black woman said. "Well let me just say that the current state of healthcare has drifted far from its intentions for either health—healing—or for caring. Healthcare in this country has failed in both health and care. In fact, by incremental turns we have developed a very sick approach to healthcare. Our dream is a long and arduous quest to guide healthcare back to its intended path. You have been selected, Nita, along with some others, to join us in the quest. You may or may not come to realize who the others are. You have met us only because the need was acute, and through no particular fault of your own, your journey was in peril even as it was just starting. This is a small example of the dangers that lurk when you try to change a system that is jealously guarded by so many powerful, vested interests. To change the system necessarily means attacking the economic and egonomic interests of many powerful people and organizations. Moreover, their ways are deeply entrenched. Even for those

who might want to change things, the way is neither clear nor smooth, which makes life uncomfortable for all."

Nita wasn't completely sure she knew what all that meant. Dr. Gravely sensed the uncertainty and said, "Let me help to clarify who these powerful, vested interests are that Sheryl is talking about." She paused and looked a little uncertain herself. "It's hard to know where to start or who is on top of the pile. Let me begin with the hospital system. Our hospitals, and I am speaking not just of this one but most of them around the country, have developed an entrenched business model by which they are run. People take that model for granted as if it is the only viable way to provide large-scale healthcare. Most of the hospitals are managed by mega-corporations. There are many people who make their livelihoods—and very good livelihoods I might note—because of the way it is. But someone has to pay for all that. It's not that it's all bad; the point is that it is very costly and quite misdirected. The bureaucracy is enormous, and the quality is not high in many cases.

"Working in conjunction with the hospitals are the countless suppliers of goods and services, including the large pharmaceutical companies. You also have all the medical schools, which are fully interlocked with the way things are.

"Then you have all the government programs. There are labyrinths of regulations and support programs woven throughout all of this. It would be a huge task to unwind those programs without doing harm to the people who depend on them. And again, they are not all bad.

"Then we get to the insurance companies and the lawyers. They are in a death dance that is taking an unbelievable toll on health. I am referring to the health of individuals and the health of the healthcare system. This is where we start. We must excise these cancers from the system. Every time I see those huge yachts out on the Chesapeake Bay, I imagine that some have been purchased by malpractice lawyers who add little value to society and drain its resources. This is not to say that there is not malpractice that must be addressed," she paused and tilted her head slightly to the side, "but the *litigation has gotten out of control. Good physicians are being chased from medicine because of fear of being sued."*

Nita's heart felt a surprising, deep terror. She had only a general appreciation of the way hospital corporations, insurance companies and government programs dictated so much of what was allowed in medicine, but even with her cursory understanding, she recognized that attacking such a fortress was folly. Add in the lawyers, and the task would border on lunacy.

Dr. Gravely stopped and looked at Nita then said, "There is much, much more to discuss, but now we need to ask—are you willing to try? Your thoughts are correct—this is folly. It is foolish to try to attack such a system. We are a band of fools," she smiled weakly and motioned to the others who all nodded. "We are well aware that we are on a fool's mission to even try. However, the futility of a task must never be confused with its importance. People are suffering every day from our sick health system. Good physicians, like you will be, can fight for their patients one at a time and live a life of frustration and, yes, futility in some cases. Or a few can join a movement to alter at the roots how things are. We can treat the symptoms, or we can treat the disease and its underlying causes.

"Nita, we are pleased to say that you have passed the first trials. Your mouth is not always your best ally, but we recognize that it gives voice to your bold spirit, and your spirit is strong and good. It will be much needed in the war ahead. And so, we ask, are you willing to join us?"

Nita's back straightened, and she nodded. "I am ready, and I am willing."

Dr. Gravely looked at the others who all signaled their assent. She stood and picked up a manila envelope that sat on the table and reached to hand it to Nita. "Careful now, it's a little heavy." The envelope bulged in the middle and was surprisingly heavy at that point, as she had been warned.

"Each of us is a pebble thrown into the wide river. We may make a small splash but the ripples that move out from us in broadening circles have

a way of changing things in simple but profound ways. Go ahead and open the envelope," she said.

Nita bent open the brass prongs on the back and opened the flap. She steadied the envelope as the heavy weight in the center seemed to shift. She looked in and was puzzled to see what appeared to be a gray rock.

"You may take it out."

She reached in and slid the stone out. It was a round disk.

"Turn it over."

On the side that had faced down were three concentric circles. She recognized the symbol immediately. It had been carved into her consciousness by the pounding of her dreams.

"Welcome to the healers' circle," Dr. Gravely said.

CHAPTER TWENTY-NINE

Nita left the building, unable to discern where reality started and stopped. When she arrived back at her cottage, Henry was sitting on the porch steps. He rose and smiled as she got out of her car. Nita shook her head in disbelief, somehow knowing that Henry already knew. They walked toward each other and hugged when they met. Without speaking they walked to the garden. Nita felt energy from each step on this special ground.

The vibrant plants in the garden swayed in the sunlight, their small shadows playing on the rich soil. A hawk called from above, drawing the attention of Nita and Henry to the sky where the raptor glided in effortless circles high above the trees.

"The circles are everywhere," Henry observed.

Nita looked at him, wanting him to say more.

"The hawk's flight is a circle that seems to have no beginning and end. You have learned that there is no gap between your thoughts and your dreams. Likewise, there are no gaps between your desires and your realities. You will discover that there is also no space between other things that you might not imagine are actually connected, like between our memories and our hopes for the future. There is wonderful depth to our world, which we can all learn about every day if we open our eyes to the wonders."

Henry waved his hand out over the garden. "The lessons are every-where. Your garden can teach you that there is no line between food and medicine, and your garden helps you grow just as you help it grow. The land can coach you in many, many ways if you let it. It will show you that most of the boundaries we encounter are of our own making. People imagine lines that are not there. When you look out at the ocean you see the line of the horizon, but when you sail out to find the line what do you find?"

Nita shook her head, and Henry continued. "More ocean. Like much of life, the more you search for answers, the more questions you dis-cover. In the end, though, there is only one answer for all the questions."

Nita looked at Henry, and her heart told her the answer. "Love?" she asked.

"Love," he smiled. "Not just love like Bessell and I had and still have, but love in so many ways and forms. We simply must help it grow, allow it to heal the many things that are wrong in this world. It has the power."

Henry helped Nita take the canoe to the river's edge, then steadied it as she got in. He gave a small push out onto the water. He waved and turned back away, limping slowly toward his truck.

Nita stroked the water, gliding across the current toward Time Island. The green craft glided silently out into the current. She stroked steadily on the left side of the canoe to turn upstream into the slow-moving

Susquehanna. A great blue heron glided above her in the morning sunlight, and its shadow crossed the water just ahead.

Adjusting her technique as she went, she made it to the long island out in the middle of the wide river. Although she missed her exact target, she managed to slide up alongside a fallen tree and grab an outstretched limb, then maneuver to the rocky shore. She beached the canoe and put the paddle in it.

Nita walked to a large rock and sat looking back at Port Deposit.

# # # # #

Special thanks to my supporters and guides including:

Bill Bosley

Clete Boykin

Kevin Brown

Ray Germann

Gerry LaFemina

Susie Meyer

Walt Meyer

so many others